Banshee's Scream

The Chronicles of Ismir Book 1

Elin Wilton

Published by Elin Wilton
www.bunimead.square.site
www.facebook.com/lonelyelin/

Cover Design and Illustrations by May Taylor (@maytaylorr)
Writing, Editing, Internal Design & Illustrations by Elin Wilton (@lonelyelin)

The print editions are typeset in Baskerville Old Face, Times New Roman, and Bunimead No.1

No AI was used in the creation of this novel

First Edition 2025

ISBN: 979-8-9935100-0-2 (paperback) | 979-8-9935100-1-9 (ebook)

To those that seal themselves away in their own world, hoping
for something better.

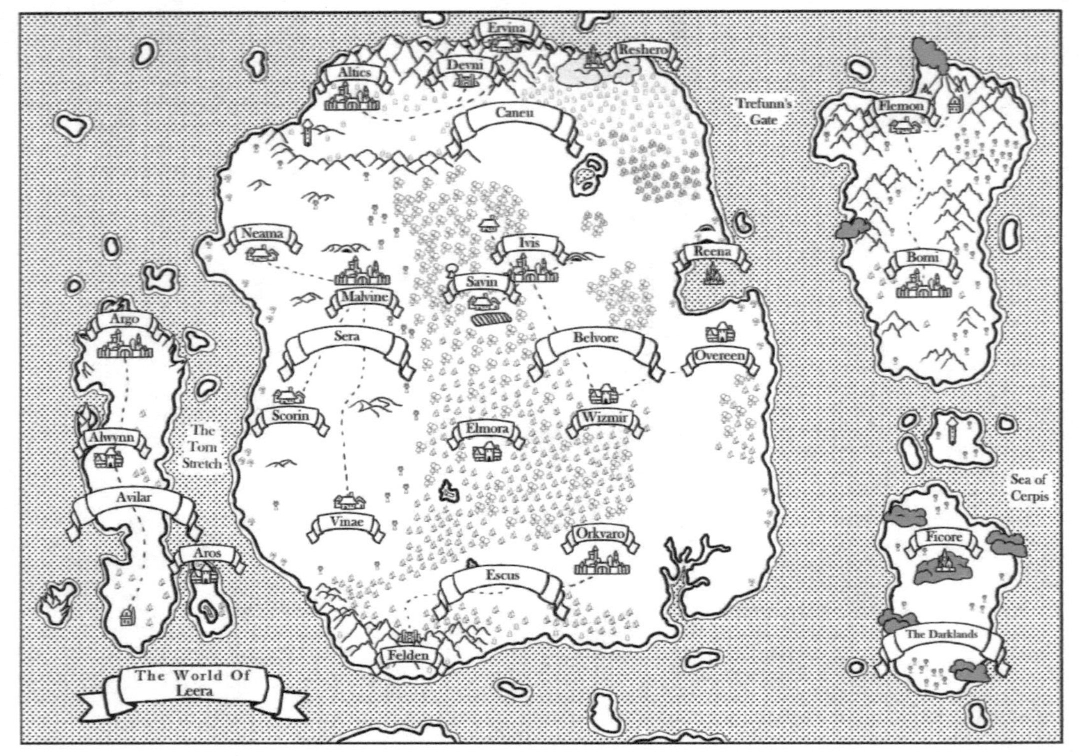
Ervina
Reshero
Devni
Altics
Caneu
Trefunn's Gate
Flemon
Neama
Ivis
Reena
Borni
Savin
Malvine
Argo
Sera
Belvore
Overeen
Scorin
Alwynn
The Torn Stretch
Wizmir
Elmora
Avilar
Vinae
Aros
Orkvaro
Ficore
Sea of Cerpis
Escus
Felden
The Darklands
The World Of Leera

Letter from the Author

Someone's perspective on the normality of daily life is often based on one's experiences.

Growing up, I often found myself entranced by the abnormal, the magic of life. I devoured the Hobbit and the Lord of the Rings and ached for a dragon to arrive at my doorstep. However, as much as I reached out into that fantastical daydream, I was always reeled back in, thrown back into church clothes, and made to learn about the *real world*. Over time, the magic of my childhood began to fade, and I turned to other books rooted in less far away worlds. Slowly some of the magic returned, with book series like Cirque Du Freak bringing to light my fixation with the strange and macabre. If Darren Shan could run away from his family and live an interesting life full of adventure and mayhem, why couldn't I? Maybe the problem was I wasn't ready to let go yet.

It wasn't until 8th grade that I finally took the plunge in a creative writing class. I left this world behind for one of my own creations: Leera.

What prompted this change in venue was Bumble, written by a fellow Oklahoman, Connie Suttle. I was inspired by her book. I loved the dynamic of having different supernatural races, all living, working, and learning together, without major strife (well, most of the time…). It was a place where everyone fits in. Well, everyone except the main character Ashe. As a late bloomer, he really comes into his own power and sense of belonging after feeling like an outcast in his society. I immediately resonated with his situation as soon as I read it. Like many others out there, I've felt like an extra piece to a jigsaw puzzle, out of place and lost. Longing for the time when I can finally find where I truly belong, and be able to take root and grow into the person I was meant to be.

It wasn't until college that I truly came into my own sort of power. I grew into myself and became better equipped to face the world around me. I found friends, but more importantly, I came to know myself better than ever before.

In our world, often when we don't understand something or when someone looks different from us, we assume the worst. Fear turns into hatred and leaves us divided and alone. I believe that people should be given the chance to show us who they are, as often this can lead to a stronger sense of unity instead. You never know what gifts someone has to offer society if you never give them the chance to truly shine in the light.

When venturing into a world of my own creation, I wanted to include as many of the creatures and experiences that line a fantasy society. In doing so, I delved deep into supernatural creatures and lore. When I was reunited with my writing in college, I took it upon myself to use biology, my major, and something I truly enjoy learning about, as a way to provide my world with life. Whether it's the magic system or the abilities of those creatures that reside there, I've tried to design everything to be cohesive and understandable.

One thing that intrigued me about all of the supernatural books that I've read over the years was that despite using the same universally known creatures (vampires, werewolves, etc.), each author paints a slightly different version. They've built around either their own lore or already established lore that others have created. In this book, in particular, I delve into banshees and how, when someone's voice is taken away, it's as though an essential part of us has been stripped away, just aching to be heard.

This book was meant for those such people: the outcasts, the freaks, the silenced—those not given a voice to speak up for themselves, instead discarded by those around them.

I hope that ***Banshee's Scream*** will inspire you to venture out into worlds of your own devising and serve as a gateway into dark fantasy and supernatural fantasy alike. To find your own power amongst the strong and the weak.

And I hope to see you again on the path of your literary journey. Whether it be in a this series or another.

Sincerely,

Elin

PROLOGUE

The night had a deathly stillness to it, only broken up by the warm summer breeze flowing off the backs of the nearby hills as it lofted in through the partition of the window. The warmth gently caressed Iona's pale cheeks as she began to toss and turn in a fit of dreaming. The curtains swayed beside her headboard as a smoky cloud drifted through the dark night, fading into the shadows of her room. Quietly, it examined her, its monstrous teeth nearly scraping against her skin.

A sharp noise from afar tore the shade's attention from her. As the sounds grew louder, Iona began to arouse from her slumber. Sitting up, she rubbed her eyes of sleep. Glancing around her room, there didn't seem to be anything out of place. Blurred lights danced underneath the frame of the wooden door. She rubbed her eyes again and her vision soon cleared. The noises persisted, luring her out of her bed to investigate. The bed swayed as her tiny body crept forward. She shuddered as the cold floor met her feet. Walking forward, she tried to parse the words from beyond the door. With her hand on the doorknob, the voices of her parents became slightly more lucid in the still-lingering fog of her mind.

"What are you talking about? You're not making any sense!" Her mother's voice twinged as she spoke, the words caught in her throat as emotion spilled through the syllables.

"Lara..." Her father's voice had an unfamiliar edge to it.

"No! Do you even know what you're asking me to do? What you're asking me to give up?" she huffed. Her words barely made sense to Iona's groggy mind. "Y-you can't just take our daughter away. I won't allow it!"

THUMP.

Iona felt a weight slam against the door. Her hands went slack as she lost her grip on the knob. Backing away slowly, Iona's heart began to pound in her chest. More and more it beat to its own jungle-like rhythm as her feet slowly pushed her back to the door. Pressing against it, she tried with all her might to break through to the other side but the weight was too much for her to command. Her chest began to feel as though it would erupt at any moment, growing bigger and bigger as she pleaded for the door to open. She needed to see them, she needed to know what was going on. *Is daddy hurting mommy?* She could smell death in the air as anxiety swelled within her, ready to burst. Her eyes welled up with saltwater as she pushed.

Suddenly the weight shifted, letting in light from the keyhole of the door. Iona rubbed her face before peering through to the other side. However, all she could make out was the outline of her father as he hovered over her mother, her body still pinned to the door.

"El-" sputtered her mother. "Wha- are you...doing?" she pleaded, gasping for air.

As Iona stood silent, watching her father, the shadowy beast began to snake its way through the darkness towards her. As it built itself up behind her, a strong gust of wind rocked through the house, extinguishing the light that had shone throughout the hall. Instead of devouring the child whole, the smoke-like creature found itself drawn outwards, towards the two adults lingering in the darkness of the home. The shadow flowed past her and out through the crack in the door. Iona, startled by the chill that enveloped her, dropped to the floor. She watched underneath as the soft light of the moon outlined the billowing smoke, collecting itself on the other side of the door to form what she could only describe as a body. It peered back at Iona with soulless white eyes, its face giving form to shadowy teeth which contorted into a horrific smirk before the full weight of her mother was reintroduced to the door. The shift impacted Iona, forcing her back.

The night was silent once more. Her heart skipped a

beat as she listened. "What *is* that?" her mother gasped.

The air stood still for a second before the sounds of her parent's screams began to echo around her. Every fiber of her being shot to life, like something deep inside her was telling her to run, to hide from the outside horrors. But she couldn't. Fear had come to consume her. Iona tried to muffle the sound, covering her ears as best as she could, but even years after the screaming stopped, she could still hear it.

Chapter 1

Iona spun around looking for a way out. *Dammit! I must have gotten turned around. I could've sworn this path opened up to a side street.* She thought to herself as she quickly ducked behind some crates in the deserted alleyway. As soon as she heard their voices she winced. Touching her side, she was reminded of her injuries from the previous week, still aching to be fully healed. Fearing what they might do this time, she shuffled back, nearly tripping over the dirty cobblestones that lined the old street as she went. They had her cornered, standing between her and the only exit. She scoffed, biting her tongue at the noise. These three always seemed to find her, and today was woefully routine.

But there was something that unsettled her further. They seemed more agitated than usual. She could hear the small squeaks of their shoes as the leader barked orders at the other two. Daring to peek out from behind the crates, she was immediately taken aback by a pair of glowing golden eyes. *A wyr? I don't remember seeing his brown eyes shine like that before.* She cringed at another pang of pain. Right. *He* didn't typically take part in the ritualistic beating she'd come to expect from these boys. *His name is Bernard, right?* Iona remembered overhearing some other kids around her age mention him in passing as they wandered through town on their way to school. He's a local, and a wolf at that. No wonder she'd been backed into a corner. The predator had cornered its prey masterfully. The glow of his eyes shone golden flecks onto the freckles that caked up around his nose. Thick tufts of wavy black hair danced as he kicked over some empty barrels nearby. Iona had never seen him in such a foul mood before. Sliding back into her hiding spot, she hoped that they would be satisfied with their destructive episode and leave her be this time.

But hope doesn't mean it'll happen. Would a hunter let go of a rabbit caught in a trap?

"Where is she?" growled Bernard, the guttural sound deepening his voice.

"I saw her come through here, I-I swear," said a boy with short blonde hair, his posture straightening up before returning to a deep slouch.

"Unless she's learned how to fly, I doubt she's gotten far Bernard," said his other companion.

"You could try her scent," the blonde suggested.

"All you'd smell is the shit she's been living in. A street-trash orphan thinks she can do whatever she wants in *our* town?" Bernard rolled his eyes at the boy's words.

Iona's heart skipped a beat as she dug her fingernails into her palm. It was the only thing she could think to do to try and keep calm.

"One can only wonder how she's survived this long, I mean, the idiot doesn't even show up to school. Not that anyone would want her there," Bernard's words barbed sharply into Iona.

As Bernard raised his head to sniff, Iona shuffled back to the nearby wall, knocking over a glass bottle that laid on the ground.

Bernard's ears perked up at the noise. A smile curled up his lips. "Found her."

Bernard's companions rushed Iona, dumping aside barrels and crates until they caught sight of her. Her ratty clothes ripped against the stones as they dragged her out by her long white hair. Tossing her to the ground, they waited for Bernard's approval to continue.

"Don't you think this is getting a little old?" Iona yelped as she rubbed her sore scalp. She looked up, making eye contact with Bernard for perhaps the first time. She noticed a faded bruise around his right eye. She couldn't tell whether it had happened recently, due to the fact that wyrs heal quicker than she would ever have the pleasure of experiencing. Bernard's eye seemed to twitch at her gaze, their eye contact broken by a punch to the head. As her eyes refocused, she was back to watching the dust as it churned above the cobbled stones of the road.

Bernard sat back on a crate, watching as his companions began to beat into her. Iona curled into herself to defend against the barrage of blows as best she could. And as they continued, a low heat began to permeate her very being. *Why do I have to be their punching bag?* Growing hotter. *Time and time again, we end up here, and for what?* Hotter and hotter. *What have I done to deserve this?* Her blood almost boiling. *Why won't anyone help me!* The more her mind began to echo around her, the more she began to feel a greater fury, a fire brewing from within her. Her skin was hot to the touch, as if she was boiling from the inside out. Her body began to reject the pain, until the only thing she could feel was the all-consuming heat, leaving her numb to the world around her. Slowly, she crept, attempting to stand despite their continued abuse.

The blonde swiftly acquainted his knee with her ribs. She doubled over as hot air escaped from her lungs. Her chest tightened, burning in agony, before she had a chance to suck in more air. She fell on her side, tears rolling down her cheeks with each gasp.

"I'm so... tired of this..." she spoke, her words haggard between breaths. Drops of bright red blood seemed to ooze out from her insides, staining her clothes as she talked.

"It's wyrs like you that give your entire species a bad reputation," she huffed. "You're just a rabid mutt."

Bernard's eyes flashed a darker hue as he bared his canines in anger. Rage blinding his entire sense of reason, his arms growing furred as he partially shifted.

The air stilled as an unfamiliar sensation flashed through her. Gathering herself off of the ground, for a moment she could have sworn that a fist was swiftly approaching her with deadly intention. Glancing upwards, she realized that her body had moved of its own accord. Her arm was outstretched, hand encapsulating the fist of her attacker.

She had caught the punch.

She looked up to find it wasn't the humans that had taken a swing at her. No, it was Bernard that had attempted to land the decisive blow.

"No way," mumbled one of the boys. At this point, Iona couldn't tell who was talking as the beat of her heart pounded away in her eardrums.

"I knew she was a freak!" said the other. Both of the boys started backing up towards the entrance of the alley as they watched Bernard and Iona in horror.

They seemed afraid, but Iona was more confused than anything. Her mind still foggy with the memory of pain. She wondered how her body could have acted so quickly, and without her input no less. *No human could have caught that punch. Not without breaking all the bones in their hand.* The fist was still entrapped in her own. Exchanging pressure, Iona didn't feel pain, but rather a new power resonating from within. She could tell by Bernard's expression that he didn't seem to share the same sensation as she did. Iona's hand began to glow red hot like a poker fresh out of the fire. Bernard tried to fight back tears as his fur began to blister and burn under the concentrated heat. Iona pressed further, his joints popping as she went. She could see the fear and pain in his eyes as she continued to slowly crush his hand under her newfound might. Just for a moment, Iona wanted Bernard to feel the pain that he and his friends had caused her, but before she could progress any further, a sharp pain emanated from her upper back and she lost her grip. As soon as she let go, Bernard turned to utter panic.

"F-freak! Look at what you did to my hand!" growled Bernard, almost baring his fangs as he held his bloodied fist to his chest and scurried off after his friends. "Gods, I can't let my dad see this."

Iona could sense her skin beginning to rise in temperature once more until it felt as though she was physically starting to burn. Her hands and arms soon seemed to be radiating with heat, hotter and hotter it continued until the final moment of ignition. It started with one large burst of flames along the outside of her right arm. Next thing she knew both arms were drenched in flames. Looking around the alley she found herself alone once more. *What's happening to me?* She wondered as she peered down at her hands to find armor-like scales covering her skin from beneath the pecks of fire. White scaly patches intermixed with gray and pink. The strangest part about all this to Iona wasn't the fire itself, but that it didn't hurt. In a way, it felt almost comforting, like a warm blanket wrapped around her on a winter evening. She couldn't even begin to understand what was happening. Her head pounded with blood and her vision began to blur along the edges.

Moments later, the fire that had engulfed her died down. Her senses slowly coming back into sharp focus.

"What the hell just happened?" She mumbled, examining the parts of her body where the fire had been just moments ago, the scales seemingly popping back underneath the skin.

"At least the scales are gone too," she said, "but my clothes are ruined," she sighed. She examined the charred white fabric and the holes and tears that had formed towards the bottom. Small dots of blood had caked around her neckline as well as at her stomach but the wounds themselves had already wound closed.

Cautiously, Iona started to make her way out of the alley and towards the street. Unbeknownst to her, a smoky darkness had began to gather at the dead end of the alley as if some kind of fog had begun to roll in across the ground. The summer air seemed to dip toward frigid as she turned around in utter dread, her heart starting to pound away in her chest again.

"What *is* that..?" she said, backing up towards the bustling city street. As her heartbeat quickened, adrenaline propelled her further towards the street.

As the smoke edged further toward her, she broke out into a full sprint towards the crowded street. A large swath of black smoke broke from the ground, lurching upwards towards her. As it swooped down upon her it caught her leg, causing her to topple to the ground. With what little strength she had left, she pulled herself up, limping towards the street, closer and closer, until she finally reached the brightly sunlit road. As she made it into the light, the shadowy entity sunk back into the alley and away from the highly populated street. Iona turned the corner and down the busy road she went. She couldn't bear to look back.

That thing... could it be the same? Hazy memories of that night six years ago flooded back in. The kitchen, all that blood, and the pain and suffering that followed. Tearing up at her overwhelming thoughts, her vision began to blur once more as she collided with a brown haired girl, causing her to drop what she was carrying.

"Hey! Watch where you're going!" the girl yelled at Iona as she ran off, scrambling to pick up her belongings before someone else did.

Iona just kept running. The memories spun around in her head as though a storm front was about to hit within her.

She ran until she made it back to familiar ground. As she entered a narrow alleyway, memories of living there burst to the forefront of her mind. She had lived in that alley from time to time since the early days of her street-bound life. The air carried scents from nearby restaurants that reminded her of better times. Hoping it might shield her once again, she scrambled over the crates that were lodged between the two neighboring buildings.

She found remnants of the shelter that used to be there. Fabric matted down from rain and made black with the soot from imps cuddling for warmth. Small cups and torn books sat in stacks inside a hollow crate. She clutched her knees to her chest, trying to calm the raging beat of her heart. However, this small comfort did little to keep her childhood memories from piling up inside her head. She held her face, her cheeks brimming with a warmth she wasn't used to.

Her temperature suddenly spiked. Her hands recoiled from the searing heat of her skin before the scales could encase her. She burned once more, fire emerged before engulfing her entirely. Iona cried out in a high-pitched shriek as the fire resonated outwards, busting through the crates as the flames made their way into the nearby street, as well as upwards into the sky, leaving scorch marks that radiated outwards from her. This time however, the fire died down as quickly as Iona had been overwhelmed by its power, and there she laid, face down on the scorched ground, swiftly falling out of consciousness.

Chapter 2

"Hey! Watch where you're going!" Maisie called out as a strange girl slammed into her, eyes flashing almost a blazing red in the morning glow. The faintest hint of something foul flowed through the air behind her.

A hint of sea-salt tears evaporated from the girl's face as she kept moving through the crowd. Maisie scrambled to pick up what was hers before someone else did. Her burnt umber hair shone in the early morning light peeking between gaps in the larger specialty stores and smaller boutiques of Belvore's capital city. Even still, the light failed to reach the ground, blocked by the masses bustling through the crowded marketplace. Turning over her loaf of bread, she noticed that the watery filth of the road had already seeped into it. Silently cursing, and less silently kicking over a nearby box, she begrudgingly made her way back up the street, garnering stares from those around her.

As she reached the bakery it was as if the day had gotten suddenly five degrees hotter. This shift in temperature was predated by a commotion off in the distance, the same direction in which the girl had run off.

People darted their heads out windows as smoke poured out into the otherwise cloudless sky above the rooftops. The dark cloud overhead made her wonder about the brazen eyes of an otherwise colorless girl.

"Gone and gotten herself in trouble no doubt," she said sullenly, looking out in the direction of the billowing smoke in the distance. Sighing, she turned back to the bakery door.

Entering, she could already hear Seamus grumbling.

"First, I get Dalians knocking on our door and next there's this explosion across town! I swear, you never know what's going to happen here in Ivis, I wouldn't be surprised if we saw a dragon flying overhead next!"

"I wouldn't jinx it Seamus, you know how coy dragons can be."

"Perhaps you do Beatrice, you old bag," said Seamus, cackling.

"Well it wasn't too long ago that that big one lived nearby. You ever seen'em?" asked a customer.

"With my own eyes? Surely not, but I've 'eard stories of 'em-" said Beatrice, before noticing Maisie's entrance. "Ah! Young miss Ardelean. Back so soon?"

"Ran into some clumsy girl on the way here, just need a new loaf of bread," she explained, holding up the soggy mess before finally tossing it in the nearby trash bin.

"Oh come now, again? I'm beginning to think you're

the one who's clumsy miss Maisie," she chuckled.

"Are you gonna make me a new one or not?" Maisie glared at her, her frustration already setting in for the day.

"No need, I made two just in case when I made yours this mornin," Beatrice turned about, gathering the second loaf into a thin paper bag.

"How thoughtful," said Maisie, nearly grimacing.

"Oh and before you leave," Beatrice called over her shoulder, "be sure to tell your mother to be careful, there are dangerous people about." Turning back to the counter, she handed Maisie the spare loaf.

"Are you referring to the Dalians? I heard Seamus mention them as I walked in."

"Yes dearie."

"Are they here to eat our toes?" Maisie replied sarcastically.

"You, outta anyone should know that's an old wives tale. I'd reckon though, they're here to do a hell of a lot worse than just toe eaten. You're young, so you don't have a lot of experience with them. *Do not* underestimate them. They're an angry people."

Setting aside the term *angry people*, Maisie's curiosity was peaked. "What'd they come looking for anyway?"

"They were looking for a girl I think, mentioned something about white hair, not much else I'm afraid. Probably didn't want people knowing too much of their business," Beatrice said.

White hair? Maisie thought back to the girl from the street. *Just what kind of trouble did she get herself into?*

"Best be on the lookout. Sooner they find what they're looking for, the sooner they'll leave for their own gods forsaken continent. Would probably be best to stay out of their way in the meantime."

"Thanks Bea, I'll be sure to let my mother know," Maisie said, replacement bread in hand.

On her way out, Maisie couldn't help but wonder about the white haired girl. Her fiery eyes still burned in her mind. *She looked homeless.* Maisie took a moment, contemplating the filthy dress adorned with ashen tears. Her matted hair akin to a feral albino Serian at first glance.

As Maisie made her way back down the bustling city streets of Ivis, she soon found herself at the far-off scene that had felt like a world away. Uniformed members of the policing guild had blocked off a portion of the road that had been blackened with a flaky soot. A few of the officers were busy shooing off some imps that thought the crime scene was a buffet. It appeared as though the small alleyway had received the business end of a fiery inferno, anything that had been in the alleyway had disintegrated, merely ash and dust remained.

Putting both Ivis and the scene behind her, she continued home, but she kept being brought back to what

Beatrice had said earlier that day. As her thoughts raced, the wind began to blow gently over her neck, lightly cutting through the shorter ends of her hair. As time passed and she found herself amongst the outer fields of Savin, she began to relax once more at the thought of home.

Passing through town's welcoming archway, Maisie made her way home for the day. Her house wasn't what most would call lavish, but it was a modest size. Anything less wouldn't fit the needs of her family.

"I'm home!" she yelled into the empty vestibule as she entered, making sure to remove her shoes at the door before wading further into the house. "Mom? Dad?" she called out as she wandered about, finally finding her parents in the kitchen towards the back of the building.

"I heard Belfast ran into Bernard and his father in town the other day, the boy looked like he had been roughed up again. It's very worrying Nic, I just hope those kids will be fi-" as her mother spoke, her voice was elated with concern while still maintaining a familiar matronly air of authority.

"There you are. I called, didn't you both hear me?" Maisie interrupted.

There was a moment of silence between them before her mother answered, "Did you remember to get everything Maisie? You took longer than you usually do."

"There was some commotion in town, it looked like someone was using unregulated magic without authorization. The guild made it a headache as usual." Maisie replied, depositing her bag of groceries on the kitchen table.

"Really? Could you tell what kind?" Her father asked, taking a sip of tea from his mug.

"Can't be too sure, maybe fire magic of some sort? Whatever it was, it completely destroyed everything that was gathered up in an alleyway. I didn't see any healers so I'm not sure if anyone actually got hurt though."

"Hmmm... that's troubling. The council is convening in Wizmir this week aren't they dear?" he looked to his wife for confirmation. Gently, he placed his hand atop hers, trying to add some comfort.

"Yes, but I don't think an elf would use fire magic, it's not in their nature nor wheelhouse."

"Actually, Beatrice and Seamus said something about some Dalians showing up at the shop today, it sounded like they were looking for a girl."

"Dalians? Here in Belvore? That's not a good sign at all," her mother said, leaning back in her chair utterly exasperated. Her long brown hair swayed behind her, nearly sweeping the ground.

"I'm sure they'll find what they're looking for and leave for Dala dear..."

"Yes, but how many lives will they tear apart trying to get there?" her mother said before getting up and leaving the room altogether.

Maisie raised a brow. "What's wrong with mom?"

"Nothing sweetheart, just old memories," Nic sighed as he got up from his chair. Maisie winced as the wood legs slid in a screech against the wooden floor as they went back underneath the table. Nic looked to her apologetically. "I'll go ahead and start getting dinner ready while your mom cools off," he said, lifting the bag of groceries from the table.

"Is it okay if I take a little walk out back? I just need to clear my head."

"That's alright. Just try to be alert, alright?"

In response, Maisie ran up to her father and kissed his cheek before grabbing her shoes.

The surrounding area of Savin was mainly farmland, but it was also home to a great swath of forest, perfect for many of the fae that lived in the area. Maisie had grown up in this forest. Its stooped branches calmed her whenever she thought of them. It was a place that she always felt at home, never lost, never afraid, never alone, always surrounded by familiarity. That day however, there was something amiss in the air, some low grueling hum of the earth that seemed out of balance with everything around it. A lot had changed since Maisie last walked this trail. It was to be expected, but this change in the air, in the earth, was unlike any she had noticed before. Nearing a large clearing in the woods, the air went stale. However, as Maisie looked around, she couldn't see anything amiss. The great willow that rested in the center of the clearing still stood, the trees forming the ring of the outer edge remained unmarked or marred. But yet there was this unnatural rhythm, this foul presence in the air that lingered. It sent a shiver up her spine.

She was about to turn back when, from across the clearing, some bushes began to rustle. Ducking behind a mossy tree trunk, she saw two strange figures off in the distance. One appeared to wear a cloak, covering itself entirely, while the other had their hood down. The one who's face she could slightly make out had long black hair accompanied by pale skin.

As they made their way closer to the willow she was able to piece together some of their conversation.

"You almost had her, but you still need to work on your timing," the long haired one jabbed, his voice low and smooth, followed by the other cloak lurching out at him.

"Woah, calm down! Trust me, you'll have another chance. We just have to pick her scent back up," he took a breath, their tone turning more somber. "You've *seen* Ivis, it shouldn't take very long."

"Why could not get sooner?" said the cloaked figure, its voice sounding as if it had drilled itself inside of Maisie's own subconscious. She held the side of her head as a twinge of pain set in.

"Patience. The Duke needs her alive, or have you forgotten that?" he replied to the shrouded figure, before being met with a grunting scoff.

The Duke? Maisie pondered the strange title. *Could those two be the ones from Dala?*

SNAP.

Shit. Maisie thought as the obscured figure's head darted towards her direction, smoke billowing out from the cloak. Getting up to her feet, she immediately started towards home, terrified of what lurked beneath the creature's outer facade. As she ran, her heart beat frantically. She could nearly taste the adrenaline as it forced its way through her body, carrying her further and further away from the clearing. She hadn't even noticed that she had shifted until she got home, her furry flesh beginning to recede as she panted on the ground, trying to catch her breath. Her claws slowly turned back into fingernails as their grasp on the ground beneath her relinquished. As her vision fluttered back to normal, she sat up, staring out at the forest's edge, looking for either hooded figure. To her relief she found neither painted amongst the background of trees.

Finally heading inside to the comfort of her home, she could smell dinner warming on the stove.

"Oh Maisie! Can you help set the table?" Nic asked as

she came in. Her father nearly dropped one of the dinner plates when he saw her, ragged, clothes torn from transforming. Her eyes still glowing gold with a look he hadn't seen in years.

Chapter 3

As Iona began to awake from her slumber, she was comforted by the soft warm sheets that surrounded her. Shifting her weight, she could feel a pillow cradling her head. Without even opening her eyes she could feel the world around her. A subtle warmth in the air from a fireplace, the faint scent of freshly made bread wafting in from elsewhere, and the sharp jittery sound of gears turning as if there were machines all around her. It was as if the world was telling her what to see without the need for sight. As her mind shifted from each scent and sound, she was reminded of what had happened in the alleyway. The crackling of fire and wood brought forth visions of flames erupting from her skin. The mere thought made her bubble over with heat as she slowly opened her eyes. She found herself in a small outcropping of a larger space. It looked as though nothing more could fit other than the bed and a few shelves that lined the walls, filled with trinkets and other, more useful, items.

There came a rustle from behind the makeshift curtain that, on second glance, appeared to be used as a partition between the bed and the rest of the room. As whomever was behind the curtain approached, Iona quickly shut her eyes again, trying to relax back into a more sleep-like state. As the figure pulled back the fabric, Iona slightly opened one eye, trying to peer through her own veil of bangs and lashes. Although her vision was obscured, she could make out the rough silhouette of a boy not much older than her, holding what looked like a tray. As he pulled an item from it, bringing it closer to her face, Iona swiftly grabbed his arm before he could touch her. For a moment they stared at each other, light refracted in his glasses as his blue eyes shone before her. He fell back as Iona shoved him with great force, the partition nearly catching him with a tear. The tray clattered against a nearby shelf as a bowl of water soaked into the bedding. In mere seconds the quilted top had become cold and damp as the liquid wet her legs. The water sizzled on her skin as steam flowed upwards from her feet. Leaping from the bed, she was met with even more strange senses as the rest of the space revealed itself to her. The room was cluttered with papers, books, and other materials. Tinkering tools were strewn about, surrounded by diagrams and notes that littered the walls. The only area free of clutter was a work table and a cot that set next to an open window, through which a cool evening breeze wafted in. A fire blazed from the hearth as it filled the room with light, illuminating the boy in further detail. His tufts of almond hair stood still around his face as he looked up from beneath her on the floor where he laid. His eyes darted around, no longer glassed over by his spectacles, almost franticly searching for them.

"Where am I?" Iona snarled at him.

"Umm... you're at my house," the boy sputtered, his hand finally catching on the wire and glass frame. He slowly placed them back on his head, trying not to take his eyes off of her.

"Where?" she asked again.

"Huh? Oh! Ivis. I-is that what you mean?" His voice trembled as he spoke.

Her eyes didn't leave him. "How did I get here?"

"To Ivis, or to my house?" he asked, staring at Iona for an answer until he was satisfied with receiving none. "I carried you. You passed out in an alley in town, after... well you know." He shuffled around on the floor, not daring to stand up quite yet. He lifted the fallen tray and sat it down on a nearby table, not seeming to care about dampening some of the papers that laid atop it. "You actually caused a huge commotion, the entire market district ended up getting searched over. I was lucky to get you out of there before the policing guild showe-"

"Why did you bring me here?" Iona continued to press. She lept down from the damp bed, her feet meeting the wooden flooring with a light *thud*. "Why didn't you just... leave me there?"

He backed up, giving Iona her space. "Um... well, would you rather be here where it's safe, or locked up somewhere for using unregulated magic? You thankfully didn't hurt anyone, or else you might have just woken up somewhere... else," he slowly brought himself up back to his feet. "Everything considered, my house isn't so bad."

She eyed him cautiously, taking a moment to realize she was no longer wearing her own clothes. She scratched at the white ruffled night gown that was a size too big on her. Pulling back the collar, she was relieved to find her undergarments still in place, albeit dirty and torn in places she wasn't sure she'd be able to mend later. "Do you know what's happening to me?" she asked, gazing up at the various diagrams of different creatures nailed to a nearby support post.

"You mean, you don't know?" he pushed his glasses further up the bridge of his nose. "Huh... well that *is* complicated. Was earlier today the first time you've summoned that fire?"

Iona nodded, watching as the boy turned to one of the desks in a hurry.

"Okay..." grabbing what appeared to be a messy notebook, he flipped it open to a newly sketched out drawing. On the page there appeared to be a generic anatomical structure, as well as some crudely drawn white hair scribbled on to it. "Now, I'm not sure how you came to be this way exactly, but I have reason to believe that you are, in fact, a dragal," he said, pointing to the diagram.

"A what?" *What is this kid on about?* She thought.

"It's not surprising you've never heard of them. They tend to be few and far between. In fact, one of the last historical accounts of a dragal was recorded during the time of the last great war about a hundred years ago."

"So was I born like this? Because, last time I checked I couldn't burst into flames." The heat in her body seemed to bubble up at her comment. Some pit inside her, churning anew.

"You can't really *become* a dragal by birth, it's more of a magical thing. Like most ambiguous things, there's a bit of disagreement whether or not one should consider it a blessing or curse." He flipped through his notebook some more, studying it closely as though it was some sacred text.

"Which do you consider it?" Iona asked, alarmed.

He stopped immediately, slowly closing the notebook. "Oh, I don't really think my opinion matters on the subject," the boy fidgeted nervously. "It really is all about optics... erm, how you see yourself," he said as he searched for something else at the table.

Iona thought back to the alley. "It did seem to help in the moment, but what happened after-"

"Okay, here it is," he said, starting to read off a pile of what seemed to be hand written notes. "A dragal is a half-human, half-dragon, hybridized creature. They're said to be extremely rare given that most of the remaining dragons are believed to spend a majority of their time in a state of hibernation. Of all the ways to become a dragal... you don't happen to be adopted are you?"

"Ahh... No."

"Ok..." he replied scanning further down the page, "then have you recently come into contact with a draconic artifact or an artifact of unknown origin?"

"Not to my knowledge."

"Ok, well that wouldn't explain your appearance anyway," he mumbled to himself, checking off another item on his list.

"My appearance?" Iona's brow furrowed. *What does he mean by that?*

"No offense intended of course! I'm sorry if it sounded that way," he said quickly, his face turning red. "But you must have noticed that your appearance must garner stares from those around you."

"Well... I guess. I mean, I do tend to stand out in a crowd..." she said, looking down at her pale skin that peeked out between mudded feet and the flowing white ruffles of the gown.

"So that only leaves one option! If you weren't adopted and you haven't come into contact with anything foreign... then you must have been blessed!" he said, slamming his notebook shut.

"Blessed?"

"Yes... by a dragon..." he said much quieter than before.

But Iona's ears perked up all the same.

"A dragon? What do you mean a *dragon*?" she asked.

As Iona's head began to spin at the mere thought of what he was implying, she couldn't help but think. *A girl touched by dragon's flames... I never had a chance at being normal did I?* As her mind refocused, she thought about her parents. *They must have known right? Were they the ones-*

"Are you alright?" he asked, breaking Iona out of her panic-like trance. His hand hovered inches above the surface of her arm.

As she could feel the heat of her skin beginning to cool down she replied, "I'll be better once I know why I'm like this."

"Well I'm sure that that can wait for tomorrow, it's already quite late and unlike you I haven't been able to rest yet."

"I'm not going to wake up in some cell am I?" Iona asked.

"If I wanted to get you arrested for using powers you did or didn't know you had, you'd already be with the policing guild. Think of it this way, I'm trusting you to not burn down my *mostly* wooden house in your sleep, and in return I, the frail human, will sleep in here, in my workshop, on the cot," he said, throwing a stack of blankets and sheets on the tiny padded makeshift bed near the fireplace. "Besides, even if you don't know how to use your abilities you could still snap me like a twig with that new strength of yours. So you got nothing to worry about from me."

"You're not scared of me?" She asked.

"Nope, not one bit," he said, making his way to the corner of the room. "In fact I find you absolutely intriguing."

She watched as he started making the cot up with sheets and a thin padded blanket. She couldn't sense any danger coming from him. To her, he just seemed like a normal boy. *But I still know nothing about him.* She thought to herself as she settled back into the bed, trying to mop up what little water remained between the sheets.

"I never did catch your name," she sounded.

He paused, turning towards her. "I'm Olyn, Crosse. And you?"

"Iona," she said as she curled back up into bed.

That night Iona was met with dreams of the past, of nights long forgotten and horrors long suppressed, a windy breeze, a fight, a struggle, and blood.

CHAPTER 4

Iona was woken up by the gentle beat of birds flying outside. The light streaming in through the window behind her illuminated the small room with an effervescent glow. She could see the shelves of books and trinkets held up along the walls more clearly than she had in the dark. It looked as though they'd come tumbling down on top of her if they were weighed down with anymore junk. *This room must be used for storage.* Iona poked her head through what remained of the curtain that separated her from the rest of the world. Surprisingly, she found herself alone. Stepping out into the larger room, she nearly tripped on a box that had fallen out of favor with the underside of the bed.

Steadying herself, she pulled back the curtain to join the two spaces. It had been so long since Iona found herself in a home like this. To feel safe by walls that for a second almost felt as if they were your own. But it was hard to fully feel comforted by the strange little house. Gears clicked into place as she examined the space once more. It didn't take a genius to guess where Olyn spent most of his time. Around the room were drawings, accompanied by meticulous notes and writing on all sorts of creatures and objects. She barely knew what she was looking at as she sifted through a pile clumsily scattered on a table nearby. The table appeared no different than the bed space she had awoken from, a mode of storage. Boxes poked out from underneath, one seemed to be filled with journals and other writing materials while the other sported what Iona would consider junk. Bits of metal were mixed with contraptions that looked rusted over and piled with dust. *If he has this many notes on other fae, I wonder just how much he knows about dragals like me. He seems thorough.* She sought out the desk that Olyn had procured notes from the night before. Sitting atop the dark wood finish was a ornate box with some sort of strange script on it. Staring at it for a few moments, words began to swirl in her mind, as if the sigils themselves were whispering to her.

Her hand reached out, nearly touching the wooden lid. Before she could touch it, a crow landed on the open windowsill and sounded off a loud, rattling caw at her. She stood staring at it for a moment before it flew off almost as abruptly as it had arrived. As her mind began to clear she turned back to the box for a moment, rubbing the palm of her hand. The box sat silent once more, but Iona could sense a faint chill at her fingertips. As if something had begun to deaden her from the inside out. Trying to ignore the box and the gnawing feeling of dread that had sprouted, she started to wonder where Olyn had run off to. The cot he had slept in seemed to have been made tidy again, blankets sat folded neatly on top while some sheets remained attached.

A breeze kicked through the room, rolling in from the nearby window left ajar to help facilitate the cool morning air. The way it blew past her sent a shiver up her spine. As the wind stirred through the room, one of many precariously stacked piles of paper crashed to the ground. Quickly, she ran over to the window, closing it with a soft *thud* before it could cause any further avalanches of paper. She turned back towards the desk in a huff, a puddle of paper sitting at her feet. Looking around, she sighed. It didn't seem like Olyn would come waltzing through the door anytime soon. Kneeling on the ground, she began to shape them back into a pile.

It wasn't long before one of the pages caught her eye. On it, were drawings of what appeared to be a ghastly creature. It was made up of thick black smoke and had piercing white eyes and teeth that could just as easily rip your throat out. There were notes scribbled about on the page. They outlined its blood lust and feeding habits, while another questioned how sentient they were, or if they were merely guard dogs meant to be commanded. At the bottom was the name *Shadow Reckoner* scratched out, but still legible enough to read. Her mind churned as the drawings reminded her of the alley, the shadowy hand that had scraped at her, in an attempt to drag her away. *Is that what that thing was? Why would Olyn have something like this? I haven't seen anything like it since that night...* Her emotions pricked with the sight of blood flashing through her. It was as if the room ran red with it dripping down the walls all around her. She shut her eyes quickly, trying to shut out the memories. Slowly opening once more, her vision caught on a group of pages that were bound together, the official stamp of the policing guild peaking her interest.

Unable to bring herself to look inside, the front door swung open to Olyn carrying a multitude of parcels. Iona's face glanced up to meet him as he entered the room, still sitting amongst the fallen pages.

"Oh dear," he said, calmly setting down the packages. He approached the pile of papers, kneeling down to meet Iona on the floor.

"The wind... I was trying to tidy them up."

"Don't worry, it happens more often than you'd think. Usually, I sleep out here if I'm working late and well, the fireplace gets a bit hot so I like to keep the window cracked," Olyn placed a pile of the remaining papers neatly back on the desk.

"Why do you have notes on those... things?" Iona cringed at another glance of the sketch.

"Huh?" he said, examining the fallen papers more

closely. "Oh. Shadow Reckoners you mean?" He glanced at the sealed documents in Iona's hands. "There was a sighting of one years ago here in the city. I was only a child at the time so I didn't know much about what happened until recently." He removed the bundle from her hands, placing it next to the rest of his notes on the desk. "They're thought to have originated in Dala so we don't see many of them in these parts of Leera. I was just making notes in case I ever came across one. Unfortunately, not much is known about them."

"What exactly happened? I mean back then, that case..."

"It was pretty open and shut. There aren't many things that come in the night and leave nothing but blood. Apparently, it happened on the second floor of a house in the residential district, two people were reported missing or killed. There was so much blood it soaked through the floor boards and down the kitchen walls on the first floor. The report did mention one survivor, but from what I could tell they were a minor, so most of their information was taken out of the case file before I ever got to see it. Didn't seem like there was much of a follow up though," Olyn's eyes locked onto his feet as he fidgeted. "I can't even imagine what that must have been like. To lose someone like that. So suddenly."

Iona's mind snapped back to years prior. A tear

stained gown and blood caked around her feet. The kitchen red with their blood, but her mother and father nowhere to be found. In a way it was almost easier, not seeing the bodies. Years later she could still imagine them out there somewhere, looking for her. Waiting for her to come home. *Why did you run away?* A man's voice whispered softly in her ear. Iona turned suddenly towards the wooden box. Her body shivering once more with a chill.

"Uh... are you okay Iona?" Olyn asked, reaching out towards her before stopping short. A light blister of heat had erupted from her hand, nearly scalding him. She turned back towards him, noticing the flames. Cupping her hand around them, she tried to drown them out.

"I'm sorry, I don't know why I reacted like that." *What was that? Did it come from the box?* She thought to herself as she tried to keep her emotions from showing on her face.

"It's okay," Olyn said, trying to comfort her. "I should have mentioned that it was a gruesome story, I'm sorry if I scared you in any way."

"Can I ask you something?"

"Yeah, sure."

"Why do you call them Shadow Reckoners?"

"Um... Well, according to what little recorded accounts of them I could dig up, they seem to only exist in the shadows. Bringing forth deadly reckonings upon their enemies, or depending on who you ask, pouncing on their prey. The more common name for them nowadays is a shade. They've actually gone through a couple different names over the years, since people have a hard time figuring out just what they are."

"I see..." Iona mumbled as she collected herself once more. "Where did you go this morning?" she asked, trying to change the subject.

Olyn just stared at her dumbfounded, his cloudy eyes trying to sift through how to answer. "Oh right, the parcels... I had almost forgotten about them." He returned back to the doorway where he had laid down the packages. As he picked some of them up, the tufts of his hair brushed past the inner crest of his nose. "I don't have much here right now so I had to go to the market in order to get us some breakfast."

Iona followed Olyn down the hall to the kitchen. Light streamed in from the front windows, revealing the large canvas blades of the windmill as they slowly cut through the scene of the city below. As Iona scanned the early morning horizon, Olyn carried the parcels over to one of the kitchen counters, making sure to pull out all the necessary cooking equipment from the cupboards.

Taking a seat at the kitchen table, she turned to face Olyn, asking, "What all did you get?" Her stomach growled at the thought of an actual meal for once.

"Let's see... I got some nemi eggs, a couple of fresh salt rolls, some beef mixture for you, and two bottles of freshly squeezed orange juice for the both of us."

Yum was the only thing Iona could think as she stared out at the feast of goodies. Her mouth began to water as soon as the smell of the meat entered her nostrils. Her hands wrapped around her mouth as the saliva began to emanate, swallowing it down. She never remembered meat being so appealing, but there was something about the savory aroma that made her almost want to gobble it up raw. The scent only stood to intensify as Olyn started to prepare the food. As the heat radiated outwards towards her from the stove, she was met with the smoky aroma of freshly cooked meat and eggs. Iona sat, waiting patiently, at the small kitchen table in the corner of the room. Before too long, the aroma started to get to her. How long had it been since she last ate? Surely the day before when Olyn found her? Or had it been longer still since she had a properly balanced meal. As she thought to herself, she could feel her body begin to ache with hunger. Gripping the edges of her seat tightly, her fingers started to dig into the wood. Nails hardened into small claws, carved into the wood bit by bit until Olyn finally brought forth the feast.

He placed before her two of the large eggs in a scramble as well as the mixture of freshly cooked meat.

She waited until Olyn had sat down at the table next to her before she started to tear into her meal, as to not seem completely without manners. As she began to wolf down her food, she could hear the faint sound of Olyn mumbling a prayer under his breath. By the time he looked up, Iona's entire plate was bare. He looked at her, astonished, as she quickly licked up whatever bits remained on the plate before starting to wipe the grease from her face.

"I take it you like my cooking," he took a sip of his juice.

"It's just been a while since I had a proper meal is all."

"I could tell that from those clothes I found you in. Have you lived in Ivis long?"

"Born here."

"And raised?"

"...Here."

"Do you have any family?"

Iona paused for a moment, "No."

"I take it no friends either?"

"No, well yes, well... why do you have to phrase the question like that?"

"Like what?"

"Like you already know the answer."

"Well if you had friends or a place to go to, you would have already left wouldn't you?"

"Not necessarily."

"Why's that?"

"Let's say I have friends, but I'm just not exactly on great terms with them right now. Besides, you still need to explain all of this dragal stuff and whatnot."

"And if I don't?"

"Don't what?"

"Help you."

"Hm, then I'll just leave I guess. But from what I can tell, you enjoy learning about stuff you don't quite understand. So *I* don't understand why you'd just let me walk out of here without adding me to your collection of notes."

A smirk began to break across Olyn's face, "I guess you might be right about that... How about this, let's make a deal."

Iona eyed him cautiously, "*What kind* of deal?"

"I help you out how I can, and all you have to do is say you'll be my friend."

"I just have to be your friend? Why? Is there some sort of catch?" her eyebrow raised.

"Not unlike yourself, I don't exactly have a long list of people I'm close with. And like you said, I *like* learning new things. I just feel that if we see each other as friends it will make this whole exchange a bit more palatable. I would be helping a *friend,* not some girl I picked up off the street, under albeit weird circumstances."

"So, its just for appearances?"

"If you prefer, but it doesn't have to be. We could actually become friends, Iona."

"Maybe, but for now I'll stick to appearances. You forget that I only met you yesterday."

"Speaking of appearances," he glanced down at the nightgown, now stained with small drops of grease, with a sigh. "I got you some items while I was out shopping this morning."

She followed him back to the workshop where the rest of the packages still sat on the floor. Gathering up the last few from the assortment, he turned back to Iona, placing a couple of paper-bound parcels into her arms. She balanced them in her hands, trying not to drop anything that might be fragile. They seemed light but bountiful. As Iona wondered as to what they might be, Olyn seemed to answer before she could even form the question on her tongue.

"They're clothes," he said, staring at her old dress that was now slumped over a chair, nearly in tatters and marked with soot.

Iona peered around the room, looking for a place to change.

Nearly snorting, Olyn led her back towards the outcropping. Making her way behind the curtain, she unfurled the packages out onto the bed.

"I had to guess on the sizes so I'm sorry if they don't fit right," Olyn called as he returned to the kitchen, resuming his morning graze.

As she tried on the garments, Iona was pleasantly surprised by how well they fit. She noted the quality of the upgrade from her typical attire. Olyn had picked out a nice pair of fitted quilted pants, the colors almost mesmerizing as she felt the soft interchanging fabric against her skin. The shirt was a nice and billowy white blouse that she tucked into the pants. The last parcel was stowed away in a paper box. Opening it, she traced the wrinkles in the leather of the adventurer's boots. Light blood stains lined the cracks on the bottom of the soles. *He must have bought these second hand,* she thought as she slipped them on over some wool socks. Making her way back to the kitchen, she was stopped by a familiar sight. She looked at her reflection in a mirror hanging in the hall. She hadn't noticed it before. She touched her face as she looked. Ash lined her facial features and dirt had dug itself into her skin, making her appear older than she was. Spitting into her hand, she tried to wash most of the filth away. Wiping her hands on her pant legs, she pulled a matted black headband from her head, which she used to tie her hair up into a high ponytail. Natural waves laid in a mess along her back.

"Oh wow," Olyn started as he came out of the kitchen, an odd look on his face.

"What?" Iona combed through some of the knots in her hair.

"Ah-nothing, just the clothes look great on you," Olyn said as he came out of the kitchen. "I'm just surprised is all."

"How much did all of this cost anyway? It doesn't take a genius to tell that the boots were second-hand, but the shirt and the pants look expensive. How can you even afford all this? Especially when you live in this weird refurbished windmill," she prodded as she cleaned up more of her face.

Olyn sighed, turning back towards the kitchen, "Why do you care? Its not like I'm running a charity or anything, even my resources have limits," he paused. "We had a deal remember? I'd do what I can to help. Basic necessities like a change of clothes are the least I can do. And if you have a problem with my living situation, you *could* just live on the street again if that's more comfortable."

"That's not what I meant... I just want to understand, how exactly do you afford stuff like this?"

"If you *must* know, *I* don't do much, other than scavenge a few of the nearby dragon caves here and there, it's my mom that makes most of the money for our household," he said, fidgeting with the paper of the leftovers at the kitchen table. He grabbed a nearby notebook and flipped through a couple pages.

"And... where is she?" Iona peered around, nothing pointed towards another person living in the house, despite how clean the rest of the house outside of Olyn's workshop was. She hadn't heard, or smelled, anyone else in the vicinity.

"She's at a magic conference in Wizmir for a couple of days," he said gloomily. "That's all..."

"Doing what?"

"She works with the council for magical affairs."

"The what?"

"Nothing, just a bunch of bureaucrats."

"Okay... And your dad?"

"He doesn't live with us anymore," Olyn said, freezing for a moment at the kitchen table.

Finally turning to face her, Olyn retorted, "And what about your parents?"

"L-let's talk about something else," Iona said hastily. "So... Dragals?"

Olyn sighed, "Well..." Olyn started as he wiped his face with the length of his sleeve. "For starters, they have some of the basics for fae and fiends, such as enhanced strength and speed based on their essence, but they also have some other abilities which aren't as common."

"Such as?"

"Well, you can control fire, but you already knew that."

"I wouldn't exactly call what I did control, but tell me something I don't know."

"Okay, well from what I can tell, the overarching extent of your powers depend on what dragon gave you your powers."

"So I was blessed by a fire dragon?"

"That's what I was thinking. The one dragal that I mentioned before was taken under the wing of Reverna the Gilded during The Great Dwarven War and could melt metal with ease using some sort of super heated breath. So not exactly the same as your abilities but similar."

"Aren't all dragons associated with fire?"

"In children's stories, sure. Although historically, fire dragons were the most common because of their combative ability in battle, but there are others that were more specialized in different areas of nature. Some even ranged into icy wilderness and underwater environments."

"Well that's a shame, I always liked swimming with toadstills when I was younger."

"You're not really missing out on much otherwise. Besides your dragon's element, most dragals seem to have similar passive abilities."

Iona nodded for him to continue.

"Oh sorry," he flipped through the pages of his notebook, "apparently, you can generate some sort of scale-mail in order to insulate your body from your element, in this case I would assume they protect you from burning yourself when using your flames. Which luckily for you, is probably what saved you from becoming another scorch mark in that alley when you had your flame out."

"Flame out? You mean when I exploded fire uncontrollably and then proceeded to pass out in a literal gutter?"

"Depends on how you look at it," his gaze rose to meet hers. "I'm sure once you get to practice using your powers in a safe environment that you'll be able to "flame out", as I so eloquently put it, without spewing fire uncontrollably."

"Yeah, right. How long will that take?" Iona said with a subtle look of defeat lingering on her face.

"It'll take time like anything, Iona. Honestly, I'm not sure how much help I'll be. There's not much written about dragals, especially here in Belvore. I can share with you my research and what I know from other sources, but at the end of the day the pool of knowledge at our fingertips is limited. I mean, it was a miracle that I found you to begin with! And sure, I know a lot more than most people about dragons, but this is still fairly new territory for me."

"At least it was you and not the policing guild..." Iona mumbled to herself.

"Speaking of, why did you flame- burst into flames in the first place? I mean, I found you passed out but since you've gotten here I've barely seen one ember off of you. What made you explode like that?"

"I was being beat up, bullies ya'know? I don't know what it was but something deep inside me just... broke. It was as if a dam had burst. Next thing I knew I was covered in flames. It felt empowering, but also scary. I had no idea what was happening to my own body. What's worse is that after I scared them off, a smoky thing tried to attack me."

"A what?"

"I- I don't know what it was... it looked like a giant hand reaching out after me. It tried to grab me, but I was able to make it out onto the street. By the time I made it to the other alleyway I must have lost it, but my heart was pounding so hard... it got so hot... and then nothing."

"How dark was it where you were attacked?" Olyn spoke quickly, Iona could hear the panic wavering in his voice.

"Um... it was indirect sunlight. Slightly shady cause of the tall buildings. Dead end too so there wasn't a lot of light other than from the rooftops and the street. It was also around late morning or so."

"I see..."

"Well, what are you thinking? I'm the one who nearly got grabbed, remember?"

"Iona, I think you got attacked by a shade."

Iona's heart skipped a beat, "It didn't look like your

sketch."

"Well yeah, its whole body wasn't able to appear because they usually move between shadows. Since it was fairly bright outside, especially for a shade, it didn't show its whole self because it couldn't. If you were attacked at night you probably wouldn't be here right now."

"Well, shit."

"Indeed."

"Do you think it'll come back?"

"It probably has your scent now. And if that's the case, I'm not sure if I'll be able to hold up my end of our deal..."

"Then what do you suggest I do?"

"I'm not strong enough to protect you if that thing comes back, but I might know of a place that can. Have you ever heard of Belgrum Boarding School?"

"I think so. Pretty sure I've seen some of those rich twits walking around town in their purple blazers."

"Well those "twits" go to a school made specifically for non-humans such as yourself. With the exception of some castors of course. It's been heralded as a sanctuary for fae for decades now. If there's any place that you'll be safe, it'll be there. The only drawback is that it's quite expensive."

"Great. Are you paying?" she asked sarcastically.

Iona could see the gears turn in his head. The click of actual gears in the building lending their voice. "No need. As soon as the Headmistress sees your *situation* she'll be begging for you to attend."

Iona picked up at what he was suggesting, "Why would me being a dragal change anything?"

"The school holds itself to a high standard as holding a diverse student body, castors get shoved into a corner, only letting in the best or those that show the most promise, while other fae are let in based on grades as well as their rarity."

"Sounds elitist."

"Well with the state of how some races have been dwindling over the past century, they sort of have a right to be. Without them, some would already be extinct."

"I still don-"

"Iona. Dragons can only relinquish their breath once every hundred years or so. You're already in, whether you like it or not."

"What do you mean their breath?"

"From what I've read, when a dragal is blessed their essence is changed entirely. In order to mimic their dragon, it's as if the dragon has shared a piece of their soul with you. Trust me, it's a huge deal, especially for the dragon, which is why they don't choose dragals lightly anymore."

"If you think it'll be safer..." Iona took a deep breath. "I guess it wouldn't hurt to check the place out, and see what they have to offer."

"Exactly! Now, it's only a few weeks away from the start of the new school year, but I'm sure they'll be able to fit you in. Here," he said, rustling through a box of his things before throwing her a travel bag. "We can go shopping later in order to get you some odds and ends you'll need, and then tomorrow I can show you how to get to the campus."

CHAPTER 5

As the light began to dim for the day, the City of Ivis seemed to spring to life. Colorful lights bathed the streets and banners were strung up, directing people to the infamous Bethel's Bazaar. The bazaar was well known in Ivis for its mysterious comings and goings. It only ever popped up, unannounced, on the days during and surrounding the Summer Solstice. Wares from all over Leera were known to be sold there, each booth appearing more otherworldly than the last.

It was the last day of the bazaar's festivities and by the time Iona and Olyn had a chance to shop around at some stalls, it was already starting to overflow with patrons. Pixies danced above, flying around the twinkling strings of lights as the crisp summer air came through in a soft gust. Iona had caught glimpses of the bazaar in the past, but never like this. To see it from afar was very different experience than being able to take part in it for once. Ivis' market district had transformed into one of the most magical places Iona had ever seen. Her mouth stood agape as she stared out at all of the brightly colored garments, magical charms, and assortments of trinkets that lined the stalls spread on the bustling city streets. Small fireworks crackled in the sky as castors performed for the masses, bringing forth both smoky horrors and shimmering wonders from their hands. Children gathered around to watch them as they performed, oohing and ahhing, before running back to their parents in excitement and glee. A few wyr children played hunter and prey with a satyr their age, growling and pouncing on one another as they play fought, laughing as they broke apart once more with a few clicks of the satyr's hooves against the cobblestone road. Looking around at the adults, it was hard to tell who was what in all the commotion. Pointed ears, strange smells, a glowing eye or two, horns or hooves or both, not to mention the occasional tail.

Iona could smell so much of the market. From the meat pies at the far end to roasted fish skewers just a few stalls down. However, her wonderment quickly waned as she was reminded of the previous day's events. She wouldn't have been able to truly experience the market if it wasn't for Olyn, and she wouldn't have met Olyn if she wasn't first thrust into danger. Thoughts began to swirl around inside her, taking away from the enjoyment of the festivities. She only snapped out of her trance when a chatty vendor's voice corralled her thoughts. His loud voice boomed in her ears before her hearing started to stabilize once more. Looking over his stall, he seemed to

that of clarity," the shopkeeper displayed to them a small golden gem wrapped in cord with a unfamiliar marking etched into it. As Iona stared at the sigil it began to quiver in her mind, but remained as it was. "As a bonus, it'll also help to clean up your aura a little bit as well. I know quite a few castors that won't even let you set foot in their store with you looking like that," he said, gesturing towards Iona.

"What's the language the sigil is written in?" she asked. "I've never seen a mark like that before."

"Oh, well that would be because it's a dead language. Some believe it to be the lost language of the gods. I *did* mention that very few know how to make these anymore," he said before winking at Iona. She just stared at him. "They also say that this charm will guide you towards your destiny."

"My... destiny?" Iona's face tilted to the side as her tone turned skeptical.

"Fate, destiny, either or. Sorry, I'm only joking with you. With your appearance, I'm sure you have many stories to tell. I also do occasional readings if you'd like me to take a-"

"We're fine, thank you," Olyn said, stepping into their conversation. He gently nudged Iona's shoulders towards the next booth.

"How much for the charm?" she asked, her feet firmly planted.

"Why for you my dear? On the house. You seem like you can sense the value I'm offering," He glanced ever so slightly over at Olyn, almost as if he was reading his aura now as well, his nostrils flaring for a moment before he turned back to Iona. "Let me just get you a bag for that." He returned to stumbling around in his drawers again.

Iona's eyes wandered over to Olyn who was standing off to the side, fidgeting with his hands. *I hope he's not upset or anything,* Iona pouted for a moment, *He's the one who was being rude to the guy.*

"There we go! A blazing red, to match your eyes ever so beauteous." Iona's face straightened back into a slight smile as her cheeks darkened for a moment. He placed the bag into her outstretched hands, making sure it was firmly within her grasp. "You do your best not to lose this. It's very special," he winked again.

"Thank you kindly," she said with a timid bow as she slowly dragged her hand away from his grasp.

As she turned back to Olyn he seemed to be deep in contemplation. His face was furled as though he'd just been spat at. Iona tried to poke at his arm, hoping that would break him out of his funk, but he didn't seem to notice her.

"Are you okay?" she waved her hand in front of his face.

His face softened as his eyes began to relax and follow her hand. He turned his face up to meet her. "Yes I'm alright, I just tend to stay clear of magic peddlers. Every one of them says they can read the path that lays before you, but each one spins a different tale," he looked down towards his feet, some of his curly brown locks falling into place over his eyes. "You never know which one is telling the truth."

"Didn't you say that your mom did stuff with magic?"

"I said she was at a magic conference, it's different" he said, staring down at the ground between them. As Olyn's head bobbed back up, Iona could feel him staring past her. "What's going on?"

The ground began to rumble. Iona could hear the crowd before they even got close. The sound of bustling people running away from someone... no *something*. Olyn soon heard the yells and screams as well. As they looked out at the hurried crowd they could see light after light being torn to shreds in the distance. Mothers quickly grabbed their confused children, tearing them away from their merriment. A few cried as the people scattered. Too many creatures to neither classify nor count skittered past their ankles as streaks of pixies and imps flew overhead, off into the night. Iona ran to the side of the bustling road, trying to grab hold of the side of a nearby stall in order to hoist herself up for a better view.

"What do you see?" Olyn yelled through the noise of the crowd.

"I can't tell. It's too dark."

Suddenly, it was as if a switch had gone off in Iona's head, dark turned to light and it was as if she was looking at the scene in the daytime. The only thing that wasn't illuminated was the creature made of black smoke barreling towards them.

Quickly she jumped down from the stall and grabbed Olyn by the arm. "Come on!" she yelled as she pulled him down a nearby alley that she hoped would lead them out of danger.

Iona usually knew the city like it was painted into her memory, but because of the bazaar she couldn't quite pinpoint where she was headed. The decorations and all the lights had lead to confusion. They barreled a right, then a left, and a left again. Dead end. A nearby streetlight dimmed before the sigil powering it sparked uncontrollably. Iona could feel the anxiety of the night swelling up within her. Was this it for her? Would she die here? Slowly they turned around, only to be greeted by an unseemly sight. The smoke-like creature had become corporeal in some parts, its body and face partially solid underneath the flickering street light, while its terrifying claws had become razor sharp. Its face appeared to be sporting a mask. A fiendish smile painted across it. It wasn't until the face moved that Iona and Olyn realized it wasn't a mask, the creeping grin was the creature's own.

Olyn didn't dare move. His body began to shake with a low whimper. It was enough to make him sweat, but not enough to cause his legs to run. He felt as though he might buckle down altogether. The weight of his body was almost too much to handle. Iona on the other hand was almost the opposite. Sure she was scared, she was absolutely terrified. But instead of feeling overwhelming doom, she felt angry. This thing must have tracked her from the market, and now with a whiff of its ash and sulfur scent she knew it was truly the full embodiment of the black hand that had attempted to attack her before.

Her anger soon bellowed into a rage as her eyes began to glow with a light akin to fire. Her arms started to spark up, beginning with her fingertips. Recognizing what was about to happen, Olyn took a step back, stumbling onto the ground with a light thud. Sensing weakness in the boy, the shade turned to face him almost if by instinct and lunged. Olyn tried to shield himself from his impending doom, but then... nothing. No pain, no blood. Peering out over his arms, he saw it.

Iona, under the duress of the situation, somehow, someway, had redirected her heat and light to the palms of her hands. He watched as she gripped the now solid flesh of the creature, holding it back from devouring him whole. The wretched creature's face contorted as it let out a blood curdling howl. As Olyn covered his ears, drops of blood began to drip from Iona's as she continued to hold it still.

FWEET! Iona heard a sharp whistle from up above. A split second later, before she could locate where the sound had come from, she was hit by a strange burst of weariness and a muddled pain that started at the back of her head. Her mind buzzed as she tried to open her eyes, she could barely make out the hooded figure as they landed on the ground nearby. The hood turned towards the shade and it let out a quick whimper. As it spoke, its horrible voice seemed to scratch at one's mind.

"Look at what she did to me A-"

"Shhh," the figure said silencing it. Their tone was comforting and light.

Before Iona could react to the scene, large bird-like wings burst from the back of the hooded one. The feathers were black with hints of blues and purples she could just barely make out in the pale light. But she couldn't keep her eyes open any longer.

By the time she had awoken the two were gone.

"Iona? ...Iona?" Olyn tried to get her to wake up, "I really don't want to have to carry you again," he groaned at the thought.

She slowly rose to the sound of his voice, her head still aching from where she was hit. After a few moments, Olyn helped her up her feet, his own legs still trembling from the whole ordeal.

She rubbed the back of her head, "Why didn't they take us, or kill us, or whatever?" she wondered as she looked around at the scene. "Why just leave us here and take off?"

"Does it matter? That shade seemed really spooked when you did, well whatever you did with your hands," Olyn replied, dusting himself off. "How *did* you know how to do that?"

"I... don't know..." Iona glanced down at her palms, the skin still pink with warmth. She thought back to the moment the shade was about to attack Olyn. "I know it sounds crazy, but it was as if... something was showing me how to."

Olyn raised an eyebrow, "Well I'll tell you what, we are definitely taking you to that school pronto," he said as he helped her trudge home.

Iona stopped before they exited the alley. Patting down her pockets she groaned. Turning back, she began to search frantically. "Have you seen the charm? I must have dropped it when we were running or something."

"Uh no. I haven't seen it. Why does it matter anyway? It's not like it sounded all that useful."

She sighed. "I guess its not that big of a deal..." Iona sounded in defeat after finding no trace of it.

They took their leave as the streetlights seemed to crackle back to life around them.

Chapter 6

The road leading to the school was strangely overgrown. If it wasn't for Olyn's accompaniment, Iona would have sworn they had taken a wrong turn somewhere along the way. The walk had taken up most of their morning, the midday sun beating down on them in its summer glory. It was as if nature stood on guard on all sides, not daring to intrude on the well worn path. As they finally made it to the end of the road, they were met with a large wrought iron gate. The warm heat of the day had left them sticky with sweat. As they took a moment to rest at the entrance, they gazed out at the school itself, which stood upon large open grounds, far from the comforts of the city. Peering through the bars of the gate they could only see the main building. Vines arched up the walls of an otherwise undisturbed mansion.

"It's a lot smaller than I thought it would be," Iona said. "You're not trying to tell me that everything takes place in that large house, are you?"

"Trust me, it's a lot bigger than it looks," he pointed to the arch above the gate, "see if you look here, you can see the runes."

Iona examined the etchings in the metal for a moment before Olyn spoke again.

"The gate has been magically attuned," he moved back some vines to reveal magical runes etched in parallel, engraved into the gate's stone foundation.

"Why all the warding?"

"It's meant to keep certain people out, in particular, humans."

"I thought castors were humans though aren't they? I thought you said some go to school here."

"Castors, naturally born anyway, are thought to have their own essence. Unlike most humans, they can be magically identified as something more isomorphic. But you're forgetting about elves and other races that can use mana more easily than humans."

"Huh... can't we just go around the gate?" Iona asked, peering around. She could see a short metal and stone fence entrenched within the bushes that flanked either side. *It doesn't look like it'd be that hard to just jump over.*

"Given the warding on the gate I doubt it would be that easy," he sketched out some of the runes into his notebook.

Iona stepped back from the gate. The wrought iron stood defiantly in front of her. The more she peered out at the runes that lined the metal the more it began to shift and change.

"Do you see that?"

"What?"

"The runes, they're moving," she pointed up at the arch.

"I don't see anything, just the runes," Olyn sat back down, looking at his notebook. "Are you okay?" he asked, looking up for a moment. "Do you need some water, Iona?"

Iona didn't answer, instead she continued to watch as the runes transformed into a more readable language.

"All monsters of man welcome," she mumbled to herself, reading the words aloud.

"What was that?" Olyn stood up quickly, turning to view the arch. "You can read that?" he pointed upwards at the writing.

"It just kinda translated itself," Iona shrugged.

"Stupid!" Olyn yelled, whacking himself lightly on the head, "I knew those runes looked familiar. They must be in Dracolith."

"The language of the dragons...?" Iona mumbled.

"Those markings are similar to some I've seen before, probably because it's not a curse but instead a form of protection," he scribbled down some more notes in his book.

"I can read it," Iona mumbled, still staring out at the

arch.

"It must have something to do with you awakening your powers. The connection to your essence must be strengthening itself. I've read a few accounts that speculated that dragal could gain knowledge from the dragon they're connected to. In this case I guess it just translated for you, psychically."

"I guess that makes sense..." she approached the gate slowly, as if it was about to burst open.

"Well it's just my best guess. You said the other night that it felt like someone showed you how to stop that shade-"

With one heavy push, the gate slowly swung open. A burst of magical energy sprung from the gateway, flooding past both Iona and Olyn. Before their very eyes the dreary mansion transformed into a robust landscape of dorm houses and training grounds. A few extensions to the main house now outcropped as well.

"Woah..." Iona took a sharp step back at the scene. As she squat to grab her things, she couldn't help but fumble to keep her eyes on the campus, in fear that it might disappear again.

Breaking through the threshold, she turned back to Olyn. He stood silent, staring out at the campus. His foot turned over a small loose cobblestone nervously. His bottom lip hid under some of his teeth as though he was bracing himself for something. "Aren't you coming with me?"

"I think you should go alone," he was quick to reply.

"But-" Iona stopped short. *Right. No humans. He knew this ahead of time, and yet he still walked with me all this way.*

"You're used to being on your own. You'll be alright."

"It's just... I don't know anyone here. Coming here was your idea in the first place."

"I know, I just can't. See?" Olyn tried to push his hand through the gate. A thick pocket of air seemed to keep him from moving forward. "The gate won't let me pass through."

Recollecting her thoughts, Iona could see that it pained Olyn to stay behind.

"I hope we meet again," Olyn stared at the dirt beneath him before turning back towards the path.

Suddenly, Iona didn't want to go. As dangerous as it clearly was out in the world for her now, Olyn was the first friend she had made in a long time.

But something within her nudged her forwards. She knew deep down that if she had any hope of finding out more about herself she had to carry on. That school contained the answers that she sought, or so she hoped.

"I hope so too," she nodded her thanks as she began to follow the path. Her heart felt heavy as she carried on without him. A not too unfamiliar feeling.

Before she made it too far up the path, she turned back towards Olyn. He was nearly out of sight when she cupped her hands around her mouth in an attempt to extend her voice. "Thank you so much for everything!" she yelled after him. She wasn't sure if the message had reached him in one piece, but he turned around all the same. A spark of determination glimmering in the distance.

Iona continued down the path with her bag in tow. It was the same travel bag that Olyn had given her the day prior. To Iona's initial surprise, it held quite a few items and didn't seem to weigh her down as much as she thought it would, making their morning trek all that much easier. As she approached the main building, she took a moment to take in the sights around her. At least three or four large dorm buildings stood off on the far side of the campus overlooking a training field that was brandished with legions of scorch marks and cuts in the concrete slabs. Bits of litter cluttered the field, remnants of training equipment that had used up its usefulness.

The main building itself was quite old, greenery peeked through cracks in the tiled courtyard, but was well-maintained on the main path. Worn footpaths wove themselves through the short grass of the campus. The monolithic limestone foundation was discolored from decades, centuries perhaps, of water running down it and yet showed no evidence of erosion. Iona noticed a series of names that had been carved into the stone towards the right side of the building, all but hidden by some tall grass. Perhaps they were the names of students long gone from the halls of Belgrum Boarding School. Vines overtook a great deal of the brick facade of the ground level, webbing their way higher and adding a splash of color to the darker wood and clay latticed walls of the upper levels. Iona imagined they would've grown on forever had nature not been curtailed by the many window ledges of the upper floors. Flowers and other herbs she couldn't even begin to identify swelled from hanging pots and boxes lining some of the stone windows.

Perhaps most imposing was the circular annex on the corner of the main building. It began on the second floor and carried up another couple stories topped with a conical roof of dark blue-gray clay shingles that matched the main roof. Huge vertical stained glass windows encircled the tower. Iona thought she saw a shadow move behind one of them but couldn't be sure.

Entering the main building, it was eerily silent throughout. Iona's ears perked up, trying to sense any sounds but could only pick out a few muffled noises up above. Looking around, she noticed a sign pointing to the main office. As she approached the door she could feel her stomach churn with anxiety. A thousand different thoughts came flooding into her mind. The bazaar, the attack. The more she thought, the more her mind drug up the past, until it was almost unbearable. Noticing that her skin had started to heat up again under the inner turmoil, she shook her head, trying not to succumb to the pressure that was slowly building up from within. Taking a deep breath, she waited for the heat to subside before continuing down the hall to the office.

As she opened the door she was baffled once more. No one. There was no one to be seen. Listening closely again, she couldn't even pick out a heartbeat, other than her own jungle beat in her chest. The office was chalk full of ornate tapestries and other foreign pieces of art. Noticing that the main desk featured a dingy teapot. She lifted it up, and feeling it empty she sat it back down again. She noticed the layers of dust caked up around its spout. She was about to turn away as the spout cover sputtered at her. Before she could investigate, it opened once more and a blue mist surged out from within. Her pulse quickened as the mist seemed to consume the room around her before condensing into a pillar-like form. After a few moments, she saw her.

It was a woman. She was neatly dressed, her blue hair tied back into sections. Her skin was a deep olive color, her features denoting some far off land Iona was unaccustomed with.

"You know, its rude to knock around someone's

house," she said, collecting herself. "I certainly wasn't expecting anyone today. You called?"

"What *are* you?" Iona was still deeply perturbed by the woman who had emerged from the teapot. As the woman shifted, it was if her aura shifted around her in odd shapes. As the mist finally settled into her, the shapes receded as well.

"A blunt one aren't you. I'm a djinn sweetie, as if you couldn't tell," she looked Iona up and down, "Well maybe *you* can't. My name is Oza, and I'm the secretary for the Headmistress." She leaned back on her desk, almost sitting atop it.

"Okay... Well," she gulped. "I was wondering if there was someone I could talk to about applying to school here."

"I see, and when were you wanting to start?" Oza said as she shuffled around her office looking for an application.

"This next trimester. If possible..."

"Oh dear. I'm not sure that'll be doable. I mean, we do have some beds available but typically we have to speak with each new prospective student's parents, and it's a whole ordeal. Not to mention, the next trimester is only a few weeks away."

"Please!" Iona roared, slamming her palms into the desk. "You don't understand. I don't *have* any other choice than to come here. I was told I could be protected here," her forearm let out a spark before she finished.

"Miss, please calm down," Oza said trying to soothe her as she backed away slowly from the desk. "Here, have a seat," she waited for Iona to calm down a little. "Now, I didn't say that it *couldn't* be done, just that it would be out of the ordinary." She meandered over to a nearby cupboard and pulled out a glass. With a wave of her hand it slowly filled with water. Setting it on the desk in front of Iona, she continued. "May I ask why you're in need of protection?"

Iona took a sip of the water. "A-a shade. Its attacked me twice so far in Ivis. I had to get away."

"I see..."

"There must be something that you can do, please," Iona was prepared to get on her knees and beg.

Oza placed her hands on Iona's shoulder. Iona could feel a strange current of air that seemed to resonate around her. She wondered what might happen if that current were to meet her flames. Instead, her body was met with a coolness as a strange sense of comfort washed over her.

"Now, what's your name?"

"I-Iona..."

"Iona, I can tell that you've been through a lot. And being hunted by a shade, that's not something to scoff at. No, it's very serious. However, I'm not the person who gets to decide whether or not you get to go to school here.

That'll be up to you and the Headmistress," Oza spun around to check the time on a nearby clock. "She should be just about done with her meeting. Once she's finished up, I can let you speak to her yourself and plead your case."

Oza directed Iona towards the top floor of the building. As Iona made her way up the stairs she started to pick up bits of a conversation. She could hear two female voices arguing from within the looming tower she saw from outside.

"After what happened last night?"

"Last night had nothing to do with the school."

"Saya, this is important. What if they make their way here?"

"I'll make preparations to revise the warding around the school. There is nothing to worry about. I'm sure they'll find what they're looking for in Ivis and then they'll leave."

"And what if they don't? What if they come here and put not only my children in harm, but all those others? Not every child has had as much training as mine have."

"I'm sure that they-"

"What if it was Melonie?"

"You know as well as anyone that I wouldn't let anything happen to her. That goes for the other students as well. Or do you think my duties start and end with my daughter?"

"How can you be so sure?"

Suddenly the door to the Headmistress' office burst forth, and a middle aged woman walked out, her piercing blue eyes darting towards Iona, taking a moment to examine her, and then back at the Headmistress. With a low growl she made her way back down the stairs.

"Sorry about that. Won't you come in?" the Headmistress said.

Iona entered to a strange scene. The Headmistress was dressed in a loose fitting shirt and comfortable looking pants. Her long black hair had been tied back while she worked in the summer heat that seemed to seep into the office through the stained glass windows of the tower. Her eyes were an iridescent purple that shimmered in the light as she moved. The office was strewn with boxes of student files and other assorted school documents. She motioned her to sit on the only chair in the room that didn't have a mountain of papers nestled into it.

Taking a seat, Iona felt compelled to ask, "What was that about? O-only if you don't mind me asking of course."

"Not at all. It was simply a courtesy call from one of our student's parents. She thought I should be aware of some local happenings over in Ivis."

"After what happened last night at the bazaar?"

"Were you listening to our conversation?"

"No, well yes, a little. It's still hard to control my hearing. It's all a bit new... to me."

"Hmn..."

"When you both mentioned the bazaar I kept listening."

"Why might that be?"

"I was there."

"So you were an eyewitness?"

"Not exactly..."

"What do you mean by that?"

"The thing that attacked the event, the shade. It was looking for me."

"Why would you think that?"

"I saw it before that day in an alley. And after it crashed the bazaar, everyone scattered. It ended up cornering me in another alleyway. I was able to fend it off, but the friend I was with got really shaken up by the whole ordeal and suggested that I come here right away. He said that you could provide asylum."

"What do you mean by *fend it off?* I'm sorry, but you must have confused a shade with something else. If it truly was a shade that you came into contact with you wouldn't be speaking with me right now. Shades don't just let their prey go. They're intense hunters and trackers by nature."

"I *know* what I saw! I was in the alley and I was able to hurt it a little, but then some guy swooped in and they just...

left."

"*You...* hurt it?" The Headmistress annunciated each word carefully.

"Yes?"

"Show me."

Iona paused, staring at her. *Is she serious?*

"Excuse me?"

"Show me how you hurt it."

"Uh... well it's hard to control, and you have a really nice flammable file collection going on here, and I'm just not sure that I would be able to," Iona could feel her cheeks starting to sting with heat.

"Well if you can't show me, then I think you need to go. I don't have time for liars."

Liars? What is she talking about? Does she seriously think I'm not in danger? Iona's eyes began to glow with heat, her hands lightly sparking like little firecrackers.

The Headmistress' iridescent eyes watched her in delight and curiosity as Iona's forearm was set aflame. A thin layer of pale white scales could be seen almost glowing beneath the embers. Iona snapped out of it as soon as she saw the grin on the Headmistress' face. Her eyes averted, as she rubbed the scales from her arm. As the heat slowly died down Iona could feel a coolness return back to her face. She was almost embarrassed by her reaction. It seemed like that was a new normal for her. Unchecked emotion. Ever since the alley she had been finding it harder and harder to keep the rage from boiling over like a burnt pot of soup.

"That was a test wasn't it?" Iona asked. Her gaze still not meeting the Headmistress'.

"You mentioned before that you couldn't control your hearing, meaning that you've only just recently come into your powers, meaning a lack of control. Anger is a great motivator, especially when it comes to showing off what you can do."

"So what now?"

"An interview."

"Right now?" The Headmistress pulled out a form from the top of a nearby pile, shuffling around for an enchanted nib to write with.

"Name?"

"Uh.. Iona. M-moran." She stuttered, still taken aback by the suddenness of her questioning.

"Parents?"

"...Dead."

"...Guardian?"

"I... don't have one."

"I'm so sorry Iona, someone such as yourself should never have been left alone."

"It's okay. It's been like this for a while now. I'm used to it." She could feel a trickle of tears forming and quickly wiped them away with a swipe of her sleeve.

"When did they? Your parents I mean, if you don't mind me asking."

"When I was six. Like I said, I've been alone for a while now." She averted her gaze to a nearby stack of student intake forms. *She's almost as bad as Olyn when it comes to clutter. I'm surprised the rest of the campus doesn't look like this.*

"Right. Let's move on then. Have you always looked like that?"

"White hair, pale skin, and red eyes? Since birth, at least that's what I thought."

"So you were blessed as a child or baby?"

"I never said-" Her attention peaked.

"That you're a dragal? Trust me, I've seen all kinds of fae, and dragals are pretty easy to point out. They stick out like sore thumbs when you compare them to most naturally occurring fae."

"Have you ever had any here at the school?"

"We had one years ago, back when the campus was based in Ivis. Sadly that was before my time working here."

"When do dragals typically awaken their power?"

"See, that's the strange part. By all accounts, you should have been in touch with some part of the dragon that blessed you starting at the time in which you both first connected. Have you ever heard voices? Or done something with prowess that you shouldn't have been able to do?"

"When I hurt the shade, it felt as if something was guiding me, showing me how to use my powers, and then today at the gate... I could read the runes. It was as if my mind could translate the text."

"But those occurrences were just within the last few days?"

Iona nodded. Her mind glossed over glimpses of *other* long forgotten events, but they remained too far in the past for her to be sure they actually happened. They appeared as blurry photographs, snapshots of things that she or someone else might have caused.

"We'll have to look more into it for you, but as it stands, there is a possibility that someone might have locked away that part of you from yourself."

"Why would someone do that?"

"Fear... maybe control? It really just depends on the person."

I don't want to believe that my parents would do that to me without good reasons. But even if my powers were sealed, it didn't suddenly make me look normal. If they wanted me to be normal, then why have me blessed in the first place? Iona took in a deep breath before quickly switching the topic of discussion.

"What kind of fae are you?"

"Excuse me?" The Headmistress was taken aback by the bluntness of the question.

"You were asking me questions, I thought it only right that I should be able to ask some."

"Touché then..." the Headmistress raised her hand to her mouth, covering a chuckle. "As you'll come to find out if you become a student, I am a banshee."

"Isn't that supposed to be like a fiendish ghost?"

"In children's tales maybe. In truth we are both a rare breed. There aren't very many of us banshees left. In fact, my daughter Melonie and I came here to Belvore when she was younger in order to see more of what the world had to offer."

"I take it you're from a small town?"

"Very small. Near the city of Aros on the western isle."

"I wouldn't know much about anywhere outside of Ivis, been there my whole life."

"Well I think you'll fit in well here. We do have some students that come from all over Leera, but most are from nearby towns and cities such as Ivis and Savin. It tends to be easier for the families if the students are still somewhat close by."

"Do you... think I'll fit in?" Iona twisted a strand of her long white hair in her hands, her anxiety starting to prick back up along her edges.

"Well that depends entirely on you. But that's not why

you came here is it? I thought you came seeking asylum."

"Asylum, enrollment, they both feel like the same thing now that we're talking about it."

"Of course, you'll have to attend classes. And I would suggest you at least *try* to pass them, we do hold ourselves to a high level of achievement for each of our students, no matter their background. Also, I might have you help out some of the teachers occasionally, given your *free* enrollment."

"What sort of help?"

"Nothing you can't handle. Things like cleaning up the practice field once the leaves start to pile up, maybe help the librarian with some of her organizing, stuff like that."

"That... sounds more than fair. Thank you Headmistress-"

"Hersch, you can call me Headmistress Hersch if you'd like. Otherwise Headmistress will work just fine."

"Thank you... Headmistress Hersch."

CHAPTER 7

Iona stood under an archway located in the courtyard of the main building. The passage overlooked a large swath of the campus. Looking out over the commons, her mind still buzzed with all that was going on. A lot had happened over the last few days and Iona hadn't yet fully caught her bearings on the situation. The buzzing felt as though someone had kicked a bee hive loose in her head, her mind darting back and forth from one event to another, to her past and her future, and sometimes everything all at once. Like a swell washing over her, pulling her down into the ocean of thoughts.

"Io...na," a voice croaked out from amidst the jumble. It was subtle and grave, like someone gasping for air. She spun around, her mind trying to resurface. Her eyes darted back and forth from the courtyard to the tree line and back again, trying to sense where the voice had come from. She turned back around towards the main building one last time to find a young girl with long black hair and emerald green eyes staring back at her. She sat in a strange chair, the sides featuring distinct wheels. Iona could hear a slight creak in the gears as the girl adjusted in her seat. Her curtain bangs seemed to flutter in the soft breeze against her forehead, strands catching in her eyelashes before she batted them back to the sides of her face.

"Iona?" she asked. Her eyes seemed to only glaze over Iona's face before returning back to the ground.

"Uh yeah..." Iona's eyes peered around the courtyard as she stepped forward, "that's me." She could feel her mind begin to settle once more.

"The Headmistress sent me to come find you," she played with the wheels as if she was rocking back and forth.

"You must be Melonie, right?" Iona asked, letting out a breath.

She stared at Iona with a peculiar look. "Saya wanted me to show you around campus, we *really* should get going." She peered around Iona before spinning the chair around, starting back off towards the inside of the building.

"Saya?" Iona pondered the name as she tried to catch up.

"Yes, well I'm sure she'd prefer you call her Headmistress Hersch."

"Why do you call your mother by her first name?"

Melonie tilted her head, confused, and laughed. "It's common for banshees. Sort of a cultural thing I guess you could say."

"Oh." Iona was impressed that the school had survived

as long as it did, hosting so many distinct fae and fiend cultures. She allowed herself a moment of wonder as Melonie continued the tour.

"I'm sure you've already seen the main building. That's where most of the classrooms are, as well as the main office, the library, and my mother's office of course."

"There's a library?"

"Yeah, what would a school be without one? We can go there first if you want."

"If you don't mind." The thought of an actual library excited her. Most of the books Iona had read she had "borrowed" or dug out of the trash.

"It's *your* tour, I can show you whatever you'd like."

Her wheels let out a screech as they came to a halt outside the library. As she reached for the door however, Melonie found it locked.

"That's strange," she said, trying to see into the dark of the room through the stained glass window embedded in the door. "I thought she was back from break already, but I guess not."

"The librarian?"

"Yeah. She goes on trips a lot. Only the gods know where, but she always comes back with the best stories."

"She sounds interesting."

"She really is," Melonie took a breath as she thought. "Well, since the library is closed, where would you like to go next?"

"We could check out the dorms?"

"Great idea."

As they approached the four towering buildings, Melonie showed her into the closest of the quad.

"This building is typically meant for wyrs, while the other three are for castors, teachers and others."

"Others?"

"That's where I live. As well as exchange students and the like, when we have some. Basically it's a space for very specific fae and fiends, as well as those with special needs, like my chair."

Making their way through the building, Iona and Melonie came to a door on the first floor. Each one featured a distinct sigil carved into the wood above the doorknob.

"More magic?"

"Each door is locked by magical means. The castors here can't even override this type of magic so it makes it very efficient when it comes to privacy."

"How do you get in though?"

"You simply place your hand on the sigil and it should open so long as you are set as an occupant of the room."

Iona placed her hand on the door, a subtle red glow flowing from the cracks underneath her.

Before Iona could ask, Melonie answered, "It reacts to

your essence. Mine always glows green, I know some others that glow gold or blue. It should be open now."

With a light turn of the knob, Iona entered the dorm. As she passed through a small hall lined with built-in bookshelves and into the greater room, she couldn't help but be taken aback by the thought of having her own space. It had been years since Iona had any sort of room to call her own. Staying with Olyn had been a nice reprieve from the years spent scrounging on the streets of Ivis, but Iona still longed for a place to belong once more. The room itself was bare but spacious, it contained two beds located on either wall in parallel to each other. What filled the space in between was a long desk that stood entrenched in the far wall itself. Bright rays of mid-day light beamed down upon the wood from the center palladian window. Iona watched for a second as the wind blew through the reeds of grass outside. Turning back, she noticed the room also contained a small bathroom and two chests, one for each of the potential students' belongings.

As Iona took in her new surroundings, there came a rustling from the hallway. With a rasp on the door, Iona opened it to see Oza holding some papers.

"Oh there you are." She was almost out of breath.

"Is something wrong?" Melonie asked.

"Oh nothing," she panted. "Sorry, I'm still getting used to being out of my teapot again," straightening herself up, she continued. "I'm just here to measure Iona for her school uniform," she said with a smile. "Care to join me dear?"

Headmistress Hersh had allowed Iona to stay for the remainder of summer vacation on the condition that she attend some summer classes. Typically, the school would have an orientation for new first-year students in mid-summer in order to figure out what classes a student was to be placed in, but for Iona, her classes were meant to help her get a handle on her abilities as well as make up for her lack of a formal education over the last decade. All within the few weeks before classes were to start back up.

The beginning of the first week was history, taught by the Headmistress herself.

"Did you get all of that down?"

"All of it except for the last bit," Iona tugged at the short white sleeves of her fitted uniform. The periwinkle bow around her neck was similarly constricting. She'd always preferred to scavenge more breathable garments off any clothesline she came across if she was in need. The one outfit she owned, that Olyn had bought for her, was fitted but breathable, unlike the boarding school's stuffy summer uniform. She had a hard enough time listening to the Headmistress without also asphyxiating from the neatly pressed clothes. "Sorry," she apologized, pulling her skirt down her legs once more. "I'm still getting used to these new clothes."

The classroom was quiet, save for the Headmistress' lesson plans and Iona's writing nib scratching across the page of her notebook. The gem embedded in the pen glowed a faint white as ink appeared on her paper. The day's sunlight streamed in through gaps in the outside tree cover, making the room feel warm and bright.

"I'll go over it again, try to pay better attention this time. Now, where was I?"

"You were starting to talk about The War of the Heavens."

"Right. It's well known that The War of the Heavens spanned several decades and cost countless lives on both sides. The war itself plunged the whole of Leera into utter chaos and despair for the better part of a few centuries after it ended in a catastrophic ordeal."

What kind of ordeal was that again? Wait, I think I remember reading about that final battle in some of my books as a kid. It was the battle that created the darklands wasn't it? The eastern islands were never the same after that.

"If it wasn't for Sirus the Moon Lord and his draconic disciples plunging Magni and his followers into exile deep within the darklands, the world would look a lot different than it does today." The Headmistress shut her textbook with a loud thud.

"Okay... so let me know if I'm getting this right. Magni set himself down the path of world destruction. And over the course of a war trying to stop him, it decimated many populations of various races, leading to one of the reasons why many are as rare as they are today. Hence where you and Belgrum come in."

"Correct. Although there is only so much that our school can do in terms of rebuilding what has been lost. We ultimately hope that our graduates will go out into the world to accomplish what our school alone never could. Unfortunately, there are *some things* that can never be replaced. The war didn't just kill humans and fae," the Headmistress' tone turned somber. "Many dragons also fell in the struggle. And many people still fear Magni to this day, I'm worried that too will never change."

"Why would they fear him? The war ended over three hundred years ago. Didn't you say he was dead?"

"He is gone, that's true. But forever? There's not a clear consensus on that. There are those that believe that he could be released onto the world once more, that he's not gone, merely trapped."

"Who would believe that load of rubbish?" Iona asked, kicking her feet up onto the desk before remembering her skirt, moving quickly to fix it once more.

"People who want to see this world burn," Headmistress Hersch stared out the classroom windows as if to appreciate the fleeting beauty of the summer day.

Chapter 8

"Eyes up front, kid. Don't get distracted."

Iona huffed as she finished her set, throwing the last remaining punch at the training dummy sitting in front of her. *Hard not to get distracted while surrounded by this circus.*

The training fields on the far side of the quad had transformed into something that resembled a war-torn battlefield mixed with a brutal playground. The course had massive pitfalls and intimidating mechanical obstacles that swept and swung through the path. Thankfully, Iona found herself in one of the many unique sparring rings. Each one mimicked a different environment. One was a swampy mess of mud and vines, with a pond with a dozen or so lily pads in its center. Another was a large sandbox complete with dunes and crests.

The ring next to Iona's consisted solely of a couple dozen upright logs which towered high into the air. They cast long shadows into the craters, cracks and scars of the concrete slab she stood on. Iona, grateful for the shelter from the sweltering summer heat, moved into the shade of one such pole and held her arms above her head in an effort to catch her breath.

While the simplest, the ring Iona stood in was by far the largest and far from featureless. The center was largely intact, some sort of metallic track forming an inner ring. Outside of it though, the foundation was split in several places with greenery reaching up through the cracks. Scorch marks plastered & darkened several areas and claw marks varied in size & depth. Many of these characteristics were shared by the dozen or so training dummies along the perimeter, though the effigies clearly had it worse. Bite marks and chunks torn out at the throat, holes blown clean through them, and faces melted from various spells cast.

It was a wonder Iona could make out any features at all. The one she was currently facing was clearly painted and proportioned to resemble some kind of demon or angel, once upon a time at least.

"You falling in love there, kid? Come on, next set."

Iona glared over at the physical training "instructor", a gangly man past his prime who reclined on top of a pile of straw mats near the bleachers that circled the entire field. The other teachers she'd met thus far had actually made an effort to appear presentable despite the school year still yet to officially begin. The ironically named Mr. Joix wore fairly casual clothing for a physical training teacher, although a light jacket set him apart from most of the other faculty members. *Who wears a jacket in this heat?* His hair also caught her eye, as a stripe of white broke through sections of jet black.

She was no stranger to cardio, but Mr. Joix pulling her from one exercise to the next was starting to kill her. *Keep him talking to catch my breath for a moment,* she thought to herself. "Why *these* ones?" She gestured at the target in front of herself.

Mr. Joix cracked a smile and peered at her. "Why? You wanna go after the wyr over there?" He nodded to a few dummies down from where she stood. Iona must have had something resembling shock in her expression. "I saw you clock it the moment you entered the ring." He explained haughtily. "Let me guess. Bad experience?"

He cleared his throat. "You know, it's not that uncommon. Lots of wyrs have problems with anger issues, comes with the territory of their nature, but not all of them are bad. Hell, some of us even get to help people."

Iona took in his scent. It wasn't the same as Bernard, but it was similar enough. A scent of musk and dirt mixed with a lingering of honey. Irritated at his insight, Iona's brow twitched and she had to remind herself to control her breathing. "I mean, why am I hitting these targets of fae and fiends, and why from like *three feet away?* Isn't that like attacking other students at the school?"

Mr. Joix snorted. "You're kids. Eventually, somebody

is gonna spill someone's secret about such and such wants to break up with whoever. Blah blah blah," he threw an uncaring hand up in the air and let it fall before hopping down from his perch. "Better you take your anger out on these guys rather than each other," he walked over to the target nearest him and traced the claw mark carved through its chest. "Besides, it's one thing for you kids to fling your abilities at a bullseye down range. You need to understand what it means to use it on someone right in front of you. You gotta remember, most of these kids have lived with these abilities since primary school. You're basically a baby with your current understanding and experience." He sighed, "Just hit the target."

Unconvinced, Iona crossed her arms. "Then where's your's? You have all these different ones, but not one of *whatever* you are," she jestered to him up and down. Her nose still unable to pinpoint what he was. She could sense something within him, but it was unclear to her just what lurked underneath his skin. "At least give me something I *want* to hit."

Mr. Joix stopped and looked at her seriously, maybe for the first time, before breaking out into a large grin. A minute later, Iona was standing in the center of the inner ring as the instructor finished installing a new dummy inside the metallic track. "This here is my favorite training tool," The effigy was a strange caricature of a wyr that someone had used to try and capture some of Mr Joix's more prominent features: the silver line running down the center of his otherwise jet black hair, a bushy tail trailing along the bottom, the evil grin and pointy horns on the forehead. Well, clearly the last two involved a degree of creative liberty, but the likeness was there. It looked like Mr. Joix for all intents and purposes, aside from the metal bar running through its center and down into the track set in the ground. Giving it an experimental push, Mr. Joix nodded, pleased when the training dummy made a complete circle around Iona.

"A couple students a few years ago had the same thought you did, so they made this and asked if they could use it," Mr. Joix seemed strangely proud rather than offended as he stared at it. "I told them they could, as long as I got to make a few adjustments first." Using a stick he'd retrieved along with the dummy, he hit one of the arms which spun on some kind of rotating axis. Iona slid back to avoid getting hit. She noted the other arm and both legs having similar mechanisms.

Noting the X at her feet, Iona smirked. "Okay, I get it."

Mr. Joix matched her cocky grin. "Good, I hate over-explaining myself. Now you'll note our handsome friend here, while lacking a fresh coat of paint, is missing the cuts, burns, and bashes our other friends have accumulated," he brushed some dust off its shoulder and pat it proudly on the head. "Our dummy Mr. Joix has never once been struck during his short tenure here at Belgrum."

Mr. Joix had begun circling Iona. She now stood between him and the dummy. "Never, huh?" she laughed. Quickly, she reared her fist back and threw it forward, only to nearly lose her balance as her hand passed through the air, hitting nothing. The back of her head stung for a moment, but quickly subsided. Spinning around, she saw that the dummy had gotten behind her, the arm spinning as an inner mechanism slowed it to a stop with a *click, click, click.*

She startled as Mr. Joix cleared his throat, and she looked forward again to see him standing next to where the dummy had been a moment before. "Never," he confirmed. "You may begin."

A small bit of steam bellowed out of Iona's nostrils as she returned to the stance they had practiced. Narrowing her eyes, Iona tried to focus on increasing the strength in her arms. Small flames flitted about as she took another lunge at the target. This time she saw him. Mr. Joix, fast as lightning, dashed around to the other side of the inner ring, first delivering a blow with his stick to the right leg of the dummy and then to the base that connected it to the track. That's when her vision blurred and she lost sight of him. A bolt of pain shot from her knee a moment after the dummy had disappeared from her vision, forcing her to the ground. "Again," she glanced up, the sun making her squint. The humor was gone from Mr. Joix's expression, replaced by something more sinister. "Come on, kid. Get up." Iona complied, and this interaction repeated itself many times with occasional advice.

"Don't just rely on brute strength. Access and act."

Growing increasingly irritated at his comments, Iona, after cursing the old man under her breath, decided to make a few of her own. "How do you move so fast? Just what are you, old man?" she spit on the ground. "I've never seen a wyr move like that."

"Didn't Saya scoop you off the street? I'm sure there's a *lot of things* you've never seen before," he hit the dummy away from one of her retaliatory strikes.

Saya? So they're on a first name basis too, huh.

"Must have been tough making it on your own." She thought she heard a twinge of empathy or respect in his voice before quickly dismissing it after receiving a kick to the rear. "The Policing Guild only offers two options for those that go in as human. You either die young, or survive long enough to retire as an unhappy old man with a few abilities. The former was taken already," Mr. Joix noticed the flames on Iona's arms grow larger.

Rolling her eyes, Iona let her frustration fuel three quick jabs, all missing, of course. *The Policing Guild is filled with sanctimonious jerks. They never seemed to have time to help me when I needed it.* A flash of a blood filled kitchen flitted through her mind. Instead of throwing her off, it fueled her punches. *They never stop to help anyone, they just blow through town every once in a while to chase down a query.*

"So you're what, here to scout out threats at the school? See which of us *problem cases* will give you headaches in the future?"

Mr. Joix's brow twitched. *Touchy subject?* He matched some of her irritation in his own voice. "Got stones in your ears, kid? I already told you, I'm retired from the Guild," realizing that this girl was getting the better of his emotions, he simmered down before launching both of the dummy's arms forward. Catching her off-guard, the blow connected and nearly pushed Iona out of the ring. He let out the kind of sigh you would expect from someone of his age. "Look, I'm here as a favor."

Iona was busy rubbing the pain out of the leg she'd fallen on, but this made her raise an eyebrow. "A favor? What kind of favor?"

"The *maybe I can bring some semblance of security to this place* kind of favor. And who knows? Maybe I can teach *you* some semblance of control in the meantime."

Hearing the emphasis in his words, Iona raised an indignant eyebrow "Me?"

"Yeah, you," Mr. Joix approached her with arms crossed. Although thin and wiry, he still towered over her, and he used his height to bore into her with his piercing gray eyes. "Let's not forget how you discovered your powers. A moment of anger that nearly burned down the market."

"It wasn't like that..." thinking back to the alley and the shade that had attacked sent a shiver down her spine. "I just- It was survival instinct. I was fighting for my life."

"Exactly!" Mr. Joix emphatically pointed. "Instinct." He spat the word out and it looked like it made him nauseous. "Kid, I've been around a lot longer than you have. I've seen good men, women, and children torn apart by that instinct of yours." He threw a thumb in the direction of the school's main building "The kids going here have been using their powers a lot longer than you. I don't have to worry about *them* burning down the school. And you know what they have that makes me think that?"

Iona raised an eyebrow. "Non-dragon related powers?"

Mr Joix knelt in front of her and took her hands. Surprised and not wanting to burn him as her arms were still alight, she tried to step back but he held her firm. Momentary panic made her flames grow which she realized caused Mr. Joix's greased back hair to glimmer in the heat. Embers were rolling off the sleeves of his jacket and floating into the air. *Enchanted.* Iona realized then and there that Mr. Joix was probably a lot smarter than she'd previously given him credit for.

Now about half a head shorter than her, she met his gaze, an almost pleading tinge to his eyes, like if she was ever going to listen to him it should be now. "Control," he corrected her. "They have *control*."

He waited for her to calm down but her flames continued to bubble up. He noticed and gently let go of her hands. "Stop the fire."

She was so intently staring at him, she had barely noticed that her scales had appeared. Surprised, she shook her head as the flames died down. "I thought I was supposed to be *learning* to control my powers."

"So show me you can control them. Simmer down, keep your temper under control. Don't let your powers control you."

Exhausted and hurting all over, Iona finished her set against the dummy. "Good, good," Mr. Joix nodded. "That's enough for today," staggering backward, she regarded her instructor as he withdrew an old fashioned pipe from his pocket and began patting himself down looking for something else. Glancing up at her, he held it out to her. "You mind?"

Sighing, Iona reached forward. Mr. Joix recoiled slightly, mocking caution. "Easy now," He said smiling.

Iona allowed herself a tired laugh. Holding up her hand, Iona stared at her pointer finger. She could feel the flames boiling and churned beneath every pore of her skin before becoming concentrated in her hand. It was a feeling she'd grown accustomed to, maybe even taken for granted. The flames had always come forth when she needed them, but also when she hadn't. Her skin glowed slightly before a small spark erupted from the tip of her finger.

She imagined the flames in her hand funneling down into the index finger, her scales appearing and disappearing as her power rolled its way through her arm. Her skin glowed slightly underneath the white scales that traveled from the knuckle to the fingertip which grew pointed and black. Pushing the heat just a bit further, Iona was mesmerized by the small candle-like flame that sat atop of the claw-like nail.

Mr. Joix cleared his throat and held out his pipe to which Iona promptly lit it with a capricious grin. He returned a slight smile.

The thought of being taught by Mr. Joix started to grow on Iona as she thought that maybe she wouldn't mind his teaching style after all. He raised an eyebrow at her hand, "You can put that out now, kid."

He chuckled while puffing on his pipe. Although his demeanor changed quickly when someone called out to them from the training ground entrance. "Ah! Iona, Mr. Joix, there you are!"

Coughing uncontrollably, he tried to straighten his attire the best he could, Mr. Joix turned to greet

Headmistress Hersch while holding the pipe behind his back. Iona raised an eyebrow at the two of them before greeting her as well.

"Good afternoon, ma'am." Mr. Joix suddenly straightened his back. He seemed unable to look at the Headmistress outside of a few seconds, his eyes glancing around the scenery instead.

"It is, isn't it?" the Headmistress smiled. She gazed softly at Mr. Joix. The uncomfortable silence that followed was enough to make Iona wince.

"Soo..." Iona said, letting out an uncomfortable shriek.

Remembering why she was there, the Headmistress continued forward, stepping into the ring with them. "Yes, I was on my way to see Ms. Heisengroph and then I remembered your next tutoring session is with her. Would you care to accompany me, Iona?"

Glancing back and forth between the two of them for a moment, Iona processed her question. "Yeah...I guess..." She noticed Mr. Joix's eye twitch, likely at having to clean up the equipment they'd used by himself, but uncharacteristically he did not let his annoyance be known. Iona began packing everything she'd brought into her bag, watching the two older adults out of the corner of her eye. *I wonder what's up with those two.*

The Headmistress, taking a step closer seemed to make Mr. Joix more fidgety, but if the Headmistress noticed, she seemed to wave it off. "The faculty and I will be dining together tonight. Can we expect you?"

"I uhm... I don't know if- Well, I wouldn't want to- Uhm..." Iona noted out of the corner of her eye the way Mr. Joix's demeanor resembled that of a crumbling wall, the bricks falling over one another in a disastrous mess. "It might be-"

"I would enjoy your presence tonight, *Axel*."

"...If it pleases you, ma'am."

Iona had retrieved her school uniform and rejoined them. She noticed Mr. Joix's defeated expression. The wall had truly crumbled. She glanced over at the Headmistress and noticed her nose twitch. She held out her hand expectantly. Iona watched as Mr. Joix complied, handing her the pipe he'd hid behind his back. The Headmistress casually took it by the stem before breaking it in half and placing it back into Mr. Joix's waiting hand. "Thank you, ma'am." He sounded like he was almost happy.

Turning to Iona, the Headmistress nodded. "Are you ready, my dear?"

"I just have one quick question about our training today, I'll catch up in a sec."

The Headmistress nodded before she started heading back towards the main campus. Once she was out of earshot, Mr. Joix growled, "What?"

They both stared at the Headmistress walking off in the

distance. "There are no cutouts of banshees." Iona stated with a smile.

"That wasn't a question."

"Nope."

Growling audibly again, Mr. Joix turned and grabbed the training dummy that held his likeness and ripped it out of the track. "Get going, kid."

Iona jogged to catch up the Headmistress, biting her cheek to keep from smirking.

CHAPTER 9

The transformations classroom was laid out differently than the others Iona become accustomed to so far. Instead of the neat and tidy rows of desks and barren walls, there were hand drawn diagrams and anatomical models of different species scattered about in a way that would make you think it was a science classroom. Which in a way, transformation was a science.

The room also featured a prominent staging area towards the front. A small changing room could be seen off to its left. Iona stopped herself as the Headmistress entered the room. The only other person, a woman with stark red hair, sat hunched over a desk facing the right side of the far wall. *I take it that's Heisengroph.* Iona took a seat towards the back of the classroom, taking the time to reorganize her belongings after being swept away from her physical training class so abruptly. Sweat was still smeared on her cheeks and forehead. Wiping a towel across her face, she couldn't help up overhear their conversation. The classroom wasn't the largest, and her hyperacusis didn't help.

"Ah, Fern. I knew I'd find you toiling about." Her voice was heavy but sweet.

"I heard the both of you on your way over. I assume it's my turn to take over?"

"Don't act like that, I know you love your students."

"I have far too many new second-years to prep for, and now you're giving me an entirely new species of fae to wrap my head around in my research," she sighed. "Sometimes Saya, I feel that you ask too much of me."

Iona bit the inside of her cheek sullenly.

"Oh come now, I only give you what I think you can handle."

Heisengroph raised her head from the desk, gathering in a large breath. *Is she smelling me?*

"Did you have to bring them straight from Joix? Could've at least let them shower."

"*She* can shower after you have have a chance to work with *her*. And in terms of new species I could have done worse," Headmistress Hersh spun Heisengroph's body around.

"Oh..." Ms. Heisengroph stared at Iona for a second before turning back to the Headmistress. "*OH,*" She sounded as though something finally clicked in her head.

"Okay, I guess we should start with the basics. Do you know the three main tenets of transformation?" asked Ms. Heisengroph, her long red hair almost obscuring her vision through her glasses. Now that Iona could get a better look at her teacher she appeared slightly more aged than the Headmistress, however Iona could sense that she was much older than she looked. Her soft features reminded Iona of Saya and Melonie, but for whatever similarities the three possessed, Heisengroph's bright hair separated them.

"Considering I thought I was human until a few weeks ago, no I do not."

"Okay... so that's where we're starting off at. The three tenets are feeling, focus, and function."

"Meaning?"

"Meaning that transformations can be caused by different... opportunities, as I like to call them. Intense emotion can cause a wyr to change and react without thinking about their intentions behind why they are changing. For example, rage."

"So they turn into monsters."

Ms. Heisengroph gave Iona a piercing glance. "What a wyr does with their power is up to them. Just being a wyr doesn't make them a monster. Some wyrs have a very easy time controlling their emotions. Like anyone, *people* can have anger issues, or abuse the power they hold."

Iona bit her cheek to keep from speaking aloud. *You've probably never been on the receiving end of that kind of abuse.*

"The next tenet is focus. When we focus, we often have much more control over what piece of us transforms, making selective transformation achievable. This is what I usually focus on when teaching second-years. However, for you we'll need to focus on full transformation first before anything else."

"What makes selective transformation useful?" Iona asked impatiently.

"It helps give the student more control over their body. For example, a wyr might only transform their eyes so that they can see better in the dark. A lot of my students find that exercise particularly easy though, given many fae do small adjustments like that involuntarily in response to their outside environment. But it's always good practice to be able to stop your eyes from adjusting, to introduce choice to your body. Sometimes you don't want to see in the dark, sometimes you do. You get it?"

"I guess... My body generates scales along my skin in order to insulate me from my own fire. Are we going to learn how to stop those scales from forming?"

"Eventually, maybe. But for now? Gods no. You'd only end up burning yourself. Our bodies create defense mechanisms for a reason, so unless you *want* to burn yourself, I suggest you don't try it. But, while we're on the topic, how hot do your flames have to be before your scales appear?"

Iona hadn't thought much about it. But thinking back, she realized that her scales didn't always surface. "Sometimes if the fire is cooler on my skin or it feels like its hovering just above it the scales don't come out. However, if I want to burn something, or I get too emotional, then they coat my body fairly quickly.

"Good to know," Ms. Heisengroph said as she jotted down some notes. Seeing her write reminded Iona of Olyn. *I wonder if the two of them would get along.*

"The last of the three tenets is function. Selective transformation in it of itself can be used for specific functions, but so can full transformation. For a wyr, it could be jump starting the healing process, and for you it could be sprouting wings to carry you."

Iona was dumbstruck. "Say again?" *Wings? What does she mean, wings?*

"Look, it's all speculative at this point. I did some digging through the archives for any mention of the last dragal that was enrolled in the school. And I found some scribbled notes about the formation of dragon-like features, not uncommonly like your scale-mail situation. But there must be more... For there to be so little written down, it's almost as if someone didn't want the information out there."

"So you don't know exactly what I can do?"

"Of course not, but we're going to try to narrow it down anyway. The faster we do that, the quicker we'll gain some information about the dragon you're connected to."

"What do you mean connected?" *Now that she mentions it, didn't the Headmistress mention something about a connection?*

"Did Saya not explain? Huh... well maybe I have better research sources than the Headmistress. Sorry, I'll walk you through it," Heisengroph drew in a breath. "When a Dragal is blessed by a dragon, a portion of that dragon's power is passed onto that being. When this happens it's known as essence synergy. Which, in turn, creates a psychic link between the holder and its source."

"And what if I'm not connected to a dragon?"

"Well, its not really heard of, but I guess it could be possible. We probably won't know for sure until we strengthen your connection to your powers."

"How do we do that?"

"With practice," Heisengroph shook her hands sarcastically.

Heisengroph directed Iona to the staging area at the front of the classroom. Grabbing a pail of water, she sat it on the floor next to Iona with a light pang of the metal against the tiled flooring that harshly stood out against the wooden floorboards underlying the rest of the classroom.

"For this first lesson, why don't we just see what you can do," she explained as she sat back down with her notebook.

"You *do* know the last time I used my whole body, I exploded right?"

Heisengroph scooted her chair back a few more feet from Iona.

"Okay then. Try to go slow. If you feel yourself starting to lose control try to breath and work through it slowly."

Easy for you to say. Iona closed her eyes in a slight chuff. Holding her breath, she could feel the air in her lungs begin to heat up. She focused on radiating it out towards her skin. Soon she could feel a light hum of flames dancing around her like tumbleweeds in the desert wind. They moved along with the air that surrounded her. It felt like she was in some sort of bubble. Her scales began to pock her skin as the heat around her grew. As she opened her eyes she could feel a crest of scales around her face. Releasing control for just a moment, the bubble seemed to pop. Hot air blew past Heisengroph. Her long skirt brushing past her ankles. Heisengroph swooped down to scratch at the fabric as it scraped her leg. Her long flowing skirt parted ever so slightly, long enough for Iona to notice long burn marks emanating up from her feet.

Heisengroph seemed to take no notice of Iona's gaze.

Iona wondered for a moment what might have caused the burns. Her mind shifting sharply back to her own callous thoughts that seemed in hindsight to disregard Ms. Heisengroph's lived experiences. *Tsk.* She looked away from Heisengroph for a moment as the heat dissipated abruptly.

"Can I try that again?" Iona asked sullenly, rubbing her wrist while it was still warm to the touch.

"Ready to try again so soon? Okay, we'll go with a different technique this time."

Chapter 10

Iona awoke to find Melonie sitting outside of her door. She was dressed in a white blouse with a light periwinkle plaid dress laid over top that reached almost to her ankles before being broken up by some thick socks and shoes that looked like they hadn't been worn at all.

"I was wondering when you'd get up."

Iona brushed her long hair in her hands. "Yeah, training and classes has really been taking it out of me. I was excited when the Headmistress said I could have a few days off."

"Days off? You mean the weekend? Everyone gets the weekend off," Melonie started rolling down the hall.

Iona stood, processing what she had said, before running off after her in a hurry, "What do you mean the weekend? What day did I get here?"

"You started training on the fifth, and now it's the eleventh."

"So it's already been six days huh..." Iona stated sleepily. She stretched her arms up over her head with a yawn.

"Any plans?"

"Sleep sounds good. Hah... I'm still sore from where Joix hit me during our sparring lesson." She massaged her sides as she tried to keep up with Melonie.

"Muscle training?"

"Feels more like anger management training."

"Really? You don't strike me as the type to burst on people."

"Before, I used to just keep it to myself. Kinda had to just put up with it. Got bullied and beat on a lot when I was little. Hell, even just last week," Iona sighed. "And, well... after my powers were awakened I've been finding it harder and harder to keep things bottled up the same way I did before."

"You heal quickly now, don't you?" Melonie tapped Iona's stomach playfully with her arm.

Iona winced before realizing that it didn't actually hurt. Somewhere deep inside her the phantom pain from years past still rang out. "Sorry, force of habit."

Melonie looked out at her, worry painted itself over her face. She wondered to herself about what kind of life Iona must have lived before arriving at Belgrum, as well as how that life might change now that she was there. Her wheels squeaked beneath her as she pondered her own life here at the school. It hadn't been perfect by any stretch of the imagination, but the school was her home, and it had been a while since anyone like Iona had crossed her path. It wasn't so much her appearance, but rather her personality. For all of the pain that she kept locked away, Melonie could sense the kindness the girl possessed. She found herself catching glimpses of it when she otherwise thought she wouldn't. She chuckled to herself at the thought of this rough and tumble young girl fighting her way through hordes of fae on the streets of what seemed like some far off city.

They found themselves back in the courtyard where they had met. Benches lined the area as shaded walkways stood as easy passage from one side of the main building to the other. The centerpiece of the yard was a glistening fountain not yet trickling with water again. It seemed everywhere Iona went on campus, things were just about ready to wake up for another year of learning. Taking a seat on one of the nearby benches, Iona made way for Melonie's chair.

"So what's with that chair thing you're always going around in?" Iona peered over at the strange mechanical contraption. "I don't think I've ever come across one before."

"Oh this?" she chuckled as if it was an unfamiliar question. "It's just my way of getting around. Ever since I was a little my legs haven't worked the same as other people."

"Where do you even get something like that?"

"Back where Saya's from, there's this place called Argo. It's a big city that provides a lot of resources for those that are interested in technological research. They have plenty of prototypes for chairs like these there. They aren't as widely used here in Belvore because of the large wyr population and other fae that can heal quickly."

"So you can't heal like I do?"

"No. Unfortunately, as a banshee our powers help keep us alive and fed most of the time, but they don't do much in the way of accelerating healing. Even so, if I could heal it wouldn't help, it's more of a condition rather than a disease. Ever since I was born my legs seem to bow inward whenever I try to walk. Even though I can feel and use my legs, I'm a lot faster and mobile using the chair. It's just how it is."

"Oh. Well, your chair is still pretty cool though. My legs get tired from walking around all day, I think it'd be nice to have something like that sometimes too."

"My legs don't ache but my arms get that way if I roll around a lot. It takes a decent amount of strength to go places. Thankfully, I don't have a lot of places to go."

There was a brief moment of silence. Iona took the time to move from the bench to laying in the grass beneath them. The sky above was bright blue with golden clouds. *I wonder what it must be like for her. To live here and only here. Melonie seems so gentle and yet so lonely. She reminds me of myself, not too long ago.* As she stared up at the shimmering scene she asked another question that weighed on her mind.

"Do you ever hear things?"

Melonie paused for a moment in contemplation. "Like what?"

"Voices calling your name? That day you met me here... I could have sworn I heard a someone calling my name."

"*I* was calling your name."

"Yeah, but it sounded different than your voice. It was slower and deeper, like an older man was speaking. It kinda freaked me out until I noticed you and I were the only two people in the courtyard."

"And that didn't freak you out even more?"

Iona shot up. "Well... yes? No? I don't know. I mean I only heard it the once or twice maybe... I don't know if it will *keep* happening."

"When do you think it started?" Melonie asked, a curious look furrowing deeper into her face.

"Maybe when my powers were awakened? But I could swear that the voice seemed familiar somehow, I just can't seem to place it."

"Did you tell the teachers about it?"

"Hah... they'd probably just think I was crazy," Iona

laid back down, arms stretched outwards. Her mind flitted back to when she was still only six years old. A blurry light danced around her, she couldn't quite remember what it looked like in detail. But the presence was remembered with a similar familiarity. *No one back then believed me. Instead I ended up locked up in a trunk at the orphanage and laughed at.* Iona closed her eyes tightly as she shook the memories from her mind. Her eyes fluttered open to the sky, Melonie's dress flowing in the breeze beside her.

As her body relaxed into the grass she began to hear the wind rustling through the trees. Focusing on the world around her, she shut her eyes, taking in the light through the pinks of her eyelids.

"Iona?" she could hear Melonie ask, but something was off about her voice. It sounded as though it was being echoed around her. Opening her eyes, she sat up straight away. Surrounding her was nothing but an all-consuming darkness.

"Io...." a gravelly voice spoke from the abyss.

"At last the monster speaks," she said sarcastically.

"Am I?"

"What?"

"A monster." Suddenly flames shot out from all around her, consuming her whole.

When Iona opened her eyes again, Melonie had her hand on Iona's shoulder trying to calm her down. A light simmering flame lingered on the opposite arm. Iona cupped her hand against the fiery skin, quickly extinguishing it.

CHAPTER 11

"Now you're getting it!" Mr. Joix yelled triumphantly as Iona launched some small balls of fire at the encroaching targets. "This time, let's try something a bit different."

"Lemme guess, a massive fireball?" Iona panted, almost doubling over trying to recover some mana from exerting herself.

"No, I was thinking more like *breathing* fire," he stood with his arms crossed.

Iona giggled to herself. "The day I breathe fire is the day I finally burn that ugly jacket of yours."

Mr. Joix bent down to where Iona felt like she was dying. Looking straight at her he said, "Nice try kid, but if you want to get stronger maybe you should learn some manners too while you're at it. Which professor is teaching that?"

"Ya' know, I know a wyr-bear twice your size that would say I have better manners than half of Ivis," Iona huffed. "Granted, most of the folks he interacts with are drunk half the time." She sighed, "Fine, we'll try your thing. But I really don't think it's going to work."

Walking back over to his position at the side of the training field, he explained. "When dragons breathe fire the salivary glands in their mouth secrete a liquid that coats their throat making it more heat resistant. If what Heisengroph told me over the weekend is true, then you should be able to do it."

"And just what were you and Miss Fern doing over the weekend? Hmm?"

"That's Ms. Heisengroph to you. Believe it or not, I do in fact have friends."

Shocking. "Okay, but where do I start though. Making fireballs is easy enough with some concentration, but I don't want to try dry heaving until flames come out."

"Well... once you start making the flames internally you'll need to release them. It's a very hard process to stop once started, and it could be detrimental to your body if you don't release the pent up energy correctly," he explained. "In terms of where to start however, I think you should have a proper handle on the process. Think about how we started with the fireballs. Focus on what you want to happen, and work your way towards that goal. Do that, and you'll easily be able to do stuff like this," as he spoke, his hand shifted into claws, his nails changing into hardened black talons.

Show off. Iona rolled her eyes as she turned away from him. Focusing on her lungs, she listened to her breathing go in and out. Back and forth. *We'll add a little heat, and then direct it towards the inside of my chest.* Mr. Joix could see flames flickering in and out down her arms, seemingly moving towards her chest before disappearing altogether. Iona turned back to face him, Mr. Joix was taken aback by her glowing red eyes that seemed to dance with the remnants of the flames that surrounded her. Her face was visibly red from the heat. *This feels strangely like vomiting.* Iona thought as she could feel the heat in her belly surge up and out, not unlike acidic bile bubbling up after tasting rancid food. A surge of thin flames spewed towards Joix. He quickly dodged out the way, letting out a sudden growl that made Iona lose her concentration. The remaining flames were instead inhaled back within her. Causing her to hack and wheeze as if her insides were on fire. She could feel the smoke rising off her lungs, the heat still hiding amongst the branching bronchioles. After a quick coughing fit, she was once again met with Joix's callous smirk.

"*Cheeky.* Better luck next time."

The transformations classroom too had changed its form over the course of the summer lessons. Seemingly sporting more and more anti-fire equipment every time Iona stepped foot in the room. A barrage of desks had been piled up as an in-case-of-emergency protection for the professor. Even though she didn't really seem eager to dodge behind them. Heisengroph looked less disheveled. This time her red hair was tied back and kept out of her face, save for her bangs and fly aways.

"This time when you focus, allow the flames to slowly overtake you."

"Isn't that a bit dangerous professor?"

"Yes, but more so for me than you. But don't worry, I have the blockade to protect me if you start sputtering out fire again," she patted the mound just as one of the desks fell loose beside her. She flashed a half hearted smile before moving the fallen desk out of the way.

"I can see that," Iona stared out concernedly at her.

"Now that that's out of the way, let's return back to the lesson. Focus, allowing the flames to come naturally, try to coax them out using calm rather than intense emotion, like we practiced."

Iona took a few steps back from the edge of the tiled stage and closed her eyes. She opened her mind to a calm vision of a warm fire. *A simmer not a spark, controlled not raging.* Within minutes, her skin began to feel like it was a pot of water heated up to a light simmer. Iona slowly opened her eyes to find that white and grey scales had sprouted up underneath the small flames that coated her body.

"Well done," Heisengroph smiled. "Now, focus your intent on increasing the intensity of your power, but keep the size of your flames the same."

"So you mean just make it hotter?" Iona huffed, trying to keep her concentration from wavering.

Fern batted a fan towards her face. The room had grown quite sweltering in all but a few minutes. "Exactly. By increasing your overall power we can see if there are any parts of your transformative abilities that have yet to be rooted out."

I can't help but feel like she's starting to treat me like a toy...

Iona closed her eyes once more and concentrated. In her mind she could see a dial, as Iona slowly turned it she could feel the heat beginning to rise. There came a great amount of pressure that began to form on her back. As the dial further turned, the heat arose and so did the pressure, small sparks of pain nipped at her until finally she fell to her knees. The pressure and pain quickly subsided. As Iona opened her eyes she could see Heisengroph staring out at her, mouth agape, as if something was wrong.

"Well, I wasn't expecting that so soon," she dashed around her desk trying to quickly grab some of her notes.

"Did something go wrong? My back feels strange," Iona said in an almost gravel-like tone.

"Oh, I wasn't expecting that either. The heat seems to

have altered your vocal pattern somehow. That paired with the scales and wings makes you the perfect candidate for Ms. Junior Dragon," she couldn't help but chuckle.

"Wings?" Iona asked, her voice still quite messy. Tilting her head to the side, she could see the overarching mass that Heisengroph described. There they were, white and grey scales adorning an otherwise fiery interior of red elastic fibers fit for flying, small flames danced around the hulking wind sails.

Iona's thoughts began to race as she felt her mind start to swim, her vision narrowing. She stared at herself in the mirror that hung on the outside of the small changing booth, the base of her wings twitched as she watched. The new appendage had torn through her button down, burning threads unable to close up once more. She reached out to see if they were real. The rubbery softness of the red inners turned over in her fingers before retching out of her grasp. *I think I'm going to be sick.* Iona braced herself on a podium nearby. Her taloned claws burning into the wood. As the heat began to boil over, Miss Heisengroph quickly gathered up her things, ushering Iona through the classroom's back door.

The cool air outside hit Iona like a tidal wave. Her mind was able to cool down and process the weight a bit better. The heat along her body subsided as drops of rain fell on her skin and her mind began to calm. Scales receded from her cheeks, still lingering around her back and her arms. Drops of water withered into steam as the rain started to pick up. Out in the open, her wings began to do little stretches as they expanded and contracted freely. Seeing how they moved while the rest of her body remained still sent a shiver down her spine.

As the flames died out, the wings returned from whence they came. Miss Heisengroph gaped at the ease in which they melded back into Iona's body.

"*SO* glad I got to see that," she said rather chipper, almost skipping back into the classroom.

Iona took a moment for herself, staring out over the training field in the distance. The sun was just about to set underneath the approaching clouds as Iona turned back towards the classroom. An aching twinge of pain resonated out from her upper back. Trying to scratch at the spot, she finished with a gentle exhale. Pulling her hand away she found that her fingernails had transformed into sharp talons. Shaking out her hand, the long claws quickly slid back into their normal form. *Accidental selective transformation?* Walking back into the classroom, she noticed Heisengroph sketching out what looked like an anatomical diagram. Peering around the room again, Iona quickly noticed the stylistic similarities between her's and all the other diagrams that hung about.

"That looks very realistic," Iona said. The piece that

she was working on appeared to be taking the form of wings. Small marks turned into scales as she continued.

"Thank you. One of my talents is that I can create drawings of anything I see. I can even manipulate them, such as turning them into diagrams."

"Is it magic?"

"In a way you could say that. It's not a common ability amongst fae like me... actually my kind tend to have all sorts of strange talents. There are definitely those with more useful innate skills, but these diagrams do make my job a whole lot easier."

"How so?"

"It allows me to create a diagram of each of my students, in both their human and fae forms, which can help them to better understand how their body changes to adapt to their abilities. I always say, transformation is eighty percent physical and twenty percent mental. I teach the mental aspect in my classes and my diagrams help me teach the physical. By allowing a student to study their own physiology they gain a greater understanding of how their body works," she explained. Her eyes glanced over Iona's shoulder. "Oh Iona dear, could you turn around for me?"

"What is it?" Iona turned so that her back was facing Ms. Heisengroph. The remnants of her shirt still laid in tatters upon her, small flecks of dried blood caked up on her skin around where the wings had burst forth.

"The whole back of your shirt is ripped up," she said as she picked at the burnt fibers. "The wings must have burnt through the back when they erupted out. I'll have to put in a request with Oza to enchant your uniform again, as well as your other clothes, but for now you should probably change out of them. They're already enchanted against tears, but I guess this kind of damage isn't exactly normal wear and tear now is it?" she stopped for a moment before moving back a piece of fabric from Iona's upper back. "Huh... that's strange."

"Stranger than wings burning holes through my clothing?"

"Well... In combination with some slit shaped marks on your back, which is likely where your wings came out, you also have some sort of birthmark squared up with your shoulder blades."

"How is a birthmark strange?" Iona moved away to grab a spare shirt from the box of extras Ms. Heisengroph kept on hand for classes.

"I've never seen anything like it. It almost appears as though it's a sigil of some sort. But... it couldn't be."

"Why can't it be a sigil? I'm blessed right? Couldn't that be it? The blessing or whatever?" Iona asked while she exchanged clothing behind the changing room divider.

"Normally, a mark of some kind is a common occurrence with curses, but this mark... I've never seen one like it, and so smooth against your skin as well! For a procedure that clean, the person who placed it on you must have been a lot more proficient in whatever magic they used than your average castor."

How did I not notice something like that before? Was it there before? Wait... "It's not a tracker is it?" she asked as she made her way out from the changing room.

"No, no, something that advanced might as well be in the form of a trinket, not a sigil. Although certain sigils can be quite powerful. I'm afraid I wouldn't even know where to begin with this. If you've fared alright this far while having it, it should be fine to leave it alone for the time being."

"So I'm just stuck with it?" Iona thought back to her conversation with the Headmistress when she'd first arrived. "Is there any chance that the sigil might be the cause of my power repression?"

"It *is* possible I suppose. I would think it's very unusual for a dragal, even in this day and age, to have grown up unable to use their abilities..."

"How, I mean *who* would have put it there?" Iona's hands began to shake. Her body felt violated. She could feel herself grow small as she receded inward.

Ms. Heisengroph laid her hand on Iona's shoulder in an attempt to ground her back to reality. "I'm not sure who did this to you, but the fact that you've been able to access your power is a good indication that whatever spell was placed on you must be starting to weaken. If you like, I can try looking into the particular sigil, but I'm not sure how much help I can be. I'm not as well versed in sigil work as perhaps some of the other facility members are."

Iona took a deep breath trying to keep her mind from racing.

"I take it that's all for tonight's lesson?"

"Iona..."

Iona brushed past her as she went to gather her things.

Heisengroph paused. "The Headmistress was hoping to speak with you before classes started. But I'm afraid she's a little predisposed at the moment with another later register. And from what she's told me, I'm going to be up to my tail in research over the last few days before classes officially start."

"Well, good luck with that," Iona said in a pouting tone, not really paying attention.

"Oh, and leave your shirt with me. I'll have Oza mend it and put in an order for the fire resistance enchantment along with the rest of your things she's prepped for you," her voice wavered sweetly, as if she was trying to glide around exploding eggshells.

"Sounds good," she said plainly, dropping off her dilapidated shirt on a desk by the door on her way out.

The way back to the dorm was fairly dark. A light mist

had formed in the humid heat of the stormy late summer night that made her skin feel tacky. *Why make promises like that when you don't know any more about the mark than I do?* She thought to herself in a twisted manner. Years of living on the streets of a bustling city had taught her that whenever everyone else around you fails, you need to rely on yourself. Feeling that independent stride again, she soon reached her room. Changing into a white nightshirt that Oza had given her, she headed off to bed for the night. But still, a gnawing feeling at the back of her mind carried on.

Later that night, a summer storm started its roll towards the coast. Lightning sprung out into the night sky and thunder roared. As Iona slept, a viscous thought drifted through the ether only to land at her doorstep.

"....Iona..." It said, ripping her from her sleep in an instant with a loud quake of thunder ringing out through the air. Her hair hung in front of her eyes. Wiping the strands from her face her gaze darted back and forth from one dark corner of the room to the next. Closing her eyes, she listened, but heard no one, not even a heartbeat. But still the voice continued, quieter now, almost as though it was whispering to her, "Are *you* a monster?"

And then it was gone.

CHAPTER 12

Hushed whispers and padded footsteps awoke Iona early in the morning. Her mind went blank for a moment as she tried to remember what day it was. A bang and a quick prance in the room next to her's quickly reminded her. Shuffling off the covers with a moan, she stared out at the desk, early light sprawled out over the wood finishing. Atop it sat disheveled packaging from a box Iona had ripped into the night before. Some of the wrapping still laid on the floor. The box had contained a fresh uniform equipped with faint runes that lined the finishings of the garment. Oza had explained their placement. The runes trickled with light against the dark purple of the fabric as she ran her hand over the uniform. They were to be the last line of defense so that the garment would not stay alight when she eventually caught on fire. The office secretary had delivered the package along with a proper map of the campus, on which, foreign buildings became all too familiar, closely followed by her class schedule. Picking up the schedule, Iona thought back to something that Melonie had said. She had let slip that Oza had been practically pulling out her hair trying to figure out which classes Iona should be placed in. They had both laughed at the thought, but looking at it now, Iona was glad to have the support she had found thus far at Belgrum. Everyone had been trying so hard to prepare her for what came next. Pulling her uniform out of the box, she wondered if it was all worth the trouble.

Iona stared out at the empty bed opposite her own. *I suppose they wouldn't be here just yet,* she thought as she reexamined the early morning light peering in through the large window. She caught glimpses of incoming students between the rustling trees, large caravans of luggage and laughter sounded throughout the dawning light. She could recognize a few swirls of horns and teeth strung about through the crowd, but most students appeared human at first glance.

GRRrrrgh. Her stomach growled like some deranged beast. She glanced around for anything she might have squirreled away to quell her hunger, but to no avail.

"I suppose I'll actually have to grab some breakfast before classes start," Iona lightly patted her stomach. Slipping out of her nightgown and into her uniform she made her way towards the first floor dining hall.

The room was filled with the warm light of the fireplace. Runes glowed along its hearth that seemed to temper the heat despite the roaring flames. Large tables with wooden benches filled the room. The fire itself seemed to captivate Iona for a moment before her stomach decided to rumble again. The soft morning breeze blew in quietly as more students found their way into the dorms. Dipping into the line of eagerly awaiting students, Iona picked up a large helping of food before finding a table to sit at. She peered out at the sea of empty seats just waiting to be filled by the arrival of new students. She landed in a spot secluded by a half wall topped with banisters. She could feel the heat begin to swell in her cheeks as more students crowded the once deserted hall. Taking a breath, she tried to focus on her meal.

She was lucky that most of the incoming students had taken both their luggage and themselves upstairs. Each in search of their rooms to change into their uniforms. Although there were still some stragglers.

"Hey watch it man!" a familiar voice rang out from the base of the staircase. Peering over at the latent commotion Iona saw exactly who it was. Distracting her, however, from the black hair and freckles was a bit of lingering plaster coiled tightly around his right arm. Iona quickly sunk into her chair, fashioning her food tray as a barrier as she forced herself out of Bernard's line of sight. *Shouldn't he have healed by now? What's a wyr doing wearing a cast?*

As her plate of food clattered onto the table, Bernard's

head darted towards the dining hall. He stood there, watching the crowd for a moment, before pushing the student he had yelled at and taking his leave up the stairs.

Iona could hear his footsteps as they faded away, but still she couldn't bring herself to check if he was really gone. Taking a deep breath, she quickly darted her head around the corner, Bernard was nowhere to be seen. She sat the tray back down with a sigh before realizing her hands had grown hot enough to warp two hand-sized indents into the thin metal.

"Really?" she mumbled as she examined the tray more. She barely noticed the dissipating heat along her body as it relaxed. She tried to reform the metal in her hands for a little bit before giving up entirely. Worried about running into Bernard in person, she swiftly scooped up some of the food still left on the plate into her mouth and then made her way to the main building for her first class of the day.

Transformation and Selective Transformation taught by the elegant Ms. Heisengroph. Entering the classroom, it didn't seem to have changed much since her summer classes, aside from the protective shield of desks that had since been decommissioned. Iona felt a hinge of nervousness wash in and out. Not out of fear of the class, but rather the students that would be encased within. This particular course was for second-years. Iona and Heisengroph had covered most of the benchmarks for the first-year class, but Iona still felt as though it had been a bit rushed. She didn't have the hundreds of hours of experience that some of the students had. As Iona stared out at the already seated students she couldn't help but feel like they were better than her. *Everyone seems so comfortable...* Iona thought to herself as she found a seat next to a student with brown hair who appeared to be napping. A light brown cardigan gathered at the nape of her white button up as she sat with her head nestled in her arms. Her dark hair covered the sides of her face, while the rest was tied up in a small bun. Sitting down, the scratching of the chair against the floor must have woken her up. The girl's head slowly rose before she parted her hair from her face, only stopping to stare at Iona.

"You!" they both said as if in unison. Other students took notice of their sudden outburst.

"I'm the one who should be saying that, not you," Maisie said, straightening up. She grabbed her book bag as if she was about to move before setting it back down again.

"Were you just napping?" Iona asked.

"I was just... resting my eyes," Maisie wiped some drool from her bottom lip, "What are you doing here anyways?"

"What's it look like? I go to school here now," Iona said, almost sullenly.

"You mean to tell me you're not here to ruin any more bread?" Maisie said sarcastically.

"To be fair, I was being chased by something, but still, I apologize for any inconvenience it might have caused you."

"Chased by wh-"

As Ms. Heisengroph walked in, the room went obediently quiet. She carried a small paper box under her arm as she approached Iona's seat. Placing the box in front of Iona, she returned to the front of the classroom. Other students around her stared at the box and then at Iona for a few moments before returning to their usual adolescent indifference. She glanced up at Heisengroph, who motioned for her to open the box. Inside contained a note and a small black velvet bag. Unfurling the note, it read:

Dear Iona,

I've kept Mr. Joix busy these past few days procuring this amulet for you. While there is only so much that we can do for you as your teachers and protectors, I thought this object might help you when you feel your body start to struggle with its newfound power. I've seen you come a long way in the past few weeks, but there is still more work to be done. You had mentioned before that you were having nightmares. Dreams can often stir intense emotions within us, both in and out of bed. The last thing we'd like is for you to burn down the dorms in your sleep. So, if they continue to worsen I hope that you'll use this. You'll find it harder to feel your fire when you wear this, but it won't be completely absent. I hope that you'll find it useful and that you keep it on hand just as a precaution.

Sincerely,
Headmistress Hersch

Iona folded the note and placed it back into the box. Moving to the velvet bag, she opened it, revealing a silver amulet with a small green gem inlay. It seemed to hum at an unusual frequency as she turned it over in her hand. An image of the food tray flashed through her mind. *I still have a way to go when it comes to controlling my emotions.* Iona pulled the amulet over her head. As she adjusted the cord underneath her collar, she could feel her strength begin to wane from her body. Iona made a fist with her hand, opening and closing it a few times before turning her attention back towards Ms. Heisengroph.

Maisie stole glances at Iona as she pondered over something.

"Good morning class. As most of you already know from first year transformations, my name is Ms. Heisengroph. Over the course of this year we will be focusing on and honing your abilities as they pertain to your transformations. One thing I like to do, especially for my second-years, is to have a sort of show and tell during the first class. How it'll work is that each student will take turns shifting into their mid or selective-form in front of the class. I do this to mainly learn about what kinds of fae I'm working with, and single out any stragglers from last year that still require more attention and practice to catch up," she explained to the class. "Now, if we don't have any questions, let's begin."

Almost immediately, two long and fluffy looking ears sprouted from beneath her fiery red locks of hair. Moving out from behind her desk, the class's attention soon drew to the fox tail that had sprouted out from beneath her long skirt. The tail seemed to sweep the ground before it disappeared back underneath. Her nails grew sharp as she stretched out her arms.

"For those of you who are new, I am what the people of Alwynn would call a kit. Can anyone tell the class what the classification of kit would be?"

Maisie raised her hand to answer, as Heisengroph

nodded she replied, "Unlike most of the races that reside in Avilar, kits have more magical attributes, despite being seen as a part of the wyr family of fae. And despite being part of that family, they cannot fully transform into their parent animal, a fox."

"Correct. Thank you, Miss Ardelean." Heisengroph sat back down at her desk to examine the list of students. "What a coincidence, Maisie Ardelean, you're up next!"

"I heard kits worship Zimm instead of Vilt. Isn't that weird?" A student whispered to their neighbor. Glancing up at the professor, Iona could sense her ear twitch but she seemed to pay no mind to the students' chatter.

The brown haired girl sitting next to Iona stood up and headed to the front of the classroom. Most other students rolled their eyes or sluggishly paid attention as she turned to face the class. *Maisie Ardelean... so that's her name huh.* Maisie took a deep breath before starting her transformation. Her ears molded to a point that seemed strangely dissimilar to that of an elf, her lower canines broke through the crack in her mouth to meet her upper lip, and her fingernails grew before their very eyes, changing into darker, thicker claws. Her eyes shot out a piercing orange glow before calming to a lighter yellow hue.

"So she's a wyr-wolf..." Iona mumbled to herself while she fidgeted with the amulet around her neck, turning it over and over in her hands. Small beads of anxious sweat glided down her arm underneath her clothing as she picked at her skirt so that it would sit right against her skin.

After Maisie was finished, she returned to her seat and Heisengroph went back to picking out the next student.

"Do you have a problem with wyrs?" Maisie asked Iona quietly as she returned to her seat.

"Iona Moran! You're up next," Ms. Heisengroph announced, looking around to check that she was wearing the amulet.

"Not exactly," Iona said to Maisie before standing up to make her way towards the front of the room.

"Better get used to it, most of your classmates are wolves in sheep's clothing," Maisie mumbled, but Iona heard it all the same.

Reaching the front of the class, Iona's heart started to pound in her chest. Her mind couldn't help but see the rest of her classmates like she had seen Bernard that day. Their eyes glowed bright, some gold, some red, some blue, all of them together more terrifying than Bernard. In spite of the overwhelming fear Iona was quickly spiraling herself into, she was able to realign her thoughts back to just her. Closing her eyes, she focused on her body, her heat, her power. Her initial response to Maisie's comment had already worked to spike her temperature, all she had to do was turn up the heat. She held on tight to the amulet.

Despite its presence, her body still began to peak. Again, her back started to swell. A wave of heat and pressure overcame her body before returning to a simmer. Opening her eyes, she was taken aback when she was suddenly met with pitch black darkness. Looking around, there was something about the space that seemed familiar to Iona.

"...Iona..."

Spinning around, she was met with a gigantic glowing red eye staring back at her. Its diameter almost matched her own. Blinking, she was brought back, gazing out at the class with glowing red eyes of her own. Iona stared out at the class as they sat staring back at her, before bursting into applause at the sight of her wings, fangs, claws, and the scales that coated her skin, not to mention the low simmer of flames and heat that covered her body from head to taloned foot. Feeling a bit caught off guard, Iona stumbled a couple steps backwards after having been snapped back into reality. In her confusion her foot caught on a piece of loose tile, causing her to fall back onto the ground behind her. She caught glimpses of students' laughter as she fell. Her wings quickly began to rejoin, clunkyly fusing back into the skin between rejoining fibers of uniform while the fire that had once blanketed her had all but dissipated. Ms. Heisengroph rushed to her side, trying to make sure that she was alright.

"Iona, can you stand?"

"I think so..." Iona said, leaning on her professor.

"Maisie, could you accompany Miss Moran to the nurse's office? Best to make sure she's alright after that tumble she took."

"Of course, Ms. H," she shifted Iona's body weight onto her own.

As they made their way out of the classroom and down the hall, they could hear ample whispering coming from the room in their absence, before stopping altogether with the sound of the professor's commanding tone.

Chapter 13

The nurse's office was prim and white. A few of the beds were made, awaiting weary students to house. Maisie had taken her leave by the time the nurse had finished her rounds. Golden curls of short blonde hair bounced towards Iona as she approached. Her ears bent to a sharp point that made Iona wonder. *Could she really be an elf? Headmistress Hersch was right, this place is a magnet for all kinds of people.* She looked a bit younger than middle-age, perhaps a bit older in terms of elf-years, as small wrinkles were just starting to form around her eyes. A warm cup in one hand, the nurse ran her other hand above the length of Iona's body looking for something.

"Now dear, this is the first time I've seen you here," she said, applying a small bit of pressure around Iona's wrist. "What's your name?"

"Iona... Moran," she looked to the nurse as if that meant something.

"Oh, I think the Headmistress was telling me about you the other day. You're a dragal aren't you?"

"I suppose."

"What brings you to my clearing in the woods?"

"I was in Ms. Heisengroph's class."

"Transformations, very exciting," the nurse said, as she moved around to Iona's feet, slowly applying pressure to their base.

"It was my turn and I tried-," Iona paused, almost wincing. "I tried to keep my power under control, and I did," Iona picked at her fingers. "But something happened and I fell."

"Something?" The nurse paused. As she peered at Iona's downtrodden face, she could tell she didn't want to talk about it. "Well, since you're not feeling well, I suggest you rest for now before heading back to the dorms."

"Wh-what's your name?" Iona felt a strange wave rush over her. She noticed the nurse's hand glowing a light green color. Immediately she felt more relaxed.

"Sorry, I noticed you were a bit anxious," the light in her hand faded away. "My name is Hazel."

As Iona's classes continued elsewhere, she instead slept. The voice that had shaken her quietly seeped in as she fell deeper and deeper into her unconscious mind. As she dreamt, the voice became clearer, and the scenery that surrounded her more vivid. She appeared to be entrenched in some sort of cave, it was dark and the cold air sent shivers down her spine. It must have been very deep under the earth. The air was steeped in moisture, and the voice stood as a wall around her, deep and bellowing.

"...Iona..." it said, although she couldn't find the source. The room was still too dark, too still to make out a figure, a being.

"Wh-who are you? Where am I?" she whispered out into the dank darkness that enveloped her.

"Child of flame... you are in my domain..." the gravely tone echoed all around her.

"Who are you?" she asked again, this time with less hesitation.

"You know my name... but you do not know me..." it sounded as though there was some grander riddle to be answered.

What does it mean? She thought to herself, trying to figure out who the voice might belong to. *Could it be the shade? No.* Scraps of unfamiliar memory flooded in and a name stood out amongst them. Finally she spoke.

"Fire... lord?"

"Ah, I see you're finally beginning to remember. I have been called a great many things... But it has been quite a long time since any mortal has called me the Fire Lord. For now, you may call me-" what came next came as a whisper as the walls around her seemed to twist and turn though the body of a white snake was descending upon her.

"Ismir!" she called, suddenly awakening from her slumber. As she sat up in the bed she found herself drenched in a cold sweat.

"Iona! Are you alright?" asked the Headmistress, rushing to her side. Iona noticed a light jacket slumped over a chair that had been pulled up to her bed. *How long has the Headmistress been here?*

"H-hi," she said looking around, the white walls around her seemed to twitch with a sense of movement. "I'm fine." Her eyes finally settled back on the Headmistress.

"Ms. Heisengroph said you took a tumble after transforming in her class earlier," her face appeared to have softened compared to the harden scowl of their history lessons. It appeared almost motherly, if Iona could even remember what such a face was supposed to look like.

"I'm fine. I just got a little overwhelmed, that's all," Iona said as she looked down at her hands gathered in her lap. The pale skin of her palms had a nice rosy tint to them.

Hazel closed her eyes as she ran another glowing hand over Iona's forehead. Her eyes shot open, quickly turning to the Headmistress. "It feels like there's some lingering psychic mana," she turned back to Iona, "Do you remember anything?" Her ears perked up.

Iona repositioned herself in the bed, trying to come up with an explanation. "I had a vision. I was in a moist dark place and there was a voice that called out to me. The same one that came to me during class. When I blinked in class, it was gone. That's when I lost my footing. That's all."

"*That's all?* How many times has this happened?" the Headmistress asked, her look of concern only deepening.

Iona paused, contemplating how much she should tell them. *No. I trust Headmistress Hersch, she's done nothing but help me.* She sucked some air up through her teeth. "It's only happened a few times before, but it's usually when I'm sleeping."

"Why didn't you tell us sooner? We could have tried to make sense of what's happening," the Headmistress said pleadingly.

"I was scared before, but I know now. It was Ismir," Iona spoke with an extreme amount of calm that seemed to catch both the Headmistress and Nurse Hazel off guard. "It was always Ismir, I just didn't realize it until now." The two adults just stared at one another, looks of concern dissolving into confusion. It was a moment or two before either of them spoke aloud.

"Ismir the *Ashen?* How can you be so sure? Or so *calm?*" the Headmistress questioned Iona.

"At first, when I was having the dreams, I was worried, but the more he reached out and the stronger our connection became, he slowly started to feel more familiar to me. Like a limb I somehow forgot I had."

"Why is he just now reaching out to you?" Nurse Hazel

asked, thinking aloud.

A shiver ran down Iona's back. It felt as though a talon had scraped across her. The sigil etched into her back flashed through her mind. "...It could have something to do with this," Iona pulled back the collar of her shirt, pressing her hand to the crux of her back.

Pulling back the fabric, the two women soon saw what she was referencing. A small pinkish sigil marred her skin like a nicely healed scar.

"Where did this come from?" the Headmistress asked.

"I'm not sure. Ms. Heisengroph thought maybe I'd had it for a while, given how set into the skin it is. But I don't remember ever seeing it before coming here. Almost like it was hidden from me as well."

"These markings appear to be old magic. Long out of practice. From what I've seen over the years, I'd say it was some sort of magic seal," Nurse Hazel retorted.

The Headmistress took a beat. "I'll have to have a conversation with Ms. Heisengroph..."

"If it's meant to seal my powers, then how come I'm able to use them *now* all of a sudden?"

"If it's truly been with you since you were a child, perhaps the mere act of you growing up has worn it down. Mixed with the massive amount of stress you've been under recently, it makes sense some of your power would leak through."

Seeing that Iona was still exhausted, Nurse Hazel sent her back to her room to rest. Iona was happy to be heading into her den of familiarity, but questions still remained. Had her parents been the ones to seal her away from herself? Had it been someone else? Perhaps someone connected to the Dalians that pursued her?

Her room was the one place she had started to feel at home while staying on campus. But even now, it was beginning to feel as though the walls of the school had a mind of their own. Watching her, crawling like the twisting wall of scales.

Exiting the main building, she walked past the courtyard, but stopped when she noticed Melonie sitting alone reading a book. The cover had an elegant inlay of ornate gold leaf as its main feature and its contents seemed to captivate the young girl's attention as she barely noticed Iona's swift approach.

Clearing her throat, their eyes finally met.

"Oh Iona! I was wondering when you would be getting out of the nurse's office."

"So you decided to replace me with a book?" Iona asked coyly.

Melonie chuckled at the thought. "No, it's just that you were taking so long. I rarely find time to read for pleasure," she raised the book so that Iona could see the cover more clearly. It read *Fae and Fiends: Classification and Findings.*

"Aren't classifications what a bestiary is for?" Iona said, thinking back to one of the books Olyn had purchased for her at the bazaar.

"If you're referring to the *Beastiarium Arcana* this book also happens to be by Cirn Sylvester. It's one of his earlier works, back when he was still just in the early stages of research."

"I see... So which are you? Fae or fiend?" Iona asked with a smirk.

"See that's a tricky question. Given the inherent nature of banshees, we're typically seen as mid-fiends, however this doesn't mean that we're inherently mischievous or evil like some higher or lower fiends. We're widely regarded as forces of nature," she gave a little nod as though she was satisfied with the book's findings.

"Widely regarded doesn't always pertain to everyone."

"You're right, some assume that we cause death, just because we happen to be near, or are somehow drawn towards it. And while our screams can cause bodily harm, it's not their primary use."

"People tend to assume a lot about me too, well, more so when I was pretty sure I was just human."

"It gets hard, doesn't it?"

"Very much so," Iona said looking down at her pale skin. Her white hair passing in and out of her view with the wind. She tried to remember her parents, but only shapes and colors came back to her, none of which matched her own hue.

"That's just more of a reason to stand up for one another right? Not everyone can be something as commonplace as a human or wyr." Melonie had her own little grin.

Following their talk, Iona wheeled Melonie back to her dorm hall before returning to her own for dinner. The dining hall featured a larger crowd of students than earlier that morning and in some small way Iona missed the silence amidst the crackling of the fireplace, but on the other hand, perhaps it was better the space be filled with something other than her own thoughts.

Full from a hardy dinner, she returned back to her dorm room where she found boxes flooded into the hall, some even working to keep the door propped open.

"H-hello?" Iona inquired, as she knocked slightly on the open door before making her way into the once unoccupied room.

"Huh? Oh hey, sorry about the boxes, my travel bags got a bit torn up so I had to have all my stuff delivered the old fashioned way," said someone from behind a nearby pile of boxes.

"Um, it's okay. It certainly is a lot though isn't it?" Iona tried to maneuver between piles leading to her bed.

"Yea, I noticed that you didn't have much on your side of the room. Are your parents bringing your stuff later or have you just not unpacked yet?" she asked.

"No it's just me and what you see." Iona finally seated herself on the bed.

"Huh?" the mystery girl shuffled behind stacks of boxes in order to get a better look at her roommate. "Oh, it's you," said Maisie, staring out at Iona.

"What a coincidence," Iona said calmly as they both started chuckling to themselves.

"Wanna help me unpack?" Maisie asked.

"Sure," Iona replied as she made her way over to a stack of boxes.

CHAPTER 14

The sound of shattering glass rang throughout the night. A small sliver of moon shone faintly on the campus as two dark figures made their way into the main building. They moved swiftly and quietly through the halls, searching intently. As they crept through room after room, they finally found themselves amongst the dusty books of the school library. The dim moonlight shone through the stained glass windows, casting muted streaks of color upon the stacks. The library seemed almost bigger on the inside than one might expect. A few too many books for such a small room. The intruders, one hooded and tall, the other intangible, wispy and effervescent, moved silently as they continued their search. The books seemed to watch them, holding their breath as the hooded one held out his hand, trying to sense what was hidden.

"Got it," he whispered to the shade as he approached a nearby bookcase.

The smoky shade lingered nearby while he worked, moving in and out of the shadows. Removing a tome, the hood revealed runes etched into the wooden backing of the shelf. Placing his hand on the back panel, it began to emit a golden white glow as the sigil engraved in it shone. As the shelf began to tremble, he stepped back. What appeared to be root-like vines began to wrap their way around the bookcase, piercing some of the books in the process. The wall began to part from the middle of the stack, an entrance. A staircase seemed to wind its way down into the bowels of the school's foundation. Moving even quicker now, they followed the stairs down into the depths below. The pathway led into a small circular room with vaulted boxes laid in the walls. In the center there it was, *the artifact.* Laying behind no visible trace of protection, seated upon a marble slab. It appeared before them as some unsung cylinder. Runes etched their way around the circumference, waiting to bring life to the ancient magic contained within. The shade, acting impatiently, reached out into the bright room with a dense arm-like appendage before being struck with a flash of light. The dark creature howled but quickly bit its tongue, trying to fight back the pain as they both examined the piece in its otherwise formless body that had turned solid. It was solid stone. The mass bubbled, growing slowly like moss trying to encase him.

"Serle... don't you ever learn?" with a sigh, the other intruder lowered his hood to reveal long waves of black hair. Scowling at Serle with reddish eyes, he rubbed the dark circles that had entrenched themselves underneath in his gaunt skin. Pushing his hair back into the hood, he pushed the shade back up the stairs before turning back to the artifact.

"S-sorry Terrigen s-sir," Serle sputtered back, still reeling from the pain in its arm.

"We'll have to get you fixed up after we give our report to the Duke through the mirror shard. I'm sure one of the gorgons will have some ideas about how to fix you before you fully turn to stone. Or you could go whimpering to Elias and see if he can figure it out."

As Terrigen turned back towards the pillar he stretched out his arm, chanting a small evocation under his breath. The pillar of marble suddenly shone brightly with the countless spell sigils that lined it as they burnt out underneath his power. Serle shrunk back at the sight of the bright light as he edged his way further back up the stairs. Having removed the hexes, Terrigen secured the artifact. It hummed in his hand, almost as if it was calling to him, coaxing them to use it. Looking at the object with disgust, he placed it in his satchel. Exiting the vault, he was careful to replace the tome he had removed before leaping back out into the night, making his way now towards the pillars of dorms.

"We only have enough time for one extraction," Terrigen explained to Serle.

"Top of shopping list?" Serle's raspy voice asked as he

lurched behind in Terrigen's shadow, the stone hand never fully entering the darkness below.

Terrigen pocketed his ashen palm, his fingers tracing the ancient sigil for clarity etched into a corded golden stone in his pocket. Relaxing, he funneled forward in determination. "He wanted a banshee's scream."

"Tasty."

"She's not for you to eat. We need to get the scream and get out. There are two of them here on campus, the Headmistress and her daughter. I take it I don't have to explain to you why finding her daughter would be better for us," he said.

"Tasty tasty."

"I'd rather not bleed from my ears again, so no tasting Serle," he commanded.

"Again?" his voice lightly scraped with disdain.

"Long story, for another time... Which building is she in?"

"Smell there," Serle pointed with the stone hand towards one of the buildings closest to them in the quad.

"Okay, let's go."

The dorm hall was eerily quiet as the two made their way down the first floor corridor. Once Serle located the room he quickly made his way underneath the door frame, unlocking the door for Terrigen and the artifact. Melonie was sleeping peacefully in her room, her chair next to her bed as always. Serle bounded towards the bed before remembering what Terrigen had said about not feasting upon the young banshee. He still gazed out at her with hungry and expectant white eyes while Terrigen moved into position for extraction.

"So the little banshee sleeps all by herself, huh. How lonesome."

A gut wrenching screech could be heard all across campus, waking even the heaviest of sleepers. Iona woke to her blood pounding in her head. Sitting up, she tried to regain control. Maisie too had woken up and was already out of bed. Iona's head pounded as Maisie tried to talk to her, unable to be heard. The pressure began to fade away as Maisie laid a hand on her shoulder.

"Iona, are you alright? I'm not sure what that scream was about, but it sounded like it came from Dorm B.

Dorm B? But that's where Melonie is. Iona tore the sheets from the bed. Opening their door, she peered down the hall only to be met with stares from the other students who were curious as well.

"Where are you going?" Maisie asked, following her through the halls of the building.

They made their way outside. Standing in the quad, it

was apparent that every student had woken up. Spinning around, Iona could see heads darting out of windows trying to figure out what had happened. Her hearing was even more overstimulated than normal, and she could hear wyrs talking to each other from different floors of her building.

Rushing to Dorm B, there was already a gathering of students and faculty alike in the dining hall. Melonie's room had been placed not far from the entrance on the first floor due to her chair. Her door was open, although none of the students dared step further towards the room. A commotion at the dorm's entrance quickly separated the crowd. The Headmistress, led by Nurse Hazel and Mr. Joix, quickly entered Melonie's room.

"Everyone go back to bed!" the Headmistress seethed with each word. Most students scurried off back to their dorms, but Maisie and Iona remained. Iona couldn't just leave, despite Maisie's tugging and insistence.

A faint heartbeat could be heard within. Melonie's heartbeat. *What... happened here?* Iona couldn't bring herself to enter the room, instead she sat outside the door. Her head hunched into her legs. Maisie silently joined her on the ground.

"She's breathing," Nurse Hazel gasped.

Iona's head perked up, scrambling to get up, she stood at the entrance to the room.

Melonie coughed, trying to take in air. As she slowly

opened her eyes, her arms wrapped around her mother. The Headmistress had to refrain from continuing the embrace, instead pulling her away. Her smooth hands inspected Melonie's face for damage. "What happened Mel?" her voice was tiny and soft.

Melonie coughed again, trying to clear her throat. "I felt something cold wash over me. When I woke up... I couldn't see much. There was so much smoke in the room. But I remember a hand reaching out. It had black feathers coming out of it, then there was this big flash of light."

"And your scream?"

"I screamed?"

"Yes dear. It woke up the whole campus."

After a faint cough, Melonie apologized, "I'm sorry."

The Headmistress just held her daughter tight. "There's nothing to be sorry about."

Smoke? And black feathers? It couldn't be... Iona's face burst with heat. *How did they find me here? Wait, do they even know I'm here?*

"Iona!" Maisie tried grabbing hold of her wrist, but was instead was met with an intense heat.

The Headmistress met Iona's gaze. "Miss Moran, please control yourself," her voice wasn't scolding, instead it was one of understanding.

"I think I know who did this," Iona bellowed.

"I think I know too," the Headmistress said as she passed by her, moving back through the doorway. Iona's heat depleted almost as quickly as it had gathered. Her eyes followed her as she walked down the hall.

Oza met the Headmistress at the front door. "We need to check on something," Oza followed in agreement.

"Instruct Joix to do a sweep of the grounds," she commanded. Oza produced a small shard of glass from her pocket. Its edges smooth like sea glass after years of erosion. Entering the library, Saya was met with books strewn all over the floor. Moving towards the vault entrance, she replaced the tome hiding the sigil and placed her hand within. In seconds, the entrance appeared once more.

As Oza joined her, she placed the shard back in her pocket. "He said there are traces of sulfur and ash near the entrance, but he can't sense the intruders," she explained, joining the Headmistress in venturing below.

She let out a small cry in frustration. Her hands covered her mouth as she nearly collapsed right inside the vault. Oza stepped around her to examine the pillar. Seeing the damage, she spoke. "There *is* one good thing."

"What might that be?" The Headmistress couldn't take

her eyes off the empty marble pillar at the center of the small room. Tears had started forming in the corners of her eyes.

"They triggered the *glimpse*." Wiping her face, she looked up as Oza's body turned back into blue mist as she filled the pillar. A small pulse of light shone brightly before receding. Oza's mist fell into place as it painted the scene. Smokey blue reached into the pillar, while another figure stood back, waiting and watching.

The Headmistress' gaze lingered around the cloaked figure. "Just *what* are you planning to do with the Crucifixer?"

Chapter 15

Melonie's scream continued to echo throughout the minds of everyone on campus that morning. As Maisie and Iona headed down to breakfast, the halls carried the meandering sounds of morning ruckus. *They sure are louder than usual.* Iona scoffed as her ears rang with numerous conversations. Everything teemed with discussions of last night's event. Some complained that they were tired and shouldn't have to attend the day's classes, while others theorized about what had happened.

"Just try to ignore them," Maisie whispered as she watched Iona's ears twitch.

Before the two of them had a chance to sit down and eat, Oza appeared in the entrance to the dorm. Her head spun back and forth trying to peer through the sea of pupils. She quickly approached a couple of older students that hung around the bubbling hearth. She spoke in hushed tones that Iona couldn't pick up over the noise around her. Oza noticed her staring and approached her and Maisie as well.

Bending over the small table, she whispered in Iona's

ear. "Can you see the Headmistress in her office after you're finished eating?" Oza backed away and Iona could see concern creasing into her face.

"Am I in trouble?" she asked, probing for information.

"No dear. Nothing like that. Headmistress Hersch just wanted to meet with a few of the students before classes begin for the day."

"Okay..."

"Does this have to do with that scream we heard last night?" Maisie asked rather abruptly. *So much for whispering.*

"I'm not at liberty to say Ms. Ardelean," Oza quickly replied before checking a piece of paper that had been folded up in her breast pocket. As she exited the building, the girls just stared at each other.

"You were way too loud," Iona scolded her. A few students nearby intent to eavesdrop returned to eating their meal.

"Quit nagging me like you're my brother. If she wanted quiet, she should have spoken with you elsewhere. There's no point in trying to hide your conversations in this dorm." Maisie peered around at the other wyr students busy wolfing down their morning meals.

Iona's shoes clicked against the stone walkway leading up to the main building. She felt a wave of déjà vu as she skirted up the final spiral staircase that lead to the Headmistress' office. Stopping just short of the door, she reached down to massage her calf, which thanks to all the summer lessons was now mostly muscle. As the soft burn of lactic acid faded away she quietly entered the room. She was met with two older students, who, at first glance, seemed unfamiliar. The room had four chairs in rows of two facing the Headmistress' desk. Peering around, it was the cleanest Iona had seen the office. She would have never guessed before that there were more than one chair hidden underneath the summer clutter. She took a seat opposite of an athletic boy. Her nostrils flared almost on instinct. His scent was familiar but featured notes of cardamom she could mistake for her roommate. *A wyr for sure, but why does he smell like Maisie?* Now that she looked at him, they did seem similar. Despite him having a lighter shade of brown chestnut hair than Maisie, they both shared the same beautiful blue eyes. *What is it about wyrs that their eyes seem to sparkle when they aren't threatening you with violence?* Her mind raced to Bernard and she shuddered. The boy glanced at her, before returning his silent gaze to the Headmistress' empty chair. She could sense a proud wolf underneath his exterior, much calmer than Maisie's own. *Well if they are related, their wolves are totally different.*

Tilting her head back, so that she could peek at the other student, she was taken aback by their attire. Their face seemed to be sculpted into that of a boy, but their uniform was all over the place. They wore a short sleeve button up with a yellow knit cardigan cascading off their shoulders, followed up by black pleated shorts from the summer uniform and some matching calf length socks that were more commonly seen accompanied by girl's uniforms. A light green bow nestled around their collar where a necktie would have sat. The scent that came off them was sweet like apples. *They don't smell like anything dangerous.* Her shoulders began to release some of the tension she didn't even realize she was holding. Shifting in her seat, she couldn't help but feel that something about them felt familiar, like an ache at the back of her mind that Iona couldn't quite pin down. They sat with immaculate posture as blonde curls masked their eyes. The sides of their head were cut short, there the hair was almost four shades darker, a nice complement to the cool brown of their skin.

The door opened once more and the wafting scent of testosterone began to entomb her. *When is the Headmistress getting here?* She took in a deep breath, trying to refocus. As she opened her eyes she stared dumbfounded at the newcomer. Her mind began to bend, trying to understand what she was seeing. It was *Olyn. But how can he be here?* The bags underneath his eyes had darkened since she had left him and his hair was rather unkempt, but it was definitely Olyn. Almost as if it was an illusion, her nose felt stuffed full with the scent of breakfast. The door parted for the last time, nipping into his side, which forced Olyn to quickly take the remaining seat behind Iona. The Headmistress, seeing that everyone had arrived, shuffled past the rows of chairs to her desk. Her hair appeared as though she hadn't gotten the chance to brush through the long and flowing black velvet that morning.

"Did you get any sleep last night?" Iona asked, breaking the silence. The older students stared at her impotently.

"Thank you for asking Ms. Moran. No, I'm afraid I didn't get much quality sleep. Or quantity for that matter, but that's regardless of the situation I find myself in," she paused. "You all heard the scream last night?" she waited for them to nod in affirmation.

"Late last night the school had a break in. Our current theory is that one of the intruders triggered a failsafe and was... dispatched. This event may have been what caused Melonie's outburst, although that still doesn't explain why the remaining intruders found their way into her room in the first place," she explained.

"Could they have been after her in retribution, or for a ransom of some sort?" the wyr asked.

"It's unclear at this time."

"What was stolen?" the blonde was jarringly blunt.

"Kipling... as inquisitive as ever."

"Well Headmistress, you wouldn't just drag us here, away from our classes, if you were going to parrot to us what most of the student body already suspects."

"An artifact from the school's secure vault was taken. Which is *why* I called the four of you here. The four of you represent the best of your respective clans here on campus. Kipling, you stand as our school's strongest castor. Topher is our strongest wyr, whose mother is not only a highly respected alpha but also an integral member of Belvore's wyr community. And as for you two, Iona here is our current sole dragal, and Olyn our only demon in attendance."

Demon? Iona's breath caught in her throat causing her to cough sharply.

"Calling on me and Topher was... an informed choice, but why are these two *children* needed here?" Kipling passed a flimsy gesture in their direction. *Who are they calling a child? They're both only a few years older than us.*

"The artifact that went missing... Is known only to a few as the Crucifixer. It has been documented to be extremely dangerous to all manner of fae and fiends, including castors," she peered at Kipling's mop of hair.

"You mean anyone with an essence," he corrected her.

"Even for those without an essence, this could be yet another shift in our very way of life. Please reach out to your family and your communities and warn them to stay on guard. Gods only know what someone would use the artifact for, especially if it's landed in the hands of people like the Dalians."

"It could be another plague all over again," Iona could just barely hear Topher's soft cursing.

Meanwhile, in another part of the building, Melonie was trying to get through her first class of the day. The black padded room contained the delicate girl, still reeling from thoughts of the night, and her teacher. A tower of beauty and grace flowed before her. Her short black hair was pert and to the point. Giving way only for two streaks of white that framed her amber eyes impeccably.

"Melonie. We don't have to do this if you're still upset about last night. Even your mother suggested you take time to rest today."

"It's the beginning of the trimester Ms. Vanya, I can't afford to slack off just yet," Melonie fumbled with her scheduling paper. The class had been written in as Scream 101, which amused her considering she had been subjected to this kind of training since she was young. Nothing about the vocal exercises and learning to harness her powers screamed *101*. But alas, it was the only class of its kind, and she the only student.

Melonie pattered about in her chair, wheeling herself up to the front of the small room. The podium was specially made to accompany her seated height. Melonie picked at the splintering wood of the stand as she flipped through some of her training notes.

Old writing sparked images, reminders of first lessons with Ms. Vanya. Her throat ached as it relived the first week of classes under her tutelage. Vanya had pushed her harder than her mother ever had, which had led to her loosing her voice for the first full week of class the previous year. Thankfully, the school hadn't been subjected to her powers at the time. The room they stood in was magically soundproof to the outside world, saving the more sensitive students from the bulk of her training exercises.

She settled on a more recent page of notes towards the back of her stuffed notebook. Taking a deep breath, she could feel her lungs expand, her ribs creaking with each extra bit of air she could muster between them. Letting it all out, she stood in eerie silence as her vocal cords vibrated within her. Ms. Vanya stood in attention at the scene. Melonie's body began to shake as the vibrations from her vocal cords turned against her. Melonie tried to hold onto the podium as tightly as she could, but it was no use. Her grip turned into a push as she teetered back from the wooden stand. A ringing sensation began in her ears before her inner ears shook with loud booms. Cupping her head, the pain jolted through her, causing her to fall from her chair onto the floor beneath her. As she gasped for help, she found that the words were unable to form. Nor could she hear Ms. Vanya as she held the girl in her arms tightly.

Oza burst through the door to the Headmistress' office. Her breathing was irregular and ragged.

"Oza! Are you alright?" the Headmistress quickly inquired.

"It's... Melonie..." she said, trying to collect herself.

The Headmistress excused the four students before making her way down to the nurse's office. Without speaking a word, Olyn and Iona met each other's gaze on the main staircase. With a glance down the stairs, they both nodded in silent agreement. Following the

Headmistress, they stopped just short of the nurse's office. Muffled voices could be heard within. Olyn sat closer to the doorway as they both tried to listen in.

"I warned you of the dangers of keeping something like that on campus," Nurse Hazel spoke to Headmistress Hersch, scoffing as she went.

"The chances of someone knowing what the artifact is *and* how to use it, let alone where to find it... I thought it almost impossible," the Headmistress' heels clicked on the tile flooring as she paced.

"The Crucifixer should have been destroyed a long time ago," Oza gritted her teeth. The old office chair beneath her squeaked as she leaned over Melonie's bed.

"It was a relic of a forgotten time. I guess it was naive of me to hope it would stay that way..." the Headmistress sighed.

"Why not have it taken to Ismir or one of the others? Surely it'd be simple enough to have one of them destroy it!" Hazel said, her voice quivering a few octaves higher from yelling with agitation.

"And take the chance that the artifact would have intrigued them enough to stash it alongside their collection? They never stop to wonder what happens to that horde when they up and disappear! We've had a handful of curse cases in just the Ivis area alone over the years because of those Old Bunker Hill caves."

Hazel turned to the Headmistress. "You *still* think the dragons are too dangerous, don't you? That's what this is about."

"It's not that simple, and you know it. For years, there hasn't been a single dragal. There has been no connection to our lives, and the lives of the many fae that they could be protecting. Nothing connecting them to *us*."

For a moment Iona turned away from the doorway, taken aback by what they were discussing. As she turned her head back, her eyes locked with Olyn's before he too returned to listening.

"So then, what is that child supposed to be protecting *us* from?"

"I would never put one of my students in danger, Hazel. But that doesn't change the fact that something is on the horizon."

"And just what would that be?" Hazel asked. Her tone turning towards annoyance.

"Magni," the air stood still around the single word.

"Oh, don't tell me you really believe all those conspiracy theories. As if Dala could really bring back that pile of ashes," She spat back in disbelief.

"Hazel, I've done the research. All it would take is a bounty of powerful magic to break the seals that bind him in slumber."

"Slumber? Saya, he's dead, not asleep. It would take

something more along the lines of a powerful necromancer, of which Leera has few and far between, if that. They're all low-power castors that like to hang out in graveyards."

"With the power the Crucifixer gives its wielder, anything is possible..." the Headmistress said as she clicked closer to Melonie's bed.

"Saya, do you know what it can do? I've never seen anything like this, not that Elmora is wrought with hard cases, but the essence that connects her to her scream is completely gone. When she tried accessing it in class the vibrations must have been there, but with no release... You're lucky she just blacked out instead of being put in a coma."

The Headmistress sighed. The skin of her palm meeting her daughter's hand before pulling away in shame. "It is said that the Crucifixer grants the wielder power over one's very essence. Allowing them to separate someone's essence from their being, utterly and completely."

"What does that mean for the rest of us?" Hazel asked, taken aback.

"It could spell the end of everything as we know it."

CHAPTER 16

Iona stared out at Olyn, their faces both white as a sheet. The treading of footsteps towards the door forced them both to take their leave, quickly gliding around a corner down the hall. As soon as the coast was clear, Iona pinned Olyn to the nearby wall with a slight grunt, her forearm bearing down across his chest. Their difference in height was slight, but she peered up at him as though she had the advantage in the situation. And from Olyn's perspective, she did. Her eyes danced like blazing balls of flame.

"What?" Olyn asked as if nothing was wrong. His arms had lifted on their own accord, as if in surrender.

"Don't *what* me, what are you doing here?" taking another sniff of his scent from outside the cocoon of the upperclassmen, she was taken aback to find the revolting stench of sulfur lingering about him. *That's strange, I could've sworn he didn't smell like that before.*

"I'm going to school... what does it look like?"

"Are you really a demon?"

"Er... um... look, it's complicated, okay? Are you going

to move?" he asked, pressing into Iona's arm without much luck.

"Are you ever going to explain what's so complicated about it?" Iona's arm was starting to gain heat, the skin pressing into Olyn began to glow with a fiery aura. "Or are you just going to leave again?" The silver amulet around her neck seemed to hiss at her as the fire inside grew steadily.

"Listen," his tone charged towards annoyance. "We all have our own shit to deal with, and we all deal with it in our own ways. You certainly didn't tell me everything about yourself when we first met," his eyes glared back at her, a noticeable twinge of pain escaping. His glasses started to fog around the edges, obscuring his vision.

Lifting her arm, Iona said, "Can you blame me? We had just met."

"And then we got attacked by Dalians." He took off his glasses. Turning them over in his hands, he used his sleeve to wipe away the moisture before replacing them.

"As if that's my fault!" Passing students turned their heads in surprise. Iona's volume quickly shifted into a whisper. "I had no idea that those two would attack us. Honestly? I still don't know why they were interested in me to begin with."

Tsk. Olyn gritted his teeth. "I omitted some information that would have changed how you see me.

That's all. Wouldn't you have done the same?"

"I've never had the privilege to. Most people take one look at me and assume all sorts of things."

"Then you of all people should understand how important appearances are."

"I suppose..."

Suddenly a messenger pixie zoomed around the hall corner, startling both of them.

"Sorry about that! Just making the rounds ya know!" The pixie chimed. "Oh yes, classes for the rest of today are being canceled! There's also a curfew going into effect starting tonight at nightfall!" the pixie stated rather quickly before zooming off towards another group of students.

"Uh... thanks," Iona said.

With the sound of the halls starting to fill up with students, Iona grabbed the base of Olyn's shirt collar, paying no mind to the countless students staring at her while she dragged the boy through the halls.

"I-Iona, where are we going?" Olyn yelled at her, trying to keep his legs from twisting into one another.

"Somewhere to talk."

As Iona propped the door to her dorm room open,

Olyn took a moment to catch his breath after almost being strangled on the way over. Entering, they were soon met by Maisie who was laying on her bed, having already returned from her morning class.

"Hey I was wondering if you wanted to-" Maisie started, before noticing Olyn. "Who's that?"

"...A friend," Iona said, moving towards her desk.

"Hello," said Olyn, motioning a quick wave before finding a seat on Iona's bed.

"Hi..." Maisie said, just staring at Olyn. The slight whiff of sulfur entered her nostrils causing her to pause. "Is he a?"

"I think so!" Iona replied, cutting her off before she could finish her sentence.

"And he's your friend?" Maisie was beginning to get temperamental.

Iona paused her rummage of the desk to reply. "I haven't exactly had a glowing experience with wyrs in the past, and yet here *you* are. If you two could just play nice for a little bit, he'll be gone soon enough."

Maisie's face turned slightly red as her eyes met Olyn's. "Fine, whatever."

As her face cooled down, Maisie asked, "Do you two know what happened? You went to go see the Headmistress and then classes got canceled all of a sudden."

"Melonie was attacked last night," Iona said, still focused on finding something.

"The Headmistress' daughter? That's a bit bold, don't you think?"

"That's Dalian's for you I guess. Aha!" Iona said, finding what she was looking for.

"No way... Here of all places? Is she going to be alright?" Maisie asked.

"As alright as a banshee without her scream can be," said Olyn.

"What do you mean?"

Iona and Olyn explained everything to Maisie in detail, starting with their run in at the market. By the time they had finished discussing the whole ordeal it was nearly midday. A bell chimed off in the distance.

Maisie's gaze wandered to the window.

"We have to get it back," Iona muttered.

"What did you say?" Maisie asked.

"We have to get her scream back," she said, speaking up.

"Well that sounds like a nightmare waiting to happen. Didn't you guys say that they have a shade? You want to know what happens when you try to fight a shade? ...No takers? I'll tell you what, it *eats you. Whole*," Maisie shuddered at the thought.

"I told you, I hurt it," Iona said.

"Yeah, but that's you, I don't have some sort of divine power I can just call forth and smite the bad guys with. Wyrs might be classified as fae but we just have the powers of a glorified animal when it comes down to it," she turned back to the window, watching as rays of light danced with dust.

"We wouldn't even know where to start looking, Iona. Her scream could be anywhere by now." Olyn interjected, painting his face with his hands.

"What about Melonie?" Iona said, her eyes staring towards the ground between the three of them. Her hands clenching her legs.

"Huh?" Maisie sounded.

"She got hurt..." tears began to form in Iona's eyes. She tried to force them back, but her efforts only appeared minimally successful. A few drops lightly dampened the wood flooring beneath her. "And it's all because of me..." Her face began to quickly heat up as guilt sprung loose like a gust of wind. The water from her eyes quickly evaporating into little trails of steam.

Maisie moved around to where Iona sat, gently placing her hand atop her knee. Staring up at her, she said, "Iona, it's not your fault when something bad happens. Is it sad that someone got hurt? Yes. But that does not mean it was your fault. Even if those Dalians tracked you here, there's got to be a reason why they went after Melonie and not you." The young dragal's eyes let loose more bursts of steam as she tried to compose herself.

Olyn shook his head, hoping they were making the right decision. "If we're going to do this, we need to know what we're up against," said Olyn, breaking up the crying. "I still don't fully buy that those two would come all the way here just to attack someone who isn't Iona. If it even was those two from the market..."

"Fair enough," Maisie said, not moving from Iona's side.

"I noticed that the library was closed for the day when I went to the Headmistress' office this morning. Perhaps you could find out why... Maisie was it?"

"What are *you* going to do?" Maisie asked, turning towards Olyn.

Olyn had noticed the book Iona had been looking for was sitting on her desk. Taking it in hand he said, "I'm going to do what I do best, research."

"Okay... what should I do with her?"

"Iona, maybe you should spend some time with Melonie and see how she's doing. We can meet back up again before the curfew tonight and discuss what we found," Olyn replied.

Wiping the remaining tears from her eyes, Iona gave a nod.

Maisie could hear the pitter-patter of students treading up and down the stairs as she made her way through the first floor corridor. She stopped in front of the large double doors that bore passage into the school's sanctum of knowledge. Before she could approach any further, Maisie caught a whiff of a familiar smell. Like ashen sulfur it permeated her nostrils and held its ground, unwilling to leave. Covering her nose from further invasion she pushed on the door. Inside were dark wooden shelves filled with colorful spines of books in various languages. Large stained glass windows spilled green light into the room and fed vines that crawled up the stone brick walls, giving the room a natural warmth. The room was eerily still. Stepping in, a familiar young woman poked her head up above a bookcase.

"Uhhh..." Maisie said, staring at her. She immediately recognized the woman as the librarian. *What was her name again? Peg- something?*

The light gleamed through the woman's glasses as her long brown hair poked out of the messy bun on her head.

"Are you here for a book?" she asked.

"Yes..." Maisie said, solidifying her footing.

Grabbing a nearby stack of books, the woman swung around the corner to better greet her. She was wearing a wrinkled light blue blouse lazily tucked into a mid-length white skirt. Maisie noticed the small metal name plate that was pinned to her shirt. *Peg Abbott.*

"I'm afraid the library is closed for the day, but if you know the name of the volume you're after I can check if we have it."

"I-I can't remember exactly what it was called but I'd know it if I saw it," Maisie looked around to see if anything was out of place.

"Hmm, well I suppose if you're quick-"

"Thank you Ms. Abbott!" Maisie exclaimed before the librarian could change her mind.

With a roll of her eyes over the blur of a girl, Peg went back to working in the stacks.

Brushing her hand over her nose to clear it, Maisie took a short whiff of the room. She could picture movements, comings and goings, as if the lingering scent of students painted a picture of the last few days. She recognized a few, but continued to focus on the stench that was burning her nose. The putrid smell of dried blood and sulfur led her towards the back of one of the adjoining rooms. *That's weird.* The scent ended at a wall, trailing off into a space behind. Looking up at the wall of books she noted faint cracks in the bookcase. Out of the corner of her eye she noticed something black sticking out. Turning towards a stack of books sitting on the floor beside her she bent down to pick up a coarse black feather. Near the base of the shaft a black liquid slowly dripped onto the ground. Maisie lightly touched the oozing goo, rubbing it over in her fingers before reaching up to her nose.

"*Blegh!*" Maisie quickly moved her hand away from her face. The mysterious liquid smelt of burnt tar and blood.

She could hear a shuffle from behind a nearby stack. As Ms. Abbott appeared again. "Find what you were looking for?"

Quickly, Maisie grabbed the nearest book, stuffing the feather in between two pages before standing back up to meet the woman's prodding gaze. Holding up the book she said, "Yep, found it. It wasn't where I thought it'd be."

"Oh, I see you're a fan of Philodandren's work as well. When you get done with that one I have a few you might like a bit more in the back."

"What?" Maisie looked at the cover of the book. It was titled *An Amorphous Guide to Pushing Daisies.* "Oh yeah... I just got into Philodandy-"

"It's *Philodandren.* That one is about a spectre and a princess, but I have one you might like that involves a wyr and a dragon if that's more your speed."

Maisie stared out at her, dumbfounded. *What is going on?* "Um... yeah I might have to take you up on that," Maisie said, brushing past her and moving towards the exit.

As the door shut behind her, Maisie could faintly hear the librarian say "Happy reading."

The door of the nurse's office shut softly behind Iona as she waded into the sunlit room. Fabric dividers moved gently in the warm breeze coming from the room's far window. Iona's heart began to pound in her chest as she inched closer and closer to the bed that held her friend. When she was finally within view of Melonie's face she took a deep breath. Warm light brushed over her cheeks as she peacefully slept. Her black hair rested pleasantly on the pillow beneath her. Pulling up a chair, Iona sat down down beside her. Raising her head, she noticed Melonie starting to stir from her slumber. Her bright green eyes had been replaced by a somber darkness that reflected back at Iona.

"Hi... are you feeling alright?"

Melonie shook her head as if to say no.

"I'm so sorry Melonie."

She slowly sat up in the bed, her head tilting up towards Iona. The bridge of her nose furrowed with confusion.

"It's all too coincidental... First the attack at the market, and now something happens here? Olyn and Maisie are trying to figure this whole thing out, but I just have this aching feeling that I already know what the answer is..." Iona covered her face with one of her hands, resting the other on the bed near Melonie.

She felt Melonie's hand grasp her own. As their eyes met, Iona felt a strange warmth well up in her face.

To any outside observer they would have seen a rosy face strung around a petite girl's waist balling her eyes out. Meanwhile all Melonie could do was stroke Iona's hair. A small smile of comfort perched on her lips.

Olyn bust through the unlocked door with an almost manic look on his face and Iona's book nestled underneath his arm. The look on his face brought Iona back to his workshop where he had excitedly scribbled notes about her. *I guess he really is that same Olyn I met before.* Her mind flickered between his abrasiveness in the hall and the curiosity and wonder he held now.

He slammed the text on Iona's desk. "I've got it!" Spinning through the open the pages, he flipped to a chapter about banshees.

"So you really did just stick your face in a book all day?" Maisie asked. "Couldn't one of us just done that?" she mumbled, still trying to shake the smell of tar from her nostrils.

"Isn't that mine?" Iona looked at the pages of the book. Some were briefly familiar.

"Yes," Olyn searched the pages for a certain passage, "I thought looking at our situation from a biological perspective might give us a lead as to how we might help Melonie. Not many people in Belvore care to study the specifics when it comes to foreign races like banshees."

"So what did you find?" Iona asked, listening attentively. "I doubt that book would mention the Crucifixer."

"Well, you're right on that point. Apparently, banshees gain most of their energy from passively feeding off the death of other living things. This could be anywhere from insects to people. I think that when Melonie's scream was taken it might have severed this connection to the world around her."

"So she's slowly starving then?" Maisie asked.

"Well, she can eat regular food, but it won't make her whole. From what I can tell, there's been certain items created by hunters in the past that remove the essence of a fae or fiend, but in most cases it also killed the subject.

Whether that was at the time of extraction or lat-"

"So she'll get worse?" Iona asked, interrupting his train of thought.

"Not if we can retrieve her scream in time," Olyn slowly closed the book. "Of course, that's practically impossible. Like I said, whoever did this could be anywhere in Leera by now."

Maisie added another book to the table, carefully opening it to the black feather. Black ooze had permeated the sheets of paper, staining the words. "And just what does your book say about this?" Maisie gestured to the putrid feather.

The smell hit Iona almost immediately. She recognized it from the market. "That's from the one with the wings isn't it?" she looked to Olyn.

Olyn's eyes perked up and darted between her and the feather. "Gods above. And here I was, really hoping it wasn't *those two.*" he said, backing away towards the door.

"What do you mean?" Maisie asked.

"I almost died once this year by Dalians, I'm not looking for a repeat." Olyn buried his face in his hands in tired lamentation, pushing his glasses atop his head.

"What happened to *we just need to find out where it is?*" Iona asked.

"That was before we knew for sure it was those two psychos. We have no idea what they want with you Iona and you're telling me you just want to stroll on up to them?"

"It doesn't change the fact that Melonie needs us," Iona's cheeks began to burst with sparks of heat. She could tell that Olyn was scared. She was too in a way, but something within stirred her heat.

"No, what she needs is the policing guild, *adults for crying out loud*, not a bunch of teenagers to go and get themselves killed."

"Cool it! The both of you," Maisie stammered. "Now, there's nothing that we can do about it today. It's almost time for curfew. So, I think that Olyn should go back to his room and we will discuss this more tomorrow after we've had some time to think about everything," Maisie huffed as her mothering exceeded new levels. Iona sensed a low growl forming in the back of her throat and sat silently.

Tsk. Olyn huffed back out and into the hall, the door shutting with a thud.

"Thanks for tha-," Iona started timidly.

"I didn't do it for you... You know, dragal or not, you shouldn't just rush into things. There's only so much you can handle, even if *you* might not think so." Maisie said, curling back up into bed, her body turned towards the wall.

Iona grabbed her book out from underneath Maisie's on the desk. Turning the other book back to the cover, her face lit up.

"Did you get this novel from the library?" She tried to fight back a chuckle from bubbling up.

"Huh?" Maisie asked, turning back around. "What about it?"

"The book you brought back with the feather, I-I used to know someone who would read Philodandren's work a lot. She had this one too. It's a pretty good read, other than the obvious sexual overtones between the spectre and the princess. Some of her other works are a bit more subtle which I like better. I think that this one was one of her first books though, so that might be why it was written that way."

Something clicked within Maisie's head, and as the gears turned she now understood what the librarian had meant about the subject matter. Her face turned red like a peach, flustered for something to say in return. "I-I just grabbed the first book I saw, I d-didn't know what it was about, don't be weird."

"Okay..." Iona's face had also transitioned a few shades redder.

"I'm going to bed!" Maisie yelled into her pillow as she tried to bury her embarrassment.

Iona sat back down on her bed with a smile and flipped open her book that Olyn had borrowed. *The Beastiarium Arcana* was an incomplete guide to the various races found around Leera. Iona flipped through with disappointment, finding there were no chapters on dragals or dragons alike. Sighing, she slid the book back onto the desk and turned out the lights.

Iona awoke to the familiarity of the dark space once more, her nostrils filled with smoke and ash and her body resonating with the damp heat surrounding her. Before her grew a flame. Slowly it transformed into a small wisp. She watched as it danced happily around her, swirling around her arms with a light heat that warmed the senses. It seemed familiar, friendly even. Then there came a shift in the air, a disturbance in the atmosphere, and the wisp vanished. The dark walls around her began to shake, the exterior flaking off like ash in a furnace. What was left behind were white and red scales with some flakes of grey still interspersed throughout. Iona reached out, softly touching the beast that surrounded her. She could sense a pulse of life flowing through it and as she pressed further on, the being began to wake. As the body unfurled she was able to take a better look at the hulking mass that lay before her. His face was the first thing she noticed. Large crests of horns curled up towards the endless ceiling as he took in a deep breath of air. Releasing it, he moved his head closer to Iona, a large eye gazed at her, almost within arms reach. A large ring of red scales encircled its piercing gaze, which was even redder still. He took a moment to examine Iona before seating himself away from her.

"Iona," he said, in a long and drawn out sort of way, the raspiness of his voice getting caught up in each letter.

"Ismir?" Iona asked, looking up at the mighty beast.

"Yes my child?"

"Have we met before?"

"I suppose you haven't." He took a deep breath before continuing. "I have not gazed upon you with my own tired eyes since you were a baby."

"So you did bless me..." she tried to focus on what to ask him but sadly came up short. "Why?"

"Did your parents not tell you? You were very sick... but that still doesn't why-" he huffed before shifting the topic. "Oh no mind now, we're finally able to speak on equal footing."

"Why, or I guess I should ask *how* are we speaking?" Iona gazed around at the darkness that encircled them.

"You've been feeling very strongly about the situation with your friend, Melonie, is it?"

"How did you-"

"We're linked, psychically. Ever since you awakened your powers I've been slowly able to learn more and more about the world through your eyes."

"That seems a little invasive."

"Do you know what happens when a dragon bestows their blessing upon someone?"

"No..."

"I'll tell you then. A dragon gives away an integral part of themselves. It's only right that we know what the blessed is doing with it. And with this Crucifixer business," Ismir slowly shook his head.

"So you know about that too?"

"I haven't seen it myself, I've only heard rumors brought up by both enemies and allies during a war best left forgotten."

"What do you think they want with Melonie's scream?"

"A banshee's scream can be quite versatile. Anything relating to one's essence can be used in a spell, but for a scream like that? It might be better used as a weapon..." he pondered.

"So how do we get it back?"

Ismir let out a low rumbling sigh. "I knew you were going to ask that... Normally, I say that its a lost cause, but I can sense the fire that burns brightly within you for your friend. I fear there is nothing I could say that would extinguish that."

"So there's a possibility we can save her?"

"Not coming out unscathed. I've been around long enough to sense when change is about. When you know the patterns like I do, you learn when to brace for the storm."

The whole room began to swirl around her as smoke engulfed the scene before Iona. She could feel a pressure forming on her forehead. A low hum swiftly turned into pounding on her temple. Iona awoke to see Maisie hunched over her as she lay caddy-corner on her bed, repeatedly poking her in the forehead with the veracity of a wyr-wolf trying to wake her up for the day.

"Can you stop?" Iona asked, unfazed. She shifted her blanket back over her face in order to soften each incoming blow.

"Did you fall asleep reading?" Maisie said, pointing to the book sitting next to Iona's bed.

"What's it look like?" she said sluggishly.

"Do you know what time it is?" Maisie asked.

"No."

"You slept through breakfast... I can't believe that you slept through your alarm," she said, her face fighting back a concerned smirk.

"What alarm?" Iona asked, sitting up to stretch her arms.

"Let me guess, you don't have a mirror shard?"

"Uh huh," Iona said, making a circular motion with her index finger in the air towards the window.

"Wow, they really did scoop you off the streets didn't they?" Maisie sounded off a short chuckle.

"Shut up!" Iona said, playfully pushing her away from the bed. "I can wake up just fine by myself."

"Clearly," Maisie said with a smirk.

"I was distracted that's all..." Iona said, staring up at the ceiling as the morning light shone through the air, getting caught in the dust as though luminescent smoke swirled about.

"Got a lot to think about?"

"Yeah... something like that."

Chapter 17

The afternoon sun's golden rays shone throughout the classroom. It was Iona's final class for the day, but with all that had happened in the last few days, she found herself utterly distracted. Peering out at the other students, she couldn't help but think. *No one seems to even notice Melonie's absence.* A wide wooden desk sat silent at the front of the class, its glassy finish refracting the golden glow of the room. *Well, except...* The Headmistress' eyes uneasily darted back and forth from the board to the emptiness Melonie typically filled.

The blackboard had scribblings of the history of Belgrum as an institution, never mind a school. Not that Iona had a particular interest in the topic. She sketched out little wisps of flame in the medians of her notebook, trying to recreate the one she had seen in her dream, before closing the book entirely.

"-dragal", Headmistress Hersch's words filtered through Iona's ears as her attention focused once more towards the lesson. Her hand shot up fervently before she could even formulate a question.

"Yes Iona?"

"Uh- um. What were you saying about dragals?"

"My, too busy taking notes?" she asked. Iona's notebook sat closed on her desk. The Headmistress' mouth slid into a slight smirk before falling back into worry.

"Sorry... again." Iona smiled apologetically. She could hear a few snickers as she opened her notebook to a new page, opposite of one that had been filled out with doodles during her last history class.

"To repeat for *Miss Moran,* the last time Belgrum had a dragal enrolled in its halls was fifty-six years ago, back when classes were still being held in the old Burn's building in Ivis' midtown district. Of course, this was back before it was strictly a boarding school so a majority of the students lived in Ivis and the neighboring township villages."

Another student raised their hand to ask what had changed between then and now. To which, the Headmistress promptly replied.

"Forty-three years ago, there was a plague unlike anything that Ivis or the three continents had ever witnessed. It was as if a dark curse had fallen upon the land. However, it was not a curse, so much as a weapon. Dead set on destroying the fragile peace between nations that had begun to blossom here on the main continent,

Dala decided to release a disease. Strangely, humans remained rather unaffected, instead acting as dispersal agents for the illness. It spread and infected those of the fae and fiend populations alike. That's when the school was moved from Ivis' walls to out here in the countryside, where its students and staff would be safe. And it was here in these walls that we fought to protect future generations from brutal eradication. But don't be mistaken, our achievements here pale in comparison to the horrors that ravaged our nation, as well as many others. So many died, not that those *bastards* cared."

The room fell dead silent as the whole class watched. Tears began to well up in the Headmistress' eyes. As Iona watched, she noticed that she couldn't bring herself to look at Melonie's desk.

With a deep and baited breath, the Headmistress finally broke the silence, "If you-ou'll excuse me, that will be all for today's class." The students remained seated as she quickly exited the classroom.

As Iona walked back to the dorms, she couldn't help but think back to the Headmistress' lesson. *They really do mean to harm us. But they can't all hate us that much, can they? No, they already hurt Melonie and they hunted me*

down at the bazaar. They've already shown the lengths they are willing to go to to get what they want. But then, why leave me there in that alleyway? With a shudder, Iona stopped walking. Looking around at the campus that surrounded her, she couldn't help but wonder who Dala might come after next. Bright streams of light whizzed through the air off in the distance as students competed in combat training, while another batch of students flew overhead. Iona touched her back, heat lightly throbbing from the base of her shoulder blades. *They could destroy all of this, and for what? What is their goal?* She thought as she continued back down the path towards the quad. She longed to find herself once again in the comfort of her room, a quiet place in which to better work out her thoughts.

Reaching it, she unlocked the sigil on the door and quickly turned the handle. She let out a billow of hot air as she tried to steady herself. Shaking herself from the door, she looked for signs of life. Maisie hadn't yet returned from her afternoon classes. Her morning books sat at her desk, but her scent of cloves had yet to be refreshed since then. Pacing back and forth, Iona's mind turned towards Ismir. *He would know what to do. But how am I supposed to talk to him?*

"I wonder if I have to say some special incantation or something. Every time I've talked with him I was either asleep or using my powers..." she mumbled to herself, still pacing, she held her hands close to her chest.

She stopped. Remembering back to the amulet that Headmistress Hersch had gifted her. She turned it over in her hand as it hang around her neck. A gleam of green mixed with her pale skin giving her a sickly aura.

"Maybe this will work," she exclaimed.

As she focused on the amulet, she could feel the dull aura of heat around her transfuse into a low hum of energy as though it was being channeled through the stone. Moving back some of the rugs that were placed on the hardwood flooring, she sat down on the cold ground. Crossing her legs, she felt almost meditative as she honed her thoughts on the task ahead. Clearing her mind, she focused only on the bonds that tethered her and Ismir together. She could feel the air around her slowly balloon with heat as she concentrated. Small bouts of flames emanated quietly from her shoulders and fingertips, small scales poked through her skin but refrained from full ascension. The fire was different than before. Instead of rising from and connecting to her body, it merely hovered above. She could feel a familiar flame a great distance away. Reaching out with her mind, she called out towards it, whispering Ismir's name, awaiting an answer.

"Well, this is a surprise *little ember*," Ismir spoke, cutting through the distant silence.

Opening her eyes, she found herself still in her room.

"I don't understand, why can't I see you?" she asked, standing up.

"You called *me*, did you not?"

"Yes," she said, looking around her room. Checking every shadow for Ismir's hulking mass. Waiting for his blood red eyes to peer back at her.

"Don't fret wrymling. Our connection is still fresh and in need of nurturing," he huffed. "For the time being, it seems your connection to me from the waking world is still a bit *fragile*."

"You mean that our connection is stronger when I'm asleep?" Iona asked, taking a seat back down on the floor, trying to refocus her mind towards Ismir.

"Perhaps, it's certainly *easier* for us to connect from an unconscious state. There are less... distractions," Ismir explained. "Why is it that you called *little ember*?"

"Right... Um. I guess I wanted to see what you knew about the plague that appeared forty-three years ago?"

"Curious..." he was quiet a moment as though pondering where Iona's line of questioning was leading. "The Dalians found quite a bit of success with that endeavor. I can sense your hesitancy surrounding them. It's strange. Before the might of one of the last remaining dragons you have no fear, but inside I sense great trepidation for the Dalians."

"You might as well just be a dream, a foreign concept,

a voice in my head. *You* can't hurt me... can you?"

A deep rumbling sounded, a dragon's laugh. "I can see how that would ring true for a human. But child, you have not been human for quite some time."

A moment of searing pain lept from Iona's mind to her hand. She opened her eyes to see the word *hello* scraped against her skin. The flesh was scorching hot to the touch. It hadn't drawn blood but the message was enough to make the skin pucker before reforming back into its normal smoothness.

"The truer question would be, why *would* I hurt you? You are meant to be a vessel for my power, and in return I am granted eyes and ears for the world beyond my slumber. I have no intention of retracting my gift all because you couldn't use it for a time."

He let a moment of silence fall before continuing.

"Dalians can be quite dangerous, but trust me when I say that not all wish you harm. Still," he sighed. "It's better to be careful. Even *I* had to relocate in order to keep from contracting the same illness that the fae folk of Ivis had fallen prey to all those years ago."

"You used to live in Ivis?" Iona scratched at her hand, still waiting for the skin to feel normal again.

"Old Bunker Hill. The site of the old dragon brumating caverns. Today it's simply a site of cursed relics and ruins."

"Do dragons curse objects? Or do you just find them that way?"

"The latter. I simply collect them. The sad things would have not a home in sight otherwise. Dragons are immune to curses you see, due to the fact that we are regarded as lower celestials."

"Does that mean I'm immune to curses too?" Iona asked, scratching the back of her neck.

"Perhaps. Although, I wouldn't assume. It's a theory better left unchecked, especially in the presence of *certain* curses. Most objects I left behind are the kinds of things that only an adventurer with a death wish would go near. If I remember correctly, most will kill or maim you as soon as you pick them up. I found such things... *amusing*," he said, the last word etched into a billowing mumble.

"I'll have to let Olyn know he's a fan of dangerous hobbies then," Iona chuckled to herself.

"I was meaning to bring that one up. His essence intrigues me, it's almost as if-"

"He's said that he'll explain himself in due time. So I plan on giving him said time. Although I'm not sure how much I can trust someone I've known for less than a week," Iona said, cutting him off.

"You've known me for even less time and yet, you felt compelled to come to me for advice," Ismir said grudgingly.

"It's different. *You're* different. Or... at least you *feel* different to me. You remind me of home, if that makes any sense."

"The home you had to leave or something deeper you keep inside?" Ismir prodded. His tone hinting that he already knew the answer.

"Are you going to help us save Melonie or not?" Iona growled, almost spitting wisps of flame between her teeth. There came another pause.

"You're not used to talking about your emotions, are you?"

"I'm not used to really having much in the way of emotions to begin with."

Another bellow came, this one sounding like a disappointed sigh a parent might deliver to a child. "Right then. In terms of the girl, even if you were to somehow retrieve what she's lost, I'm worried about the amount of danger you'd be putting yourself in."

"I mean, you and I both know *those two* are probably the ones that went after her, but I've-we've dealt with them before right? Like in the alleyway when I saved Olyn."

"This time is different. Before, I could whisper secrets in your ear, force your powers to react the way you *needed* in the moment. But now they have access to the Crucifixer, not to mention a banshee's scream... I really have no idea what would happen to you if they tried to remove my flame from you."

"What do you mean?"

"You were such a sickly babe..."

"Ismir what does-"

THUD. The door swung open to reveal Maisie carrying a large stack of books.

"Sorry!" she yelled over the mountain as she sat them down on her desk. Iona quickly gathered herself back to her side of the room so as to not be stepped on.

"...Whatcha doin?" Maisie asked, peering over at Iona. Maisie's eyes then found their way towards the small pile of rugs that had been left by the wayside. Her face baring more confusion.

"I-I was talking to Ismir, or well trying to. The connection broke when you came in," Iona explained.

"Oh... Sorry. How exactly *were* you talking to him?" she looked at Iona puzzled.

"We have some sort of psychic connection, I was trying to-"

"Okay, you could have just said magic and left it at that."

"Well it's not exactly-" Iona stopped, her eyes caught on the spine of one of the books Maisie had brought back with her. *Tales of Merodin: The Deep Trenches of Melin huh...* Iona's face couldn't help but turn a bright shade of peach.

"So, you read the book, didn't you?"

"Read what?"

"The Philodandren book you hid the feather in."

"Ohhh... that. Well, you see I started to clean it so that I could return it and then, I just sort of started reading it. Around all the gross black ooze of course," she sat down the stack on her desk, parsing through thoughts and books at the same time.

"And?"

"And what?"

"And what did you think about it?"

"It was alright... I really liked the action scenes when the princess gets rescued."

"Sure, so you went back and got another one huh?"

"SO! What were you and Ismir talking about?" Her face deepened a shade of red.

She's trying to change the subject when it was just about to get good... Iona shook her head swiftly, forcing herself to refocus back on Melonie.

"I was trying to figure out if we could somehow get Melonie's scream back safely."

"Hmm, and what did Ismir say to that?"

"That it would be more dangerous then last time when the Dalians attacked in the bazaar. They have the artifact now, and we have no idea whether they plan on using it again soon, or for what purpose they took it for to begin with," Iona did her best to hide the fear in her voice.

Maisie paced in front of Iona for a while before stopping and scratching behind her ear. "Fear is the killer of hope, and without hope there's no point in trying, now is there?"

"Did we have much hope to begin with?" Iona's face fell.

"Sure you did. As soon as you walked through those gates."

"You really think we can do it?" Iona sounded unsure of herself. Ismir's words echoed in her head, spinning her gears towards more unanswered questions.

"You've seen how the adults have been acting, they sure as hell don't know what to do, if anything they're waiting on *other* adults to do something about all this. We don't know how long Melonie has before all of this is made permanent, one way or another."

"Right..." Iona's mind flickered back to her crying spell underneath Melonie's understanding arms. She could almost feel her again right there in the room with them. *Seek the scream,* she whispered over her shoulder as tendrils of jet black hair mixed with her own albino sheen. As Iona turned, Melonie was nowhere to be seen. Turning back to the window, she glanced out at the rest of the quad. "So when do we leave?"

Maisie's ears perked up in surprise. "Well, as soon as

possible would be ideal, especially with an uncertain timetable. We'll also need to pick up Olyn."

"Olyn? You still want him to come with us?"

"You both have gone up against these people. You two know more of their tricks than I do. I know he wasn't crazy about the idea of heading out before, but he could prove invaluable. As for me, someone has to look after you and make sure that boy doesn't try anything. Fiends usually don't stick to fae for very long."

"Why is that?"

"They're like oil and water. A bit of separation does them good, but unless you add something else into the mix it usually doesn't end well."

"Surely not all fiends are like that," Iona thought back to her and Melonie's long talks in the overgrown courtyard.

Maisie seemed to catch Iona's thoughts. "Of course, not all fiends are like that. It's just that demons in particular tend to lean more towards malevolence. Though, there are definitely those that don't fit that description." Maisie huffed. "That being said, if he *does* try something, I'll rip his throat out with my bare teeth." She seemed to be talking to herself more than Iona.

"Well let's hope it doesn't come to that. Olyn doesn't seem too abrasive unless you confront him about lying to you," Iona trailed off. Maisie winced slightly at her discomfort.

"Either way, if we end up needing him we'll be happy we decided to drag him along. Even at our age, I've heard demons can be pretty powerful. He could prove invaluable, especially against other Dalians."

Maisie and Iona began to pull together clothing and supplies for the journey ahead. With packed bags, they trotted towards Olyn's dorm building. It was the same building as the Melonie's, Dorm B. Entering, Iona's eyes lingered on the first floor hall of rooms. Hoping to catch a glimpse of Melonie rolling through her door. Shifting her focus back on the wooden banisters of the staircase, they ascended to the third floor.

Iona stopped short of Olyn's door. Moving the long waves of her hair away from her face, she placed her ear to the door. Hearing nothing but a heartbeat, she knocked thrice. The room filled with the sound of someone rising from their bed, the frame shifting under the lack of weight.

Olyn's hair was disheveled and heavy on his face as though he had just been asleep. He wiped his eyes with his hands, blinking at the two girls as he put on his glasses. Peering further down the hallway, Iona caught glimpses inside. The soft light of the evening shimmered against the clutter of his room. It was as if a piece of his workshop had come to school with him. Papers coated the walls, with diagrams and notes plastered to them.

There came a sigh of relief as Olyn finally broke the silence that had gathered.

"What do the two of you want?"

"I told you we'd talk again about our plan, didn't I?" Maisie interjected, fighting back a curt smile as soon as the words left her mouth.

Olyn shut the door part way. "I know that look. I don't get a say, do I?"

"What look?" Iona replied, turning to Maisie who had gone straight faced. Rolling her eyes, she wedged her foot in the door. "Don't you at least want to hear our plan?"

"You mean you actually have one?" Olyn pushed against the door to no avail.

"We're going to get Melonie's scream back." Iona stated proudly. *THUD.* Olyn had quickly punted her foot back from the door frame and slammed it shut. A few of his neighbors poked their heads out from their own rooms before returning back to their own peace and quiet. "Well I talked to Ismir-" Iona prattled on a bit louder, hoping his name would make it through the thick wood.

Olyn's door quickly opened wide. His head darted up and down the hall once more, before herding the two girls within the secrecy of his room. "What did he say?" he spouted. His body had turned towards Iona entirely, casting Maisie to the wayside. Olyn's eyes gleamed at Iona. The version of Olyn she had met in the summer came rushing back like a strong gust of wind. *This is who he is. Not that pretender from the Headmistress' office.* Iona took a deep breath. She could barely sense the lingering sulfur from the previous day. What remained mixed with the smell of leather and oil underneath his fingernails. She wondered if he smelt this way the first day she met him. If he had, she'd been too distracted to notice.

"He called you an idiot," Iona said with a huff as she landed on his bed.

"Huh?" Olyn was taken aback.

"I'm paraphrasing. I think the line was something about how prancing around dragon caves leaves for one hell of a death wish," she retorted, only half-joking.

"I do know what a curse looks like you know," Olyn's shoulders hunched back into a sulk. "And here I thought you were being serious."

As she peered around at the room, her eyes caught on something familiar. On Olyn's desk laid a wooden box with sigils carved into it. The same one that had been on Olyn's desk at his house. However, this time it remained eerily silent. Iona scratched the back of her neck. The sigil Ms. Heisengroph had found still weighed on her mind. Her thoughts wondered towards mentioning the mark to Olyn before an unexpected heat rose from her lungs causing her to inhale sharply with a cough.

"Are you okay?" Maisie asked her. Her hand wrapping

itself around her shoulder.

"I'm fine." Iona wiped her mouth. The heat settled down as her mind turned back towards Melonie. "Ismir expressed some... concerns regarding this particular endeavor."

"Such as?"

"Well, we have a pretty good idea of the people who took Melonie's scream, but it may prove quite difficult to get it back considering we don't know where they went with her essence or what their plan for it is. Not to mention they have the Crucifixer now."

"So you want to throw yourself into a hopeless suicide mission?"

"We could *really* use your help Olyn," said Maisie. She *gently* elbowed Olyn's stomach, his face feigning a sharp pain before turning back towards Iona. Her face shown up at him, expectant eyes pulling him in. "I suppose I could tag along... but if we can't find any leads then it's back to school and you can wait for the grownups to figure something out. At least then, if she-" Olyn choked the words out. "You can be with her." Olyn's face fell. "Let me grab a few things and then we can head out."

"Hold on," said Maisie, interrupting. "If we leave now then someone will notice. We'll have to wait until after nightfall."

"What about the curfew?" Iona asked. "Surely we

should leave before the school gets put on lock down."

"There are ways around that. After all, most magic can't withstand a bit of celestial mana. So, if you're up for trying, you technically should be able to deal with the sigils yourself, Iona," Olyn said.

"What do you mean?" It was Iona's turn to be taken aback. "I can't do magic."

"What do you think happens every time you conjure flames? You're accessing *mana,*" Olyn explained.

"What is she supposed to do? Burn the door down?" Maisie asked teasingly.

"Fire isn't just used for destruction."

A soft chime tolled in the distance as the last bell for curfew sounded. Heading down to the first floor of the dormitory, they were soon blocked by the splintering frame of the front door. What had during the day been seen with welcome reprieve from the monotony of classes, now etched a more somber tone on the three. The dark wood was finely carved with sigils set in the frame. One sigil seemed to glow, it's light growing brighter still as they drew closer. It was as though the sigil meant to act as a warning to those that, not unlike these three, might want to venture off for a midnight stroll. Iona slowly brought her hand towards the wood, placing it along the sigil. Trying to concentrate, she pictured it as an unlit match. The match sat in her palm before igniting itself. The flames burned, withering away the wood until only ash remained. As the ash fell, her palm remained unscathed. Opening her eyes, the sigil had turned from a bright white glow to a much redder luster as the spell died and faded away, becoming one with the wood again. Pressing on the door, it now opened with ease.

Leaving the dorm behind, they made their way across campus and towards the front gate. The soft light of a crescent moon flitting between the shadows of the buildings and trees helped to hide their presence. None of them dared speak until they were on the other side of the boundary. Sealing it behind them, they each let out a heavy gasp. Tension fading, they began the long walk back towards the walls of Ivis.

Take care little ember. Ismir whispered to Iona as though the wind itself carried his voice to her.

CHAPTER 18

The golden dew of the morning rolled in as they finally reached Ivis. The stones that made up the overgrown walls of the city stood solemnly, a protector of the people. The wooden gate creaked as they pushed their way through. On the other side they were met with two guardsmen. Dark circles filled in their eyes as they stretched before the young travelers.

"Where're you three coming from?" asked one, who eyed Iona suspiciously.

"We're arriving from Belgrum Boarding School. We've come back to visit our families in town," Olyn explained to the guards.

"Okay then," the other said with a huff. They both moved out the way, allowing the three to move further towards the town.

"They've gotten a bit more twitchy since what happened at the bazaar," Olyn whispered.

The other two remained silent as Olyn led them on the familiar path towards his house.

"Why are we going here?" Maisie asked. The old sail

on the windmill teetered around counterclockwise. It looked precarious, as if pieces could fall at any moment.

"You're both tired, aren't you?" Olyn shook his head at her. His sleep deprived brain wasn't in the mood for anymore of Maisie's critics.

Stepping inside the old mill, the space was quiet and empty. Groaning ever so slightly, Maisie plopped down onto Olyn's bed. Exhaustion took over and she was soon fast asleep. Iona joined her, pushing the young wyr aside in order to have her own slice of the bed. Olyn took up residence once more on the cot that still remained in his workshop. However, the amount of sleep gained was minimal. The day was only just beginning.

Bang! A pan full of food hit the ground, spilling onto the kitchen floor. Stirring from the sound, Iona and Maisie quickly found themselves staring back at each other. Noticing that their bodies had somehow become interlocked during their slumber, they quickly broke away, getting up from the bed to investigate the noise from the other room. Entering the kitchen, they saw an older woman staring at Olyn. Her dusty brown hair was interwoven with grey and contained in a braid. A loose fitting robe sat on top of a long nightgown that fell right about her calves. *So that's where he got the night wear from.* Her pale blue eyes hidden behind glassed rims turned to the pan that lay unmoved from where it had dropped beneath her. Steaming heat rose from the food. Iona caught a whiff of the mixture and her stomach growled furiously. Maisie and Olyn continued to stare at the woman until Olyn finally cut through the thick veil of silence.

"Hi... Mom."

Silent, his mother rushed to hug him, her slippers digging into the mound of food on the floor. In the short time that Iona had spent with Olyn that summer, he had never mentioned his mother. Looking at her now, she shared a similar demeanor. Her hair was tied, but her bangs still curled into her face. Her eyes were tired and old, but a sense of warmth remained within them.

Pulling away from Olyn, she asked, "Where have you been?" Her hands grasped tightly onto his shoulders.

"I've been... around." Olyn replied.

"Young man! I was left in an empty house for a week without so much as a note! What do you have to say for yourself!"

Olyn sighed. Glancing towards the front door, a piece of paper stuck out from the wood. "I *did* leave a note," he pointed.

Her grip started to loosen, "Oh. I must've missed that,"

she said, releasing him. She ventured over to the door, plucking the piece of paper off the wood. Reading it, she turned it over in her hand before quietly crumpling it up and stuffing it in her pocket. "How's your new school been?"

She sure switched up quick. A sly voice slithered through Iona's mind.

"It's going alright so far... these are two of my friends, Iona and Maisie," said Olyn, motioning to the both of them.

"Hi..." Maisie and Iona both said shyly.

"You three didn't all sleep together did you?" Olyn's mother exclaimed. She gave a quick wink to Olyn that caused Maisie and Iona to do a double take. "Just make sure you use protection." She turned to grab a towel to wipe off her feet.

"Oh, gods no!" said Olyn blushing. "They took the bed while I slept on the cot."

"Good. I wouldn't want my son to be having kids of his own so soon. Look atcha! You're still a kid yourself," she said, chuckling to herself as she bent down to clean up the spilled food.

"Oh trust me, we're *just* friends," said Maisie, her eyes flashing Olyn, practically burning a hole in the side of his head. "*If* that." She muttered under her breath.

"Well, it's always good to have friends. Apparently, it's

important to have people you can depend on and walk with through life's journey, or so I've been told," said Olyn, skulking back to his workshop.

"Still, ever the dramatic one I see," said his mother.

"I take it you don't get to see him all that often?" Iona asked, bending down to help her with the mess. "Olyn mentioned that you work for the Council for Magical Affairs."

"The Council *does* like to keep me busy. It's because of my duties that I don't get to see Olyn as much as I should, I'm afraid. But Olyn's got the same tenacity his father had, that same independent spirit. Truth be told, he often makes better decisions than I would've at his age." she paused for a moment, taking in a deep breath. "Still, I do worry about him, he's always been so reserved... it's nice to see he has friends," she said, dumping the spilled food into a nearby bin.

"So what do you do on the Council?" Maisie asked.

"I'm a castor." She waved her hand and the bin pulled itself back into place. "I'm not as talented as some, but I have a lot of experience with magical artifacts. I mainly work as a historian."

"Excuse us," Maisie followed as Iona absconded back into Olyn's workshop that lingered at the end of the hall. As they entered, they found him nervously pacing in front of his workbench. The floorboards creaked lightly underneath following each round he made.

"I'm confused," Iona said.

"That makes two of us..." said Maisie. "Let me get this right, your Mom, she doesn't seem or smell for that matter like a demon, and you?" She took in another deep breath, scents of soiled food still wafted through the air but the lingering sulfur had long been sweat out from Olyn's pores since leaving the school behind. Amidst the stacks of papers he almost smelled like ink and wood. "Sulfur one minute and then gone the next... How does that work? Was your dad-"

Suddenly Olyn stopped pacing. Iona winced at his reaction knowing that Maisie had struck a cord. "No! No... you've got it all wrong," he sighed, taking a seat in a nearby chair.

"Then what?" Maisie sputtered back unfazed.

"I-I'm actually... I'm not a demon."

"Well that was anticlimactic," Maisie huffed.

"Can you explain a bit more? I still don't understand why or even how you would begin to lie about something like that. Olyn, if your mother is a castor, why couldn't you have just attended the school with me like I wanted? Why go through all of *this?*" Iona pleaded at him.

"I can't use mana. Not like her at least. There are basic spells most people can use, I can do those. But when it comes to something worthy of getting into Belgrum, those other kids leave me in the dust. I'm nowhere close to their talent."

"But what about your cavern delving? Isn't that dangerous without mana?"

"I use tools, or other cursed objects to work around curses. It helps when you've studied the languages they're written in. There's nothing castor about it."

"So what? You got cursed to become a demon part-time? Cause that sounds ridiculous," Maisie rolled her eyes.

"In short, I found something that helps me *mask* the fact that I'm human." Olyn stood, arms splayed out on one of his desks as he turned away from the girls.

"*Masking*? Don't make me laugh. Do you even know half the shit Iona goes through everyday at school?" Iona looked at Maisie with a confused squint. She tried thinking back to her last few weeks at school, and other than being referred to as a child by an upperclassmen and blaming herself for Melonie's condition, she couldn't think of anything else particularly happening. Nevertheless, Maisie continued. "Everyday, I have to hear the litany of gossips talk bad about her because of what she looks like, because of what she is, and because of what she acts like. As her *roommate* it almost makes me sprout fur right now just thinking about it! And *you!* You *choose* to come to school masquerading around as a *demon* of all things. You're just asking for someone to take their anger out on you. Do you know the years of torment peoples' families have gone through? Whole generations wiped out, because of Dala this, Dala that. And you don't care. At least have a bit more respect for Iona. You lied to her for gods sake." Maisie gestured towards her, but Iona just stared back at her confused.

Olyn recoiled further into his desk with every growl from the wolf.

"I'm sorry, okay!" Olyn yelled, his back arching above his shoulders, startling both Iona and Maisie. "I only meant to look after her. Not pretend to be some bogeyman," he turned to face them. "I've spent so long learning about dragons, it was just so... *hard* to let you just walk away. I didn't know if the Dalians were going to find you, I didn't know if I'd ever see you again. And there you were," he thought back to the Headmistress' office, "You looked so at home, and I wondered if I'd made the right choice to follow after you."

Iona let out a short sigh. "So pretending to be a fiend was your only option?" she asked, her voice quiet and timid. She was trying to understand his words as they formed in her mind. Still lost on how he could mask something as big as one's essence.

"You saw my Mom. Even with double her level of mana, it still wouldn't be enough. I *had* to be something the

Headmistress couldn't overlook." He looked deeper at Iona's features, "Something like *you.*"

"You still haven't explained the how of it all," Maisie remarked. "You can't just smear sulfur on yourself and walk through the gate, the school grounds have to sense that you're something more than human."

"Depending on how this journey goes, you'll both find out soon enough." Iona felt a hint of aggression in his tone, like a small ember bubbling up against the skin, but it quickly receded as though it wasn't supposed to bubble in the first place. "What you two should be focused on is Melonie. Her health is still in decline." Olyn shuffled some papers about as he mindlessly tidied up part of the workspace.

He's avoiding our questions, but he's right about Melonie. We need to focus on her right now. Iona thought to herself. "Olyn's right, it can wait... for now," she spoke pointedly. All that matters is that you can handle yourself in a fight."

"Better than I could at the bazaar," Olyn retorted.

"Great, then what's our next move?" asked Maisie.

"Right," Olyn turned back towards his workbench, clearing out some papers he picked up a few and then turned back towards the girls. "Now then, there's a type of spell we can use in order to find something that's been lost."

"You mean a locater spell?" Iona asked, interrupting Olyn's reading of his notes.

Olyn looked up from the pages, "Yes, and how did *you* know that?"

"You really think I was going to let you buy me a book about basic magic and not read it cover to cover?"

"You read all of that?" Olyn asked, his mouth gaping. "Did you even understand it?"

"I got bored in-between training sessions. Of course, I didn't have a lot of the stuff needed to actually practice any of it, but I understood enough. It outlined the components of casting, as well as how to execute some basic spells, a simple locater spell included."

"Yeah, see that simple one isn't going to cut it. Most of those kinds of spells are for finding missing items within a few kilometers at most. There's no telling how far these Dalians have gone, not to mention that there are people out there that actually specialize in this kind of magic," explained Olyn.

"How specialized can you really get?" said Maisie, scoffing.

"So specialized that you could find anything in Leera so long as you have something powerful enough to focus your search."

"Wow, that's a really large distance," said Iona.

"Yeah no shit, but how are we supposed to find

someone with those capabilities?" said Maisie. The trio sat scratching their heads for a moment.

"I actually might know someone who could help," said Iona, snapping her fingers.

"And who might that be?" replied Maisie.

"Oh you'll love him. We go way back." Iona waded back into the hallway.

"You actually know other people?" Olyn called out as Maisie joined her.

Walking by the kitchen on their way out, Olyn's mother stopped them part-way. "You three must be starving," she said, waving them into the kitchen.

The smell of a freshly prepared breakfast wafted towards them as they gazed inside to see mountains of food. Olyn's mother might not have had a lot of mana, but she had perfected what little she could concoct within the kitchen. There was more than enough for all four of them. Family cooking at its strongest, even with Maisie and Iona's strong appetites accounted for. Almost in unison, their bellies grumbled loudly.

Ms. Crosse pulled Olyn aside shortly after the mountain of breakfast had subsided. "What exactly are you getting yourself into with those two?" she asked, a look of concern tightened up around her temple, knitting a line of wrinkles together.

"We're off on some grand adventure, just like Dad always talked about."

"Olyn... Fine, keep your secrets. But please don't forget that your father would want you to be safe, first and foremost," she paused, "That's all I want too."

His face contorted into a sad, almost forced, smile. He couldn't stand making her worry, but he knew the truth would only stand to fracture the peacefully sane facade that currently held up between the two of them. It would have shattered long ago if he told her a portion of what he got up to during her out of town council meetings. But she trusted him, and he didn't want to lose that just yet. Taking a breather, he let his face relax.

"I can-" he wanted to banish the thoughts of impending doom that he was sure were swirling around in his mother's head, but he couldn't bring himself to say the words *I can take care of myself.* "*If* we happen to find ourselves in trouble, I have a headstrong wyr and a fledgling dragal to back me up."

"Dragal? You don't mean-" her hands cupped her mouth in disbelief.

Olyn looked towards the kitchen before carrying on their conversation further down the hall, "Yes."

"Your father never, in all his years. You?" She held her

son's face in her hand, a proud smile beamed back at him. Her other palm pawed at her eyes before returning to her side.

"It was mostly luck to be honest. If I hadn't found her, she probably would have been taken in by the policing guild, or worse," he shuddered, trying to refrain from saying more.

His mother peered back towards the kitchen, "Is it the young lady with the white hair? I was wondering what she was," she paused. "It's strange, despite her appearance, she seems almost *ordinary*. I guess sometimes we forget myths can get hungry too."

"Well, Iona hasn't exactly had an easy life from what I can tell. She doesn't have many people she can depend on." *Or at least that's what I thought.*

"So where are you all off to now?" Her eyes wouldn't leave the kitchen door frame.

"I wouldn't stare if I were you," Olyn's face flashed a facade of seriousness as her eyes darted in his direction.

"And why's that?" Ms. Crosse said, turning back to Olyn.

"She might burn the house down. She's very temperamental."

"Why would you bring her here then?" said Ms. Crosse, taking a slight nip to his shoulder with her fingers.

"Relaxxx," Olyn stepped back, rubbing the red out of

his skin. "I'm only joking, Mom."

"You little-" she knocked him back slightly with a gentle fist to his arm. Olyn braced himself, tightening the muscles against her. Gentle or not, that woman didn't really understand the idea of holding back. The fist made contact, leaving a light sting. Olyn was honestly surprised it didn't hurt more than it had. He rubbed the skin around where the pain faintly resonated before it disappeared completely.

He shook himself away from the strange thoughts he found floating around him, "We should get going. We're supposed to be meeting someone Iona knows in town."

"Well, don't do anything too dangerous just to impress them."

"I'll stay safe," he blushed. "Please, try not to worry about me."

"Sorry kid, worrying is sorta in the job description. Even if I don't always live up to my other responsibilities."

Olyn reunited with the girls in the kitchen. Double checking their supplies, they headed out into the greater expanse of the city.

As they waded through the market district Iona's eyes wandered to a familiar scene. Boxes still lined the alleyway where Iona had faced off against Bernard earlier that summer. Bending down, she could trace the outline of deep scratches etched in the stone. It was hard for her to tell if they had come from the wolf or the shade's large claw that had almost dragged her back into the dark that day. She shuddered at the thought of either. Standing back up, she rejoined the disjointed group as they trailed off further into the market. The leaves of nearby trees had just started changing colors, perfectly in time for the beginning of fall, not yet expelling themselves from their toothy branches. She breathed in the smells of fresh morning bread and pastries as the early go-getters wandered about filling their bags with errands, and leaving with a lighter coin pouch than when they had arrived.

Chapter 19

As they neared a stone brick building in the market district, Olyn noticed a wooden sign hanging near the front door. The sign featured a distinctive animal print, any text having been long since smudged into obscurity. The slight scent of booze filled his nostrils as he thought. *What is Iona doing taking us to a pub.* Iona led them around to the alley nestled beside the establishment. It was a dead end, save for some doors that lead further into other shops and restaurants. Small bits of trash blew past, getting caught in the windless tunnel. A few crunched underneath Iona's leather boots, while another squished out some soiled food from its paper packaging. Iona noted the mess and scrapped her soles clean along the jutting cobblestones of the road.

"Why are we back here?" Maisie asked.

Iona turned to one of the doors. "It's more fun this way," said Iona with a sly smile before climbing on top of some empty crates in order to get a better vantage point of what appeared to be the window of the pub's stockroom.

Maisie took a few cautious sniffs around the alley. Most

of what was back there entailed of trash and filth, but there was something more, some scent the trash had hidden. It was a lingering presence that was unlike anything Maisie was used to smelling back home. As Iona propped open the window, she quietly climbed inside.

"Uh, Iona? Are you sure this is safe?" Maisie asked, but Iona had already disappeared behind the window pane.

"Why do I get the feeling she's done this before?" Olyn mused.

After a moment, Iona's alabaster head poked back through the window.

"Don't you trust me? The coast is clear so come on," Iona beckoned them before disappearing again.

Maisie made her way in with ease, emanating her naturally superior reflexes as a wyr. Olyn, however, had less luck. Sticking his leg through the window was his first mistake, which he soon realized when he clumsily fell into some boxes. Landing with a thud on the dusty ground of the stockroom floor. Maisie and Iona looked at each other, both trying to hold back a nervous fit of laughter from seeping through their hands. The ground shook beneath them as a force came barreling towards the inner door. As it flung open, an older looking man with salt and pepper hair and a well kept beard walked through. His body clogged the door frame, his bicep muscles bulging against the thin fabric of his long sleeves. The air quickly filled with the same strange scent from the alleyway. The man's eyes glowed a bright blue as he let out a guttural growl that resonated throughout the room. Maisie's body began to shift on the ground in a panic. Her legs began to shake. Noticing Iona, the man's eyes dimmed as his face transformed into a familiar scowl.

"Been a bit, hasn't it, Tuck?" said Iona with a cheeky smile painted across her face as she played nervously with the ends of her hair.

"Kid, I thought you were dead, you know that!" He boomed before coming over and picking Iona up by the scruff of her shirt collar. Olyn and Maisie watched as he carried her off into one of the other back rooms. Concerned, but cautious, they silently followed Tuck, making sure to keep their distance.

"You know ya don't have to carry me ya big lug!" Iona chuffed, as she hung like a kitten in Tuck's grasp. "I'm not a cripple, I can walk!"

"After what you put me through? I should do a whole lot more!" said Tuck, finally plopping her down in a chair in what looked like to be his office. "And you two! Get in here!"

Maisie and Olyn quickly closed the gap between them, joining Iona and Tuck. Their backs were practically glued to the wall closest to the door.

"Now," Tuck took a seat behind the office's desk,

"where have you been?" he asked.

"Hmmm... It's a long story," Iona replied, but she could tell Tuck wasn't in the mood to be left in suspense.

"Well, we got till I open don't we?" Tuck growled.

She sighed. *We don't have that kind of time to waste.*

Iona explained what had happened in the market district the day Olyn found her, as well as where she had been since then. Tuck listened intently, about what happened with her powers being released to what happened to Melonie. After Iona finished speaking, Tuck couldn't help but fight back a chuckle.

"So you mean to tell me you can grow wings, just like that? Where do they even come out from?"

"Is that all you got from that story?" Iona said, reaching over the table to slam her bare hand into the top of his head.

"Owie... hah hah looks like you *have* gotten stronger. That would've probably left a bump if I wasn't so damn durable," he said, rubbing his head.

Looking at Tuck now, his presence at first glance appeared much more menacing than he actually was. Maisie could see the gentle softness of his face and his gestures. Not unlike her own father, he appeared tender and caring towards Iona. It was a stark contradiction between his burly appearance and the way he carried himself around her. *How does this girl get people to open up like that?* Maisie thought to herself as she pondered over their strange encounters with one another since meeting by chance on the streets of Ivis earlier that summer.

"Oh, I forgot to mention that Tuck is a wyr, didn't I?" Iona cocked her head to the side, staring back at Olyn and Maisie.

"What variety?" Olyn asked, thinking back to the blue glow that had come from Tuck's eyes.

"Right, a bear. Sorry. Sometimes I forget people can't just tell from their personalities," Iona turned to Tuck. She could always sense the animal inside him. Even before her abilities had begun to awaken. Turning to Maisie, she too could sense the baring fangs beneath her flesh, but she tried to not concentrate too much on her wolf side.

Maisie let out a deep sigh, her shoulders finally releasing from the wall, her legs nearly toppled beneath her. Catching her breath once more she said, "And here I was thinking he was going to eat us back when he found us in the stockroom."

She turned in her chair towards Maisie. "Eat you? That's a bit much, even for Tuck. Sorry for worrying you both, he really is a big softy at heart."

"I think you're missing one apology," Tuck huffed from behind her.

Turning back to him, Iona said "I'm so sorry for

worrying you. Everything just changed so quickly, I didn't have a lot of time to think everything through. A-and I didn't want to get you into trouble like before…"

"Before?" Olyn was intrigued by whatever history the two shared. Iona could tell from his face, he had more questions than she cared to answer.

"It's a long story, for another day. Now, mind telling me why you three were breaking into my stockroom? Other than trying to cause my fur to sprout early."

"Oh, um, so… are you still in touch with Elleanna?"

"You've got to be kidding me *Io*," Tuck's hand brushed back the hair from his temple in some small show of discomfort.

"What's his problem?" whispered Maisie to Iona, venturing forth from the safety of the back wall. Her hands latched onto the back of Iona's chair as Olyn still stood off to the side.

Iona whispered back, "They used to date."

He huffed, warm air breezed past Iona's cheeks and chin. "We didn't just date. We were engaged, or did your flame scrambled brain forget that part?"

"Well… I was kinda hoping that you were a bit… past that part, by now."

"*Io,* how does one exactly move past the love of their life ditching them mere weeks before their wedding all so that she could, and I quote, '*hone her craft*'?"

"That's cold, but not uncommon," explained Olyn. "Most covens won't take female castors with romantic attachments."

"The kicker is that she's not even *in* a coven," Tuck was now visibly lamenting from beneath the hands that covered his face.

"Please, Tuck, it's important. I just need to know if she can help us or not."

"Help you all do what exactly?"

"Maisie?" Her hand outstretched towards her for something. Just as fast as Maisie had placed the grotesque feather, its ooze visibly permeating the cloth draped around it, into her hand, Iona slammed it down on the table before Tuck with quick fervor.

"Now that's just gross Io..." Tuck said, plugging his nostrils. The smell of sulfur and rot filled the room in a burst.

"Ah-Are you sure you didn't break it?" Olyn barked as he covered his mouth. He looked as though he was going to be sick.

Plugging her nose with one hand, Iona carefully inspected the feather. Nothing had changed. The rachis of the feather was still more or less intact than before, its vane matted down with ooze. Flashing a thumbs up at Olyn, he couldn't help but shake his head, his hands lowering from his face before being plastered back.

"We need a large-scale locater spell," Iona's nose was still plugged, creating a strange reverberation within her voice. She wrapped the feather back up in the cloth tightly, the smell slowly following it back into its slumber.

"Io, don't tell me you're going after whoever this thing belongs to. Do you even know what this is? This isn't from some demon or other fae, that's a feather from one of the Fallen."

"Fallen?"

"They're beings that abdicated from the rest of the angelic celestials when Magni rose up, and were cursed for it," Olyn rattled off.

Maisie and Iona stared at Olyn for a moment, stunned.

"What? I read up on some of Dala's history after our recent encounters with them. I don't like being unprepared," he pouted.

"Tuck. Can she do it?" Iona said, turning back to the burly man.

"Io... she'll just tell you what I have. That it's too dangerous, newfound strength or not."

"Tuck... Melonie," Iona choked up, "is one of the only people who hasn't shied away from me at first glance. She was kind to me, even when, coincidence or not, these Dalians showed up at her door. She forgave me, even when I could be the reason that she dies. I have to save her."

"Even if you die?"

Iona sat there, stunned. She hadn't thought much about what would lie at the end of this journey. Was it one of many? Or perhaps the last in a long line of survival situations. Living on the street had deadened the fear of the end, but had she truly considered it before? Had she bargained enough? Or too little? She had faced death in a head-on launch numerous times over the course of her life, but none had taken her. Would this time be any different?

"Yes," she spoke clearly and confidently before taking a breath to start again. "I have friends to guide and protect me. Olyn and I have already handled them a few times before with moderate success. They haven't even had to deal with Maisie yet."

"Even so," Tuck took a strong inward sniff, the remaining sulfur in the air causing him to gag slightly. "You have a wolf and a human that smells funny. What's the boy even meant to do against high dark fiends?"

"I'll have you know that I can be quite useful," Olyn retorted.

"You good at flying?"

Olyn's face turned puzzled.

"Cause you three ain't walking all the way to Wizmir."

Iona's face lit up at Tuck's comment, "Does that mean you'll help us?"

"You'll have to find your own way there, but I can give you directions to her shop. I know it's been a while since

Iona traveled that far away from Ivis."

Maisie's brain had been rattled with thoughts of the journey, she contemplated the path ahead before a thought hit her. "In terms of transportation, we could always try Savin. They have plenty of horses and there's usually a caravan or two around this time of year for selling wares and transporting goods to the Festival."

"Festival?" Olyn inquired.

"Yeah, the Fall Festival in Wizmir. It's the perfect cover, right? If anyone asks, we're just a small group of kids going to the Festival," Maisie suggested.

"Sounds like you three have it all figured out, huh?" exclaimed Tuck. "But Io... I want you to promise me that you'll take care of yourself. I know it probably doesn't mean much to you, but it would at least give me some peace of mind to know that you're doing alright. After you disappeared, I began to fear the worst had happened to'ya."

"I promise to do my best. I'm sorry, but that's the most I can promise, Tuck," she looked into his downtrodden eyes, filled with sadness and a small glimmer of hope for what once was.

"If we leave now, we should be able to make it there before nightfall," said Maisie trying to do some calculations in her head.

Nodding in agreement, Iona began to rise from the small back office table. Tuck's hand gently grabbed Iona's arm, a shoot of worry washed over her. She shuddered before turning back to Tuck, his face still downtrodden. Placing her hand atop of his own, his face appeared as though drops of relief had warmed it. He finally let go.

The three exited out of the back of the pub, making their way back onto the main road of the market district. They soon departed from Ivis towards the small farming town of Savin. The road wasn't long, but it wound through dense woods, broken up only by the vast farmland that made up Savin's township.

Chapter 20

Savin was historically a farming and logging town, home to plenty of wyrs and humans alike. However, unlike other farming towns, it sported robust houses and a lively town community brought together under the authority of the local pack. As they traveled, Maisie also explained that they tended to do business with local cities such as Ivis, and even places as far as the country of Caneu.

As they neared the edge of town, Iona started to notice the townspeople more and more. At first it was a wave, or a stare, but the further they entered the town, the more people came up to greet them. As Iona watched, she realized they weren't greeting Olyn and her, but Maisie. As they continued on the path, Maisie stopped outside of a large family house, white stucco walls lined with a dark timber only seemed to further accentuate the subtle elegant homeliness of the building. The chimney bellowed smoke out into the sky as small imps zoomed through, sucking up their portion before moving on to the next house. Others clung to the sides of chimneys, their plump bellies releasing flakes of ash from the small slits along their sides that seemed to burp as they consumed the smog.

"You live here I presume?" Iona said, her eyes following the imps.

"Is it that obvious?" Maisie replied, her face turning a shade redder, but only for a second.

"It *has* been a theme today," Olyn muttered.

The moment passed as the front door swung open to a middle aged woman carrying a basket full of what appeared to be sheets. Her long brown hair was tied back in a sweeping net of strands. Bound towards her lower back, it swayed as she hiked up her the basket. She made her way down the stairs before noticing them.

"Maisie?" she exclaimed. "Well, this is a pleasant surprise. Is it time for your school break already?" she asked, wiping away some sweat from her brow. "Oh, and you brought home friends, how marvelous," She turned back towards the house, leading the three of them into the cottage and through to the kitchen.

"Here, make yourselves at home, I'll just go put the kettle on."

"Mrs.-" Iona started.

"Oh please! Friends of Maisie can call me Mali, enough with the Miss this or that," Mali did a double-take before turning back towards the kettle. "Say, you're that young girl I ran into back at Belgrum a month or so back weren't you? I'd never forget those eyes, and that hair!

Gods that must be hard to keep up with. Just how do you keep it so white?"

"It's actually my natural hair color, well... sort of, but it's a long story," Iona was surprised to sense a different kind of wolf in Mali. Her's was strong and brave, without the need for gnashing teeth like Maisie. It was maternal, a protector, a beacon that filled the room. Iona could see its light in her smile.

"Oh don't mind me dear, I've heard all sorts of stories, young castors playing pranks and the like, it is *quite* a beautiful shade of white though."

"Th-thank you..." Iona's face turned a bright red color. She wasn't used to receiving compliments, especially from an adult who she'd just met.

"So how do you two know my Maisie?" Mali asked as she stirred something into the boiling kettle.

"Well, I'm Maisie's roommate for this school year. My name is Iona Moran," she said, nudging Olyn to answer.

"Oh! And I'm Olyn Crosse, I sort of know Iona more than your daughter, but we've all become fast friends."

Maisie's eyes scowled at Olyn with a certain reluctance.

"Hmmm, Moran you said dear? I don't think I've ever did meet a Moran. Is your family from Belvore originally or did they immigrate here?"

"Um... I'm not quite sure, sorry."

"Pay it no mind, I'm just fascinated with names is all, family roots and whatnot. Now Crosse, I think I have met one or two of those. Not a very common last name."

"It's from the Reconstitution Era. Back when lots of people were picking new names," Olyn explained.

"Of course, that whole ordeal does make tracing back lineages a bit harder. But when you're a pack master you tend to pick up a knack for these kinds of things."

"So, I take it you're the alpha in your marriage too then," said Olyn, rather bluntly.

Maisie tried to hold back a laugh, resorting to a big grin painted across her face before finally bursting like a bubble. "You have no idea. She's the only reason my dad is a wyr in the first place," her distant, quiet, cackling was stopped abruptly by the sound of her mother's voice.

"Maisie! It's bad form to exhaust lineage with strangers..." she said with a pause, "But since it's already out there, it's true, my husband is one of the bitten," she looked quite solemn, as if that thought bothered her.

"I didn't realize that you all still followed those practices. I'm sure you're well aware of how dangerous the change can be for humans, even if they're consenting," Olyn prodded further.

"Yes, but-" Mali started before a tall man came bursting in through the back door, his hands full with freshly pulled produce from the back garden.

"Maisie, you're back!" he said, hugging his daughter tightly.

"Hi. Dad. Can't. Breathe," Maisie gasped.

"Oh sorry hun! Sometimes I forget my own strength," he said, moving over to his wife to kiss her on the forehead.

"Mr.-" Iona started.

"Oh no need for formalities! Call me Nic."

These wolves sure are two peas in a pod, Iona thought to herself.

"So what brings y'all back from campus so soon?" asked Maisie's mother, reorienting the conversation around her daughter. A serious look had taken the place of Mali's cheerful demeanor. It was almost as if she had tuned into something else. Her words edged towards barbed.

"There was a break-in at school, so the Headmistress thought it would be best to send the students home for a few days while the faculty had time to look over the security measures that are in place. That way, the school can better ensure the students' safety when they return," explained Maisie.

I haven't heard anything about new security measures. Iona thought as she stared at the back of Maisie's head intently.

Olyn glanced over at Iona for a moment, looking for

any sort of reaction.

"If that's so, then why isn't your brother back from school yet?" Mali retorted.

There was a pause as Maisie contemplated her next move.

"We decided to come back a day early in order to make it in time for the Fall Festival in Wizmir," Maisie was wearing the biggest smirk Iona had ever seen.

"Yeah, Iona's never been before!" Olyn broke in, trying to help.

"Actu-" Iona started in before shutting her mouth.

"Oh! So you'll be showing your new friend around! How wonderful. I remember my first Fall Festival..." Nic said, reminiscing. "The city's best castors really go all out, don't they hun?"

"Yea they really do..." Mali spoke in a more monotone voice than her husband, still focusing on her daughter. "I suppose y'all will be needing a ride?" she inquired.

"Well I just thought-"

"You thought there would be a caravan heading to Wizmir for the Festival."

"Yes."

"You should count yourselves lucky then, a few of the boys ran into a few problems with the last caravan's wheels so they had to wait a few days for repairs. Isn't that great Mali? They'll be able to make it to the festival," Nic said, nudging her slightly.

Nic had seemingly brought down Mali's defenses in one fell swoop. With a defeated look on her face, Mali let out a sigh.

"It leaves in a few hours. Guess you three should get ready to head out by then," she grumbled.

Chapter 21

Their nightlong travel towards Wizmir was hazy. All three of them had been running on what little sleep they had gotten that morning at the windmill. One by one, they all fell fast asleep in the back of the caravan, the cool autumnal breeze brushing against their skin as the carriage carried them further and further towards their destination.

As Iona slept her mind drifted.

"Iona?" a familiar voice called out.

Opening her eyes, she found herself in one of the classrooms at school. It was hard to pinpoint which one as the scene seemed to shift if she looked too hard at it. As desks blurred together, they carried sounds from far off.

"Iona?" the voice called again. It was sickly sweet, like someone with a wet cough, straining to speak.

She turned a corner and saw her. Melonie appeared before her in a black dress. A veil cascaded down her face and ruffles at the bottom of her hem seemed to slowly wrap themselves around the wheels of her chair. She turned, pushing the spokes as they became more and more entangled. She did not speak.

Iona followed her intently down the hall. A right, then another right. Until they were at Melonie's door. Her hand lifted, her index finger pointing like some mute ghost towards the frame. The wooden door shuddered before parting softly. Iona peered through to the empty room. She entered slowly, unaware of what might be awaiting her inside. As she reached out for the wall of the entryway she was met with a cold wet feeling. As she examined her hand she found that it was coated in water. Looking back at the room around her, it was not a room at all, but a rocky tunnel.

A small light emerged at the end of the tunnel. Another wisp of flame. It danced and twirled in the darkness, taken in by its own beauty. Iona carried herself forward, as wet rocks were gouged by torrents that attempted to thwart her forward projection. As she made it to the end, the light faded back. Waiting for her in the dark of a now open cavern. The wisp's light dared not reach anything but Iona.

Suddenly the wisp ignited, filling the room with a sanctimonious light. Iona couldn't stop herself from looking away.

Iona's eyes flitted open to find the sun shining around her. They were no longer moving, instead the crisp morning air carried the sounds of laughter and playful exchanges from nearby. The Fall Festival. She looked out over spires that towered around her. Ornate glass windows catching and bending the light of the day. The caravan had been parked in a small outlet along with other empty carts. Reds and golds flitted on the walls around her as castors flew by overhead on brooms and other enchanted objects. Pulling herself out of the wagon, Iona ran to the archway of the courtyard. Peering down the street, she was soon overwhelmed by the loud crowds of people funneling further into the city. A small spark caught her eye, a few children danced around with crackling sticks. Sparks flew towards the ground as they were wildly swung about in excitement. The small embers brought forth memories of a time long forgotten. Ahead of her, almost as if mist had formed into a tangible memory, she saw herself as a child, father's hand in tow as they walked down the street. But there was something wrong with the scene, the memory, or whatever it was that she was gazing into. Her father's face was replaced by blank mist. Had it really been that long that she didn't even remember her own father's face? His frame towered protectively over her as they walked. Iona watched herself. Her hair had been braided by her mother that day, her eyes a soft red, still contrasted greatly against her plump pale skin. She watched as her younger self pointed towards the children, gazing up at her father, as if she was asking for permission to join them. Her father patted her on the head before picking her up into his arms. She watched as he pushed back down the street in the opposite direction of the children's laughter. The younger Iona's face grew long and ragged. Pouting on her father's shoulder, before even her father's shoulder faded back into mist. The scene dissipated as they marched further and further through the crowd, till eventually even her red eyes were nowhere to be seen, leaving Iona alone once more.

"What was that?" Iona mumbled to herself.

"Iona, you alright?" Olyn said, coming up next to her. "I was trying to get your attention, did you not hear me?"

Iona was still watching the street, trying to catch another glimpse of herself. "It was nothing, I just thought I saw someone I knew."

"Really?" Olyn said, sticking his head out onto the street. "Well, it'll be hard to find them again in a crowd like that, was it anyone important? You didn't see Elleanna yet, did you?"

"No... it was just someone I haven't seen in a long time," she turned back towards the carts. "We should get going." Olyn followed closely behind.

Returning to the caravan, Maisie was still sleeping in its bed. Iona gave a quick flick to her forehead, Maisie's head bobbed before she woke up with a yelp. Rubbing her forehead, she looked around.

"Is it morning already?" she asked, stretching.

"It's still early. The festival only started a hour or so ago," Olyn said as he lofted a bag of potatoes over his shoulder.

"You could have woken us up," Iona nudged him as she peered into the cart. Most of the wares had already been moved out.

"Those two said to let you sleep," he pointed to the wyrs that had driven them. "Something about this being *man* work. Honestly, I think they're just scared of your mom."

Maisie let out a yawn. "Perks of having a pack master mother who's also a township leader I guess." She lifted herself out of the cart and onto the ground, dusting off some of the dirt that had kicked up onto her clothes. "Still, they should have let us take some loads instead of making a human do a bunch of heavy lifting." She grabbed the sack from Olyn's shoulders and lifted another out from the cart. "Where do these need to go?"

Olyn pointed to a nearby building with a sign that featured a rose. "That shop right there. You can enter in through the stockroom over there," he directed.

All three of them helped to unload the caravan's remaining cargo before taking their leave of the wyrs.

Iona reached into her pocket, pulling out some directions Tuck had scribbled down before they had left Ivis. Guiding Maisie and Olyn through the bustling streets, they soon found themselves on one of the less busy side streets of Wizmir's bustling market district. The shops were highly adorned with banners and other fabrics etched with magical sigils and other writings. Following the street, they soon found Elleanna's shop. A large wooden sign was carved with gilded letters that read *Elle's Bits and Bobbles.* Iona could see a light resonating from behind the frosted window of the front door. Knocking gently, she stood back from the door. It had been a few years since she had seen Elleanna. A twinge of anxiety perked up at what awaited her behind the glass. Taking a deep breath, the door swung open. Behind it appeared a tall and slender young woman with dark brown hair that seemed to absorb the light, darkening in the morning rays. As her eyes drifted down to Iona, they grew wide. The door slammed shut just as fast as it had opened a moment ago.

"Uh... Elle?"

"Why are you here?" she said, the door muffled her voice to a whisper. "Did Tuck send you?"

Iona wondered for a moment if she should answer honestly. "Uh.. No," she said unconvincingly. "Well, he gave us directions, but I need your help Elle."

The door parted open, but this time only just a crack. "So, Tuck didn't send you here?"

"NO!" Iona was beginning to grow impatient. She could feel heat begin to lick at her face as it kicked up its boil inside her. She tried to keep it contained. She couldn't remember ever getting that upset with Elleanna before and it upset her, causing her insides to churn even more.

Elleanna slowly opened the door up a bit more. "What do you need me for Io?"

Iona took in a deep breath and the heat began to subside. "We need help finding something."

"Why didn't you just have Tuck go sniff it out for you?"

"Because its not something that simple... It's something that's really important. Something that we'd need a long range locater spell for."

"Io I swear, if this is another book you left somewhere..." her head quickly bobbed towards the sky in dismay, but she stopped herself short, gesturing them into her shop. "Oh just come in before I change my mind." Olyn noticed her checking up and down the road before quietly shutting the door behind them.

Entering the shop, they were immediately assaulted by a variety of different fragrances. Peering around, it was abundantly clear to the three of them that Elleanna liked to light multiple incenses at once. The aroma almost suffocated the air around them, even Olyn was choked back as he tried to find even a bit of fresh air for his lungs. *Maybe this is one of the reasons they didn't end up working out,* Iona thought to herself as she pressed on, her shirt sleeve heaving as she tried to breath through the fabric in order to filter out some of the smell.

Entering one of the back rooms, the air finally seemed breathable. Looking around, they appeared to be in some sort of storage room, not unlike Tuck's back room they had snuck into the day prior. Tall shelves of ingredients in bottles lined the walls. Another bookshelf in the far corner of the room housed a quaint collection of books, some of which Iona immediately recognized by their ornate spines. *Secrets of the Mell, Journey to Angriva,* and *House of Revelry. Elleanna... You sure do love a good Philodandren book. Same as always.* Iona scoured over the new titles that she hadn't seen before. Jokingly, she tossed one to Maisie who blushed upon realizing what she had been handed and glared back at her. Iona chuckled between wefts of white hair that cascaded over her face.

Elleanna paid them no mind as she pulled out a large map from underneath the rectangular table that filled out of the center of the room. It rolled smoothly over the table's surface, the paper's thickness appearing almost light and airy. Olyn peered out at the map of Leera. It looked slightly different from the maps that he had seen printed in his books at home. This one featured another landmass just out of sight. It stretched far and wide across the Sea of Cerpis, almost out of Dala's reach. He felt as though it was wrong, as if it shouldn't be there. Something tugged within him in a spat of panic.

"So, how exactly does this work?" Maisie asked Elleanna. Olyn's mind attempted to refocus on the others.

"Depends on what you are trying to find," she said, placing various stones and candles towards the outer reaches of the paper, putting weight along its edges.

Iona turned away from the bookshelf. Joining the others at the table, she tried to find the words to explain. "My friend, Melonie. She's a banshee who's lost her scream. We don't know what will happen to her if we don't get it back..."

Elleanna seemed equal parts impressed and repulsed by the notion. "Hmm... well that's a tricky one. How long has it been since she lost her essence?"

"This should be the third day."

"She must be getting pretty hungry... Without her essence she'll die soon. I don't know much about banshees, but from what I do know about essence, the sooner you reunite her with her scream, the less long-term effects she'll have to suffer through."

"So can you find it?"

"If the scream is being contained in something then you still have something left *to* find. Though rare, devices that extract essence usually include a way of storing it since it's more or less intangible. Question is, do you have something that belongs to her?"

Iona instinctively grabbed at her chest. As she turned

the amulet over in her hands the metal was still warm to the touch since her outburst at the door. *I doubt something like this would even work. It needs to be something that belongs to her, not something given away by her mother.*

"I don't think we have anything of Melonie's," Iona sighed.

Maisie perked up, as though she had just made a connection in her mind. "Will this work?" she asked, placing the tar-like feather on the table, careful to keep it wrapped.

"What is it?"

Right, the feather. "We think it belongs to one of the people who stole her essence. That should work, right?" Iona asked.

"But what is it?" Elleanna asked again, plugging her nose slightly to the foul smells that had begun to escape its binding.

"We'd really rather not open it," Iona said, as she quickly tightened the cloth's hold around the feather.

"Well we can try, whatever it is..." she grabbed a few ingredients from a couple of shelves and then returned back to the table. "Do you all know how to preform a spell?"

"Basic household ones," replied Olyn.

"Oh I know this one," Iona chimed in excitedly. "For bigger spells you need three ingredients right? Well depending on the spell. There's the focus, energy, and transformative property, if needed," Iona replied, whispering the last bit.

"Close, but not quite. You need an essence ingredient, which I'll admit works a bit like supplying energy, so close enough I guess. For this particular spell, we'll use your mystery item as the focus since it's connected to its owner, some dirt from a far away land as the transformative property and a bit of my own mana to power it." Her hands hovered over the other two ingredients as they watched the dirt lift up into the air. Slowly it burrowed into the cloth, releasing bits of foul odor as it moved, meeting with the tar-like substance that had sprung from the feather's vane. Melding together, it slithered back out of the cloth, the tar becoming pin pricks, then bubbles, then a thin stream of black. The liquid spun above the map, almost as if it was alive. Iona could sense it sniffing out the location, moving from north to south then west to east before finally landing with a splat. Foul drops hit skin, Maisie almost gagging at the thought of the sulfur and tar smell being anywhere on her. The ooze on the table had formed a near-perfect ink blot encircling an area near the coast. *That's not far at all*, Iona thought.

"Why does that area look familiar?" Maisie asked.

"It's near Overeen. See, here's were the inland harbor would be," Olyn said pointing towards the coast.

"Well great. How are we supposed to get there?" said Maisie. We aren't exactly flushed for time."

"There also aren't many people going out of town right now cause of the Festival, so it'll be pretty hard to find anyone to take you," explained Elleanna.

"We're in the magic capital of Belvore, *right?* I remember my mom saying a while back that they'd been having trouble with people abusing the teleportation scrolls you could find here..." Olyn said.

"Yeah, they cracked down on a whole lot of vendors who didn't have the proper permits. Trust me, the last thing you want is to teleport your boat onto land. Sounded like a bunch of total amateurs if you ask me," Elleanna said.

"Are there any stalls still left up?" Olyn asked.

"Should be. I always see a couple of the old geezers hanging around the marketplace in the transportation district."

"Then it looks like we know where we're going next," Olyn said, looking up to Iona. Maisie and him grabbed their stuff, shuffling back out of the back room towards the door of the shop. Maisie, slyly grabbing one of Elleanna's Philodandren books from the far shelf as she made her exit.

Iona held back, waiting to speak with Elleanna alone. "It seems like you and your friends have your course charted," she slammed a small sheet of vellum down on the spell, before folding it and handing it to Iona. "This should help the rest of the way Io."

"Elle..."

"Don't. You're still a child, but you won't be for very much longer. So I need you to know... I didn't leave because of you. Me and Tuck, it just wouldn't have worked out."

"But why?" Iona paused. "When you left, Tuck cried for four weeks straight. He could barely get through orders at the bar without getting his tears in the glass. He loves you Elle."

She paused as if she was about to say something, but decided against it. "I've never been good with goodbyes kid. And after what happened with your family, I wanted to be there for you, I did. But in the end it became more about staying for you than staying for myself. I'm where I need to be. And look at you, opening up, making friends. You're changing and growing in ways that I never could have dreamed of," her voice lowered. "You'll be fine without me. I don't have anything left to give you."

Iona pushed past her, but stopped short of the door to the main room. "I'm not the one who needs something from you."

Venturing out into the bustling marketplace, it was hard to tell one ware from another. Banners strewn from one side of the street to the other danced about in celebration in a breeze that seemed to pick up randomly. Children ran past, laughing and cheering at the crackles of fire as they popped in their hand. A young girl, with their head turned around, ran straight into Iona, her sparkler launching straight into Iona's arm. Dull white scales quickly pricked up along the skin, cutting off her nerves before she could even feel the heat. The child stared up at her from the ground in a daze. As she watched, the scales popped themselves back below the skin. Iona, finally noticing the child, reached down to help her up. But before she could even touch her, the child ran away in a screech, her friends following closely behind. Iona let out a sigh before turning back to the group.

"What was that about?" asked Olyn.

"I think my scales freaked her out."

"It could be that you're also a stranger," Maisie chimed in.

"Maybe she wouldn't have been afraid to even touch me if I looked like you," Iona sighed. She'd never had a good track record with other fae, even before she knew she *was* fae. Other children would often scatter or even pick fights with her. *Children fear what they aren't taught. What they don't understand.* She told herself, hoping it would make the pang of the child's fear sting less.

Maisie gazed out at Iona, her lip bearing itself against her cheek. Looking down the street, her eyes caught on one of the district signs.

"I think we're nearing the end of the market district," she pointed towards the new symbol. "That boat must mean that's the transportation district. They might be able to point us towards the right scrolls."

Elleana had spoke true. It seemed few had interest in departing the city, what with the festivities coming to a climax for the day. The worn cobblestones told of much foot traffic, but this corner of the town seemed almost deserted. Still, there remained some merchants, ever hopeful of a sale with all the tourists flooding the city elsewhere.

"That one looks promising," said Olyn, pointing towards a stand helmed by a grey old beard. The booth itself was disheveled and ratty. Scrolls were strewn about and boxes were piled up alongside it.

"You three look like you're in a hurry. Know where you need to go?" a voice called out to them from underneath the beard.

"Is he talking to us?" Maisie asked.

"You all won't find a better deal in Wizmir, no on this side of Belvore!" he called out again. His stature was tiny compared to the bulk of his stall. Maisie wondered if he might be a dwarf underneath his hairy exterior.

"Oh great. He *is* talking to us."

On closer inspection, the stall had a wider assortment of goods than they had been able to see from down the road. In particular, small enchanted ships cut through stormy waves in bottles meant to house them. Iona stared out at the glass microcosm, the storm appearing to mimic her slight movements as her fingers danced along the bottle's surface.

A familiar sigil stuck out to her as it sat carved into the bottom corner of the wooden stall. It shaped into the same name as before at the bazaar. *Zimm. I guess he really does have a following among merchants. I want to say I've read something about him being the patron God of Travelers so maybe that has something to do with it too.*

"You get a lot of sailors out here?" Iona asked the beard, her eyes not leaving the sigil.

"My business revolves around transport. We see all kinds of sorts around here. Especially with the kinds of business castors get up to," he made a motion as though he had rolled his eyes, but it was only signaled by the movement of two large bushels of eyebrow. "Do you know where you're needing to go?" he repeated.

"We need to get to Overeen as soon as possible," Olyn replied.

"That's doable," he said, riffling around a stack of scrolls. "I do a lot of business in Overeen, good people them. The merfolk are a little fishy... if you know what I mean. Oh, here we are, I knew I had a few left," he said, placing a slip of paper in Maisie's hand. "That'll be 60 ler."

"60? For the three of us? That's absolutely ridiculous!" replied Maisie.

"New stand ain't gon build itself."

"Please don't mind her sir," Olyn said, pushing past Maisie. "Fifty-eight, Fifty-nine, Sixty. There you are," Olyn said placing the coins on the table.

"Nice doin bidness with ye," he smiled widely, revealing *some* teeth.

"60 ler my ass! I only ever get 10 for my allowance, I've never heard of anything so ridiculous," Maisie pouted as they walked away. "Crazy old merchant..." Maisie mumbled underneath her breath once they were further away.

"I heard that!" he yelled back at her.

"If you can hear so well why don't you buy yourself some new teeth!" she called back.

"Shhh... Maisie, that doesn't even make sense," Iona said, trying not to burst out laughing. "Come on, let's see what we need to get this to work," Iona led them back towards the Festival.

In the distance, the old man's head darted to and fro,

before the whole of the stall burst into a fast paced hustle of movement. A moment later, a beard with a huge pack was seen by Festival attendants running through the nearby alleyways.

As they made their way back through the bustling marketplace once more, the draw of the crowd seemed even more overwhelming than before. Olyn grabbed Maisie and Iona's hands as they waded through the sea of people, searching desperately for a less crowded area of the market. After a bit of searching, they finally found refuge in a small alcove not unlike where they had woken up earlier that morning. They could hear cheering and laughter from beyond the walls. The volume was stifled by the distance but still remained ever so, alive and abundant.

Catching a break, Maisie handed the piece of paper to Iona. Turning it over in her hand, she read through the instructions for the spell. It appeared to only require a small bit of water as the transformative property, meaning they had all that they needed. Gathering around, they took a seat on the ground and got to work on the incantation.

"A bit of water," Iona poured some water from a pouch around the outside of where they sat, forming a circle. "The scroll for the focus," she placed the paper at the center between the three of them. "And lastly, a bit of my mana as the essence," she held her hand over the paper. She could feel the heat begin to rise from the base of her palm. The paper's words resonated with a low light.

"Now for the words. *Hal eh kantin Overeen locatium*," she whispered gently. As she finished, the paper burst forth into a flame. In a few seconds it was gone.

"Well that's bogus," said Maisie. "Are you sure you didn't break it?"

Suddenly a curtain of water sprouted up from the circle around them. Colors started to mix as their vision blurred. Blues and greens mixed together to form pinks and purples before everything just went dark. Before they knew it they weren't in Wizmir anymore.

CHAPTER 22

SPLASH.

Cold saltwater met Iona's skin as she sunk deeper and deeper into the ocean, gasping for air, she tried to break for the surface but couldn't. As she flailed her arms about in the water, trying to pull herself closer to the surface, she suddenly felt a hand grab her from above. Latching on to it, she was soon met by Maisie staring at Olyn and her with a slightly peeved annoyance in her scowl.

"Lemme guess, the two of you don't know how to swim?" she asked. Olyn clung to the side of the dock, hanging on to some loose rope for dear life.

"I see what went wrong," Olyn said, spitting out some saltwater. "The old man was selling scrolls for transporting *boats* to Overeen, not people," the cold water cut through him, making him shiver.

"You think he could've mentioned that?" asked Iona as Maisie helped her up onto the dock.

"Let's get you two out of the water before you almost drown again," Maisie reached out her hand to Olyn, pulling him up.

Catching their breath, Iona waved her hands over Olyn and Maisie, radiating her heat outwards through her palms. In mere moments all three of them were more or less dry and ready to continue the journey inland.

"How'd you think of that?" Olyn asked.

Iona tapped the side of her head. "Something leftover from Ismir. I get the feeling there are even more uses for these powers he just hasn't shared with me yet."

"Has he said anything lately?" asked Maisie.

"No, not since leaving campus really. It's almost as though our connection has started to weaken. Hopefully it's not a permanent change," Iona scratched the top of the sigil etched into her back. It met her with a faint glow of feverish heat before dissipating.

"Where are we supposed to go now?" Maisie looked around the harbor.

"Here, Elleanna transfered the spell onto this so we wouldn't get lost," Iona said, pulling out a damp map made from hide. The vellum appeared to be a small replica of the larger piece at Elleanna's shop. The locator's magic still seemed active, the black ink ebbing slightly.

"Where is it pointing to?" Olyn asked.

"It doesn't look like we're that far," Maisie chimed in. "See? This is the harbor, so it's just right up the coast."

"Hmm..." Olyn grumbled.

"What is it Olyn?" asked Iona.

"Nothing, it's just that... where the map is heading, it's a place that my Dad used to take me when I was younger."

"When you were younger?"

"I used to live here for a bit before my Dad took a job in Ivis."

"What does your Dad do?" Maisie asked.

Iona held her breath. She knew Olyn's father was a sore spot. He never seemed to mention him lightly.

"My Dad *was* a member of the policing guild. And an amateur spelunker."

Maisie seemed to notice his implication and didn't press any further on the issue.

Mr. Joix's words echoed in Iona's head, *You either die young, or survive long enough to retire.*

"Well, since you're the only one of us who has been here before, you can be our tour guide, can't you?" Maisie gave Olyn an encouraging nudge. "What sort of place is it anyway?"

"I-its the Moriander Caves. No. Yes. Well. They're located right here near the cove, but the spell seems to be pointing further out to sea. Meaning that they're either by boat, or they've entered the caves... and I don't see any boats off in that direction," Olyn said, gazing out at the vast ocean horizon. His stomach felt as though a knot was slowly twisting itself into a tangle at his side.

"You're afraid, aren't you?" Iona poked at him.

"They're just caves aren't they? You've explored plenty of caves before."

"Funny that. There are these stories that always float around, how rumors usually do. I never paid them mind since it always seemed safe enough when I was with my Dad." Olyn seemed nervous. His fingers tapped along his arm.

"What kind of stories?" asked Maisie.

"Well... there was one about dragons, apparently a water dragon used to live in those caves. Plat, no Plaities, yeah that was their name."

"Did you and your father ever see them?" Iona asked.

"Nah... it was abandoned by the time we set foot in there. A bit of treasure left but not much else. Big, massive brumating room too. Perhaps even bigger than the one near Ivis... Oh! There were other stories too, more tawdry though, ramblings of flesh eating fish that wash up into the caverns at high tide and other scary creatures lurking within its many chambers."

"I think we can more than handle a couple of fish," Maisie scoffed.

"They're just stories Maisie, I've never seen the fish or whatever people talk about. What I'm more worried about is why people from Dala would be in those caves. What could possibly be down there that they need?"

Olyn thought back to his own study of banshees from

Iona's bestiary. Something clicked in his head as he darted down the pier and out towards the cove, in the direction of the caves. The girls didn't have to exert themselves too much to keep up as they jogged after him. Finally they stopped on the beach.

"Why did you just take off in a hurry like that?" Iona asked, waiting for him to catch his breath.

"You- You can't kill someone with a scream, at least not most people. But what else can a banshee's scream do if not kill?" A moment passed. Iona and Maisie both stared at him with a puzzled look. "You can wake something up."

Almost in unison they said "Like at school..."

All three of them stared off down the beach towards what one could only describe as a small jagged opening in the ground. The entrance to the Moriander Caves.

"I thought you said Plaities had moved out a long time ago?" Iona asked. "What could be big enough that they would need something that powerful?"

"They might not know about the dragon's relocation. Or, which honestly might be worse, something else might have moved in."

"Well whatever they're doing, they aren't going to wait around forever, let's get a move on. Maybe we can stop them before it's too late."

They quickly approached the cave entrance. Its rocky maw had been smoothed over by the high tide of years past. Iona noticed Olyn messing with some driftwood nearby. Tearing off a piece of his shirt, he wrapped the cloth around one end and pointed it towards Iona.

"What's that for?"

"Well, Maisie has night vision and you presumably something similar, but I'm still just a human, Iona. So, if you would?" he pointed the unlit torch further in her direction.

She placed both of her hands together applying pressure. After a moment she opened them to reveal a small flame. Olyn carefully dipped the cloth into her hands before moving to the opening of the cave.

"Ehm," Maisie retorted.

"Right, sorry, I guess you both don't need the light. Feel free to go first," Olyn said, letting Maisie lead the way down the rocky corridor.

As they traveled further inside the caves, they could feel the cool ocean breeze as it brushed up against their necks ever so often. After a while, it began to slow and then stop altogether, as though they had been cut off from the outside world completely. The walls of the cave had turned from sandstone and gravel to stone that had been unusually cut by water over the years, allowing the walls to ebb and flow into one bend, then the next, until finally it found its home. There was something else to the walls though, small divots, almost like holes.

"Guys are you seeing this?" Iona asked as she placed her hand on the wall to better examine the grooves.

Then came the rumbling. It started low, like an old house settling on stilts, but it soon grew. Maisie's ears perked up as she sensed the coming barrage. Before they knew it, a horde of creatures came spewing out from the darkness, barreling towards them.

"Run!" Maisie yelled as the small bug-like creatures overtook their untrodden path.

"What are those?" Iona asked, almost yelling as she ran in order to be heard over the scurrying beetle-like insects.

"Milithians... I think!" Olyn shouted back at her.

"You *think*?!" Iona yelled back.

Finally, they came to a fork in the tunnel that they had passed not too long ago. Quickly changing direction, they attempted to hide behind the break.

"What do they want?" Maisie asked.

"To eat us... most likely," said Olyn panting.

"What do you mean eat us?" asked Iona.

"Remember when I said flesh eating fish? What the townspeople were really talking about were the Milithians I guess, aka flesh eating bugs," he said, finally catching his breath. "This doesn't make sense though, they're usually found around town, but just a few, mostly scavengers, never this aggressive," he chuckled to himself. "Lucky for us though, they really hate water."

"You have a plan or something Olyn? Cause last time I checked I can only create *fire*," said Iona, her voice erratic.

"They're attracted to light and heat," Olyn said, chucking his torch back down the corridor. "I know we're both not huge fans of water, but I think I can actually help."

"How?!" Maisie called out into the dark as she focused on the entourage of bugs headed towards them.

Olyn moved his bag around to face him. He produced a small wooden box from inside.

"Now is not the time Olyn! They'll be on us any second," said Iona. He just scoffed at her.

It was the small wooden box carved with sigils. She paused. Olyn quickly opened the box to reveal a pair of gauntlets. *Where did he get those from?* Iona thought back to his workshop, trying to shake the uneasy feeling the box had left her with. *Just what curse has he brought with him?*

Iona couldn't wait any longer. Standing up, she blasted fire through the corridor as much as she could. The bugs seemed unfazed, moving as though they were soaking up the heat from the flames. The fire quickly dissipated as if it had been snuffed out by the moisture.

As Olyn put on the gloves, dark smoke began to rise and surround him as his very aura began to shift before them. Iona was taken aback as she watched. It was almost as if his very being was corrupting, changing into something unrecognizable. The only thing Iona thought to compare it to was that of the shade, an unholy corruption of essence. As the dark power flowed through him, his appearance began to falter. Small black horns sprouted from betwixt his brown curls of hair. And even his hair seemed to banish the chestnut brown from his head, leaving him with a more sandy coloring. As he neared the end of his transformation, his eyes finally opened to reveal a burgundy red coloring, a deeper hue than Iona's own fiery luster. Like two glasses of fine wine.

"Stand back," he said, his voice noticeably deeper than it was before.

As the milithians neared their standing ground, Olyn calmly made his way back through the tunnel to face them head on. Concentrating, Olyn pictured a rush of water in his mind. Calling out with all his might, he could feel his magic begin to latch onto the water from the ocean depths above them. As the milithians moved closer, they suddenly stopped. It was as though, try as they might to get around him, they couldn't move further through the corridor. Iona watched as small pools of water had collected around Olyn's feet, extending outwards towards the small bugs. Recognizing the barrier, their tiny bodies retreated back into the cave system. Olyn began to relax for a moment, thinking that it was all over.

Iona heard a scurry, deeper into the dark out-cropping they had turned off into. It was almost as if the small creatures were burrowing new holes. Pouring out of the walls, Iona and Maisie ran towards Olyn.

Olyn regained concentration. This time, his mind worked to pull harder than before. He could feel the force starting to put strain on him. His head began to grow painful. Iona caught the strong scent of blood as it began to seep from one of his nostrils.

This time, a loud rumbling from above them ended with a sudden burst of sea water raining down from above. But the water didn't touch them. The flow from the roof of the cave seemed to dance above as it moved directly towards the milithians. It was like a tidal wave flowing down from the heavens to save them. The milithians that hadn't immediately met the water, had turned shell and scurried back off deep into the stone as fast as they could. Cordoning themselves off from the flow of water. The salty brine continued to travel, deep down into the cave system. The small chirps of the milithians soon stopped, whether by the water's hand or their own.

As soon as the flow ceased, Olyn nearly collapsed. He panted for breath as he tried to rip the gauntlets from his hands. Maisie bent down to help him. As she touched them however, a strong feeling washed over her of being watched. Her spine tingled as she placed the gloves back in their box. Her body still lightly quaking as she slammed the lid shut. Maisie peered up towards Iona with a look of concern. Iona could feel the tension as it washed over her. Soon dissipating altogether as if it was never supposed to be there. They both remained unsure what to think about it all. Olyn was helped slowly up to his feet by Iona. His body still ached heavily, but they continued further down into the cavernous world beneath.

"You seem to have reverted back to normal," Iona said to him. His chestnut curls bounced as they walked. His horns all but wisps fading away into the darkness of the cave. The fresh scent of sulfur still hung in the air, this time intermixed with sea salt that seemed to linger along the walls.

"Yea I, uh, I change back pretty fast after I take them off," he said, still gasping for air occasionally as he hobbled along.

"Are you sure you're alright?" Iona asked. "How much have you used those things?"

"I should be fine in a bit. This is the first time I've used the mana they grant me in such a large amount," Olyn panted, clearly out of breath.

His staggering alluded to larger problem, however not one that Maisie or Iona could help in their current situation. Maisie let out a silent prayer for any god still listening as they continued further into the cave, still fighting to shake off any lingering feelings of dread brought forth from touching the gauntlets.

CHAPTER 23

As Olyn helped guide them further through the cave system, their nostrils began to flare. The putrid smell of tar and decay grew more and more robustly foul as they found themselves nearing the blot of ink on the map.

As they clambered up a sharp incline they found themselves basking in the darkness of a gaping cavern. The dark was all consuming. Even for the young wyr and dragal, making out so much as a shape in the void was a struggle. The rimmed edge of the brumating cavern beneath them was the only form visible. Past that, the domed shape morphed into a steep cliffside they dared not test. A dry heat radiated out from the center of the void, the change in temperature putting Iona at ease. It felt almost familial to the young dragal as she took a deep breath in, her lungs shaking off the cold of the sea caves. Iona could hear Olyn huffing, his breath had become ragged as his heart beat in tune with his anxiety. His torch had been lost to the scuffle with the Milithians, but now the girls' sense of sight was no better than his.

"Can you sense anything?" Iona whispered to Maisie,

her scent of earthy cloves still going strong.

"Shh..." Maisie's nose perked up towards a familiar scent. "They're here," she whispered.

"How far away?"

"If we assume this place is curved, they're about a couple hundred meters in that direction," she held Iona's hand outstretched towards the curved ridge that led to their left.

Olyn huffed once more, having regained some of his stamina. "There should be braziers lined around the outside rim of the cavern." Iona and Maisie waited for more explanation, but it never came. The scent of sweat welled up from Olyn's face. *He's not doing well,* Iona thought.

"I can take the brazier closest to us. You two should stay here," Iona said.

"You're not going to go towards them are you?" Maisie asked.

"Of course not," Iona replied.

As Maisie set Olyn down near the entrance, Iona ventured out following the right side of the outer rim. After walking a few meters, Iona quickly came upon a large brazier. Sigils etched around it called out to her as a low crackling heat vibrated from within. Without thinking, Iona reached out towards the pillar. Sigils began to burn around her as she got closer. Light exploded throughout the darkness as she found her hand placed upon the brazier's stones. Iona's eyes flashed with light. Adjusting, she saw that not just the brazier in front of her had been lit but one by one the countless others that lined the cavern. It took a moment for her eyes to refocus on the large creature that now filled what was once a void. Mere yards away from her a large white beast slept. Heaps of treasure gleamed around it, shimmering in the light of the pyres. The behemoth's scales formed a mixture of red and grey flakes painted across the bare reptilian canvas.

"Ismir..." Iona muttered to herself as all three of them gazed out at the dragon.

Maisie's eyes caught hold of the two dark figures in the distance. They stood next to another entrance of the cavern. The shade hid behind the cloaked figure as it tried to escape from the light, letting out a few scratchy growls in retreat as it went. The other figure had long black hair that protruded from the hood, covering part of his face. In his hands he held a glowing green orb.

"Iona, look!" Maisie said as she pointed towards the sphere.

Iona jolted back to reality as she glared towards the snapping maw of the shadow. She reached for the amulet that still hung around her neck. Ripping free the chain, she let it fall to the ground. Something sparked within her as she could feel the full berth of her power returning, it willed her feet to turn and run, but not away. No, she was running straight towards the two interlopers.

"Iona! Don't!" Maisie yelled as Iona brushed past her in force, but it was no use. Iona was upon them in seconds. Before she could strike, the hood raised the orb, releasing a gut-retching scream. Iona was pushed back as the screech pulsated outwards along the walls of the cave. Fighting back with all her might to not be moved, she caught a rare glimpse of the face underneath. Ruby red eyes framed by deep onyx hair peered down at her, striking her deep within. What appeared before her was a gaunt beauty of a boy who didn't appear to be much older than she was. A chill ran down her spine as she fell to her knees. Her ears were ringing with such violence. The look of the strange boy deepened into one of pity. Taking his free hand, he cupped her face, and as he pulled it back it was stained with the blood that had begun to trickle down from her ears. As red began to pool along her neck, she fought to keep her eyes open. The scream continued to echo throughout the hollow, the ground beneath them shaking as the dragon began to stir from its slumber.

Glancing at her again, the boy ran his ashen hand back along the orb, silencing it. His arms dropped back towards his center. Iona's very being was overwhelmed, the scream still echoing through her head even as her eardrums had started to heal. She felt as though she had been locked into place. The ground shook, as though it had no intention on stopping anytime soon. Rocks from the sea cave walls began to knock loose and fall to the ground. Some fell on Ismir before tumbling off like pebbles against his massive scales. The ground suddenly crumbled beneath the cloaked figure. He faltered as their footing gave out, the orb tumbling from his hands as they slid down into the horde of treasure that laid beneath the ridge. Iona took a deep breath as her body started to move again on its own.

Before she could chase after the orb however, the shade lept out from the shadows, pinning Iona to the ground. It's low guttural growl scraped against her neck as something inside her began to awaken once more. A large burst of light swept out from underneath her as the creature quickly faded back into the shadows. Her back glowed with a radiant light as her wings glimmered around her. The heat was contained, the flames dancing closely along the webbed fibers of flesh and fire. Her eyes glowed with a similar light as if a wisp of flame danced from within.

"Where did it go?" Iona growled, holding tightly onto her arm where the creature had gouged her. Blood dripped down onto the ground before the wound coagulated, stopping the flow.

"I think it disappeared into the shadows, I couldn't get a good look with all the light. Iona, are you alright?" Maisie asked as she ran up to her slightly injured friend.

"I'll be fine, it was just a scratch," she said staring at the long cut along her arm. Maisie watched as it slowly started to close. "What are you going to do?"

"I'm going after the other one." Maisie glared down at the treasure horde, the different metals glinting in the light of Iona's flames.

Iona grabbed her arm as she was about to start off, her blackened nails wrapping around skin. "Be careful."

Iona let out a screech as the shade darted out from an overlap in the girls' shadows, slicing open Iona's other arm. Maisie fell back, watching her friend quickly try to staunch the bleeding, the shade nowhere to be seen. Giving Iona a quick nod, she turned, scrambling to her feet before she headed off in the direction of the fallen.

Maisie made her way towards the edge of the cavern. Below, the fallen angel was frantically searching for the orb. In all of the confusion their hood had fallen back. Maisie couldn't make out much of the person's face, as their long black hair still obscured it, but their skin had a pale, almost green translucency. Almost as if they were sick. Rocks continued to fall around her, making it hard for her to stay steady on the ridge, her feet shifting with each shake. With a rumble, a large rock broke into pieces above her, freeing itself from the ceiling. Down the shards tumbled, straight towards her. Maisie quickly jumped out of the way and down into the horde of treasure she went.

Opening her eyes, she found herself stopped just short of the tip of a sword sticking out from the shining rubble. Slowly looking around, she noticed something gleaming green in the distance.

The shade had disappeared again, this time leaving Iona racked with the lingering effects of blood loss. As fast as her body could heal, it still took a toll on her both mentally and physically. She tried to parse together some semblance of a plan. Her mind raced as the screams of her dead parents echoed in her head. *It was there that night, I know it.* The shade's snarl corralled itself amidst the screams, shadows plummeting the room into darkness around her. She tried to refocus, this time her mind drifted to the night of the bazaar, her legs had burned as she ran from the terrified screams of the townspeople. The lights had burst as the shade tore its way through the bazaar... and later in the alley the streetlights had struggled to come to life before being snuffed to a whisper. *It's scared of the lights. No. The light hurts it?* Iona had lost herself within her own head, only snapping back to reality at the distant sound of Olyn gasping for air.

The shade had him by the neck. Olyn's arms scraped at the smoke. trying to prevent the beast from snuffing out his own light. His arms were still weak from before, so much so that his clawing motions barely left a scratch on his own skin.

Quickly, Iona pounced towards the entrance of the cave, her wings making her movements light and almost effortless. Her hand glowed with a bright searing heat as claw-like talons forced themselves out from her fingertips. With a large swing, she pierced the shade, slicing it down its back. As the light touched it, the smoke-like creature seemed to turn solid. Black sludge dripped from her hand before evaporating back into smoke. With a horrendous screech, Olyn dropped to the ground, the shade retreating back into the nearby darkness of the entrance corridor.

"Olyn, are you alright?" she asked, his body weight leaning on her as she helped him return to his position by the wall.

He coughed, his hand revealing a splattering of blood left behind. "I'll be okay... I think. It has a really strong grip."

Iona knew he was holding back. Touching his shoulder, a familiar unsettling wave flowed over her. Pin pricks started to pop and move along her body, as if there was strange mana at work. The sensation stopped as soon as she let go. Olyn noticed her expression, but didn't move to speak.

His eyes grew wide as he called out to her. "Watch

out!" just before a sharp pain bloomed down Iona's back. Turning around, she saw the shade. Its face lingering a few inches from her own. A hideous smile danced about in the smoke, sharp teeth bearing down towards her. Then she fell. Not a second later, she found herself laying on the ridge, her arm draped over its edge, rocks still falling all around them. Her body was paralyzed. All she could do was stare out at her beautiful beast, Ismir. As her eyes began to close, she noticed a light gleaming from beyond the ridge. A small pyramid-shaped copper box. It called to her, like a siren's song to a group of sailors. It wanted to be held. The shade danced about the defeated girl, snarling at her face before gloating again. Iona didn't understand why it didn't just kill her. She already couldn't move, why was it waiting? Turning her attention back towards the box, it had changed position. Impossible or not, it had moved. Something shifted amongst the horde of treasure. Patiently watching, it soon revealed itself. A small golden snake, with swirling eyes of red. She couldn't decide if it was truly alive or not. Nudging the box, the snake clearly meant to bring it to her.

"Ioooonnnaa…" a voice appeared. It sounded sleepy, wavering in her mind as if she couldn't be certain it was real. But a familiar cadence sounded again, "Usssee tthhee boxxx."

Iona fought back tears of pain as she slowly reached out towards the snake. Finally the box was within reach.

The snake wrapped itself around her arm, using its body to pull the copper box into the palm of her hand. It was much lighter than she had expected. The sigils danced with light when she touched it. One in particular glowed red. Without thinking, and as the shade turned back towards her to growl, she flipped over onto her back. The tip of the box was pointed at the shade, and she pressed her finger against the red sigil. The box opened like a blooming flower. It took a moment before the shade knew what was happening. Quickly its body, all of the smoke and shadow began to fill into the box. It swirled and bubbled and lashed out as it went. Its claws scraped at Iona, one nipping her cheek as it went, down and down. Once it had disappeared into the box, one of the panels remained open. As a bit of smoke began to putter back out, Iona launched herself, or what little of her would move, onto the box, sealing it shut.

"I'm done being afraid of some stupid shadow," she said, the box lay on her stomach. She laid on her back, staring up at the ceiling as it continued to crumble away.

"Looking for this?" Maisie called out towards the flustered fallen angel in the distance. His neck careened towards her. Their red eyes shone out in such a way that even the surface of his pale skin appeared to glow as well. Maisie fumbled backwards a bit at the sight. It was almost as if the boy was looking through her, not seeing her, but rather the orb. Maisie had come face to face with many animals who shared that same look on their face. It was a look of hunger, of single mindedness. All he cared about was the scream, and Maisie had just clued them in on where it was. In less than a second, they were face to face. Feathers molted, falling slowly to the ground as the wind caused by the sudden rush forwards cleared Maisie's face of all impeding clumps of bangs. Save for what had already been matted down by sweat against her forehead. Fur prickled along the skin as she stood, half-formed before him. Their eyes met for a moment, a glow of bloodied amber reflected all around them, but then came pain. His hand grabbed hold of Maisie's forearm now flush with dense brown fur, their own skin was ominously painted black as if the sludge they had seen come from the discarded feather back at school truly was a part of him. For a moment, it seemed as though the light was being absorbed into the skin like a black hole. It took all but a second for his hand to crush her arm. A strange burning pain caused Maisie to release the orb from her grasp, dropping it to the ground. The smell of burnt hair filled her lungs as she choked out a cough. As her knees buried themselves in the treasure below, she watched as the winged boy turned their back to her, bouncing the orb up and down in his hand. Hot tears streamed down her face as the pain became unbearable. The water fogged her vision as her assailant's wings carried them to back to the outer ridge, and further on to safety back within the corridors of the cave system. Wiping her face, she examined her arm. The major breaks of her bones had already started to set beneath the furred skin, but there was something more. A lingering smell of toxic sulfur remained in the air, and around her wound. Her fur receded, the pain forcing her back into her human form. The skin continued to heal and blacken, until there was no pain left. There was nothing.

She was soon met by Olyn and Iona who had healed enough to venture out from the entrance. The two of them seemed to lean on one another as much as they helped the other down the mound to where she laid.

"Maisie!" Olyn called out as he scrambled to meet her. He quickly examined her, placing his hand on her forehead and then noticing the black patch of skin along her arm. "What did that guy do to you?"

Up until this point, Maisie had stopped moving. Something in Olyn's voice brought her back, her eyes blinking. Her mouth finally closed, taking in a gulp of saliva.

"Maisie?" Iona inquired this time. She rolled her shoulder with a wince of lingering pain.

Maisie's head peered out at her, not really seeing her.

She swallowed again. "My arm, I thought he just broke it, but..." she held it up to her chest, almost as if it was missing. "I can't feel anything."

"What exactly did that *thing* do to you?" Olyn asked again, looking over the discoloration of her skin.

"I was partially transformed, so it started to heal, but then it stopped. Whatever happened, I don't know what to do," Maisie explained calmly as though she hadn't been fighting just a few minutes ago.

A hot gust of wind caught them, as shifting weight caused even more damage to the cavern. The ground shook with the movement, bellowed with it, as if it was going to break apart the earth and swallow them whole. Turning back towards the dragon they had all but forgotten, they were met with glowing red eyes swirling with heat and magic. Nostrils flared as he took a deep breath in, releasing yet another hot gust of wind from his lungs. Water that had collected in the cave seemed to bubble and boil, leaving behind only traces of what once was. The steam seemed to ease Iona's aches and pains for a brief moment.

"Well," he bellowed, his mouth ceased to move but his voice was loud all the same. Iona was used to this sensation. Ismir talking without really talking. The others were less so, causing them both to freeze in place. Ismir's face came closer towards them, his head turned so that one eye could better gaze upon them. "I'm pleasantly surprised to find you three in one piece. More or less," he said as he gazed upon Maisie's char-like skin.

"Ismir..." Iona approached him further, her arm reaching out to glide along the ridges of scales that lined his face. The feeling of his smooth skin felt pleasant, a gentle warmth filled her from within, a warmth that she hadn't felt in a long time. A twinge of pain brought her back to her knees. Olyn ran to her, trying to make sense of what was wrong. She clawed at her back, unable to reach the culprit. Olyn slowly pulled back what remained of her shirt collar. The sigil along her spine burned brightly.

"What is this?" Olyn asked, almost demanding of Ismir.

Ismir peered down at the girl, letting out a low guttural growl. "I've seen those markings before... A binding spell," he chuffed, sending bits of ash flying from his nostrils. "I haven't sensed her this strongly since she was just a child. From the way that spell is coiled around her, I'd say it's been slowly wearing down for quite some time."

"What do we do?" Olyn pleaded.

Ismir spoke directly to Iona, drowning out Olyn from her mind. "*Iona.* Focus on the sigil, on the pain. Burn brighter than that pain. You've removed sigils before... this one is a part of you, you don't need to touch it." Iona's hands drooped down to her sides. Her body shook with the occasionally new burst of pain. As she tried to focus, she could sense the magic surrounding the sigil. Like a parasite, the mana had embedded itself into her, counteracting her own. Its dark tendrils of power etched deep into her. Raising her body temperature, her skin soon felt like it was burning from the inside out. Olyn returned to Maisie's side, trying to escape from the heat. Slowly the sigil seemed to burn away from her skin, small embers of the markings were all that remained, rising slowly into the air before they too, flickered out. Gasping, Iona's mouth released flames that spewed over the shining treasure beneath her, fusing some of the gleaming metal with one another. Wiping her mouth, she took a breath before finally getting up.

"Iona?" Maisie started.

"I'm alright," small sparks of pain still remained, but soon dissipated.

"My child, were you able to recover the scream?" Ismir pushed the words gently towards her.

Her head throbbed with each syllable. Iona's eyes grew wide. Looking around, then back towards Maisie, she didn't see the orb. "Maisie? Did you?"

Maisie fumbled around in her bag for a moment, struggling to use her non-dominant hand. She pulled out a small orb. The inside danced with a green and white mist as if the ball contained fog. *So, this must be the power of a banshee,* Iona thought to herself. The orb grew a little larger as if it was taking on air before Olyn took it from her grasp. Maisie's arm returned to rest at her side.

"How'd you get the fallen angel to leave if you still had this?" he asked her.

"I found an orb that was around the same size. He seemed a little too preoccupied to realize it wasn't the right one. It was like they were in a trance."

"They didn't seem to notice a lot," Iona grasped the small copper box she had trapped the shade within. "They left without their friend."

"Talk about disposable," Maisie chuckled, before grasping her arm tightly, trying to activate the nerves with her touch.

"Shades aren't exactly rare, at least in Dala, but here they're harder to come by. Maybe we're wrong, maybe they did notice that the shade had been captured and just decided to cut their losses," Olyn theorized.

"What are we going to do with that by the way?" Maisie pointed to the box.

"I'm sure your Headmistress is more than capable of dealing with that," Ismir replied.

"Right... after all, she *was* the one who had the Crucifixer in the first place," Iona said. "Melonie! How could I forget! Ismir we need to get back to the campus as soon as possible! Can you help us?" Iona asked pleadingly.

"I've been asleep for a short while," he said, starting to shake the rocks and treasure off of his wings. "But I think I should be able to manage a short cross country flight."

His head bowed towards them, his nostrils flaring as they took in air. Arching his back and wings, he burst through the ceiling of the cavern. Water rushed in through the large opening, quickly flooding the basin in which Ismir had slept. He extended his front talons towards them, entrapping them within a cage-like grasp. Holding on for dear life, they watched as Ismir scraped his way through the hole, his wings extended and fluttering along the ocean-side breeze. With a gust of wind, they were flying, Ismir's wings flapped at unsteady speeds as the flitting fibers got used to being active again. Flying over pastures and forests along the coast, they could see the glistening sea and a gathering of dark clouds that loomed in the distance off towards Dala.

Iona thought she could see the dark figure of the fallen flying off in the distance, but she couldn't be sure. *It could just as easily be a bird,* she thought to herself as they flew, wondering why the Dalians had fought so hard to reawaken Ismir. Reaching back, she touched as close as she could to the spot that had housed the sigil. *Just who put you there?*

CHAPTER 24

Down below, they could see every inch of the school grounds. Ismir's body cast a long and winding shadow over the campus. Coming in to land, they could see the speckled faces of students glued to windows, watching in wonder as this hulking behemoth of legend landed in front of them. As soon as Ismir released his grip, Olyn fell to the ground with a *THUD*. He was panting, not only from the panic of being so high up, but the lingering exhaustion of his mana as well. Iona helped Maisie down, who had her arm placed in a makeshift sling around her neck. It still remained as it had been, almost petrified, the nerves deadened by the magic that had wound itself into it.

Turning towards the school, they were quickly met by stares from a congregation of the faculty, headed up by the Headmistress herself. The commotion of a dragon flying over campus must have brought them out to investigate.

"*Miss Iona Moran!* Would you care to explain why there is a dragon on the front lawn? And the three of you! Where have you been for the last day and a half?" Headmistress Hersch was unabashedly hysterical. The fact that three students had up and disappeared without so much as a note had taken its toll on her. Dark circles entrenched themselves underneath her eyes, refusing to dissolve back into her normally bright disposition.

"Well you see-" Iona brought her hands together behind her, almost in an attempt to appear smaller than she was.

A voice rang out from behind her. Radiating out of Ismir, "It was my fault Saya. I warned the children that it might be more dangerous than they could handle, but Iona cares deeply for your daughter. So much so... that she sought after the one thing that could save her, despite my warnings."

"You're lucky you three weren't killed... or worse," she looked at each of them, noticing Maisie's arm and Olyn's panting on the ground. Her face changed for a moment, further processing what Ismir had said. She gazed upon the pale dragon, "Wait... does that mean?" she asked, taking a step towards them.

Iona sped towards Maisie, reaching her hand far into her bag, she pulled back out a small green orb. It slowly wavered in size, growing and shrinking as it sat, engulfed in Iona's palm.

As the she saw the orb, the Headmistress collapsed to the ground, sitting there as hot tears began to stream down her face. Her daughter would be safe. Wiping the tears from her face, she met Iona at the bottom of the stairs leading to the lawn proper. As she collected the orb from Iona it shone brightly in her hands, almost as if it recognized her.

"Let's get you back to where you belong," she spoke with a teary-eyed smile.

Suddenly, a shorter, brunette woman pushed her way through the court of teachers and staff, appearing before them. "Oh, don't tell me they're getting off that easy!"

"Mom?" Maisie squeaked, confused as to why her disgruntled mother was standing before them.

"And you-" she started before noticing the sling wrapped around her daughter's arm. "What happened, are you alright?" Mali rushed to her side, keen on examining the blackened patch of skin.

"Yes, well I'm sure there will be some punishment for you three. We *cannot* have students running off to their possible demise," Nurse Hazel pouted proudly as she spoke on behalf of the Headmistress who had already headed upstairs to see her daughter. "Makes my job a lot harder, y'know."

Peg approached Olyn as he laid out on the lawn, her long hair blowing gently against her cardigan.

Bending down, she asked "Are you alright?"

"No, not... really," he spoke in between bids for air.

She reached down to touch his forehead. It was as

deathly cold, despite the sweat that had gathered on his brow. "I might have something that can help, just wait right here," she said, before rushing back into the school building.

Emerging once more, she had in her hands a small blue vial. "Here, just what you need," she said, handing the potion carefully into Olyn's shaky grasp.

"What is it?"

"It's a mana potion that I made. You have all the signs of mana exhaustion, so what you need now is an influx. The potion should help."

"Should?" he asked.

"Heh... it *will* help. Now, bottom's up!" she said encouragingly.

"Oh what the hell," he said before downing the entire vial of blue liquid without a second thought. For a moment his arms began to spasm with raw energy he was unaccustomed to. His joints popped as he moved before settling back down again. A slight pain radiated in his lungs, followed by a searing headache that would last well into the next day, but the sweating had ceased. As he laid back in the grass, looking up towards the bright blue sky, a smile painted itself across his face. For the first time since using those gloves, he could finally breathe easy again.

Iona found herself with the Headmistress, staring out the row of windows in the second-floor corridor that overlooked where all the commotion had taken place just mere hours ago. Ismir was out of sight, taken somewhere he wouldn't distract the students from their studies.

Taking the place of the dragon on the front lawn instead were new visitors. Iona wasn't too familiar with their garments, but recognized some of the styles in the clothing she had seen the Headmistress and Melonie wear on a separate occasions. They walked in lines of two, each one wearing long, flowing robes of purple and white. Black veils covered their faces, giving off the feeling of a funeral procession as they walked towards the main building.

"Who are they?" Iona asked as she watched them move in unison.

"They are called the Motherhood. They're like us, Melonie and I."

"Is that what they're here for? To take her away?" Iona asked, her voice giving off a pleading tone.

"They know more about banshees than even I care to admit. If anyone can help my daughter it's them."

"You didn't answer my question," said Iona, skulking. The last thing she wanted was to lose the friend she had just saved.

"She's starting to get better you know? Because of what

you and your friends did. Being around her scream has allowed her to eat finally. However, her condition hasn't fared much farther yet towards recovery."

"So she's going with them?" Iona asked again. She *had* to know. Perhaps the Motherhood had room for her as well.

"While I do think that sending Melonie off to live with my sisters may be the best course of action, I don't feel as though taking her out of an environment in which she finally has people around her that care about her would be wise."

"So she's staying?" Iona asked, trying to hide her excitement as it threatened to boil over inside.

The Headmistress gave a slight nod. "Yes, she will be staying. The Motherhood will be here for a while as they work out how to best reunite Melonie with her scream, during which, she'll most likely be confined to her room until she fully recovers," the Headmistress took in a deep breath, "You know, it's funny. I never felt like I could truly protect her here, not with the life of every student being my responsibility as well. But... seeing what you did for her, something that I couldn't even do myself, makes me feel a little better that she has people like you and your friends to look after her."

The two just smiled softly as they watched the precession of banshees.

EPILOGUE

Dark feathery wings carried Terrigan towards the rotting tower. Weathered stones of the spire laid bare after years of wear. A large set of windows at the top sat open. He flitted about as he made his quick descent inwards. Landing, his wings shot back into him alongside his shoulder blades. Several black feathers landed on the ground beneath him. Using his foot, he scrapped them all into a small pile, and with a snap of their finger, the pile burnt to ashes in an instant. Walking further into the tower, he saw a man standing over a table. Papers strung about, bottles and other ingredients laid around him. The small runed cylinder of the crucifixer gleamed amidst a pile of junk stacked up along the walkway.

The man was tall and muscular. His mid-length layered hair a mix of white and deep brown that seemed to ebb and flow in the light as though it couldn't decide what color to be.

"Duke, sir. I've returned from my duties," he said, kneeling down. Terrigan's long hair nearly scraping past his knee.

"Terrigan," he paused for a moment. "I see you don't have that guard dog with you?"

"No sir. Serle was... captured."

"How exactly does one capture a shade, Terrigan?" he sighed in frustration.

"I believe a Helicath Box might have been used. I didn't get close enough look to be sure... sir."

"Why did he allow himself to be captured? I thought the idea was to kill anyone who got in the way, was it not?"

"It was the girl, again. Serle was only acting on your orders not to kill her sir."

"Were there any others with her?"

"Her friends I believe, but I thought it best not to kill them in the case that it... affects her."

"Oh? Getting sentimental, are we?" the Duke tapped his fingertips along his hand, thinking. "And after all this time... I suppose we can work with this. Now, what's more important is the overgrown lizard."

"The Ashen one was successfully awakened, sir."

"Good... good. And what of the scream?"

"Yes, right sir," Terrigan handed the Duke a golden orb, slight indentations of runes filled its surface. "But sir, if I may, I was wondering. Why did it have to be the Ashen one? Wouldn't any other dragon have worked?"

"It's true that awakening *her* dragon might provide them with some advantages, but trust me when I say...

we're only just getting started.

"Sir I still don't-"

The orb glowed white in the Duke's hand. Eyes popped open out of the sphere, a maw following soon after. The orb shifted and shaped itself into a small golden monster, gnawing unsuccessfully at the Duke's hand. "Damn it!" he yelled, trying to shake the beast from his arm. Grabbing a dagger lodged in the nearby table he quickly stabbed it into the beast, leaving the dagger once more entrenched in the table. A golden ooze bubbled out over the wooden surface before stopping altogether.

"Sir?" Terrigan said, careful not to illicit another outburst.

"You brought back the wrong orb, you damn idiot!" he yelled at him. Adjusting his attire, he tried to calm himself down. "I suppose it doesn't matter, Ismir won't risk brumating again anytime soon. Not while Iona might still be in danger."

"I'm still not sure if I see what you were getting at sir..."

The Duke gazed at Terrigan with an irritated look. "I'll spell it out for you then. Asleep, dragons are sturdy, almost indestructible, *but awake...* their limited energy and their hubris tends to get the better of them in the end." He walked a few paces from his desk to a tented sheet, "Isn't that right, Mr. Sylvester?"

There came a scrambling from underneath. As the

Duke pulled it back, a cage was revealed, housing a disheveled old researcher with pointed ears.

The End

Acknowledgments

Banshee's Scream has taken a long and arduous 12-year journey to reach completion. It started with a dream and blossomed over the years as the draft slowly grew over time. A whole world was born and it will be in my head until I can get it all out onto the page. So I'm grateful to all of my friends that encouraged me to keep coming back to the manuscript draft even when I was afraid it'd mean starting over completely.

Firstly, I'd like to thank May Taylor, my amazing cover artist who took my hodge podge ideas and ran with it. It wouldn't be a complete book without you. And now, I can bask in the warm green glow of my debut novel as it sits on my shelf. I sincerely hope I get to work with you again in the future.

Next, I'd like to thank my friends. Whom I might not have had the courage to publish without. They've helped me in so many different ways that I'm not sure I'd be able to list them all. You have no idea (or maybe you do) how much work goes into self publishing, but I've loved (almost) every minute of it because of them. I think my manuscript would still be sitting in a box somewhere without their advice and help.

Dad, Jacob, I haven't asked you both for much support,

but I appreciate any you've given regardlessly. Whether it be silently or to my face, I love and appreciate you both so much. I only wish we lived closer to one another. And Noah, my loving husband and one of my best friends, as well as an early reader and fan of my work, I hope you brave the horrors long enough to write some of your own stories you keep locked away inside your head. I'd really like to read them.

Lastly, but most certainly not least, I would like to say thank you to all of my beta readers: Vanessa Lowe, Aiden Bollinger, SalYue (they/she), Noah, Charlotte d'Andriole, and Nikki Larkey. You all did an amazing job to help turn my manuscript into an even better book.

I'd also like to acknowledge the wonderful backers for this book's Kickstarter pre-order campaign who backed at the Wisp tier or above, in no particular order:

Tiberius, Maeve, and Chomper, Hannah Portenier, Loving Husband, The Schmitt Family, Ali Suchy, S.R. Cantrell, Ashley Smith, Adrian Cruz, Vanessa Lowe, and Veronica Dowty.

About the Author

Elin Wilton is an author who was born in Oklahoma and who fell in love with all manner of monsters and beasts from a young age. They earned their BS in Biology from Wichita State University in 2021 and likes to incorporate that scientific edge into their writing. Creating monsters we wish we could become, as well as those we'd sooner force onto others. Elin lines their notebooks with marginalia of all the ways different creatures could exist given the right nudge. Find them on Instagram or Threads @lonelyelin. And check out their online shop's Instagram @bunimead for eBook and Paperback copies of her books and exclusive merchandise.

If you enjoyed reading *Banshee's Scream* we'd love it if you'd consider leaving the book a review either where the book was purchased or over on StoryGraph/Goodreads. Reviews are a vital part of the indie author ecosystem as they help would-be readers better find our books and provide a space for feedback.

Appendix

Races in Leera

Human: One of the most basic races, but also the most modifiable. A human is born with an essence that is very susceptible to other fae and fiends alike. One bite, a scratch, curse, or a blessing can easily cast you into another race classification entirely. Despite being easily influenced, they also have one of the shortest lifespans, made even shorter by how fragile they are to the strength of wyrs and other races.

Castor: A being with a large pool of mana, usually due to lineage. Humans with a few elven ancestors may find themselves imbued with mana not found in their closer relatives. Some choose to hone that power and go on to become proper castors, while others let the mana simply fade away back into the blood. But holding on to too much mana can be detrimental, leading even normal citizens of Leera to expel pent up mana on occasion.

Wyr: A very common race in Leera. Wyr's are beings that can shift between two separate transformation stages and are associated with an animal ranging from the common wolf to rats to cheetahs. There are large studies of different wyr colonies and species breakdowns performed yearly which have all but replaced where scientists would have studied animal migration patterns and population statistics. Wyrs are versatile fae, being able to infect and breed with most of the humanoid races. Their long lifespans, enhanced senses, and ability to quicken the body's healing process through transformation only underline a few of the reasons their lineages are so prevalent today.

Kit: Seen as a subspecies of wyr, the kit is different in the fact that its lifespan is about double as long as a normal wyr and is born with a large pool of mana at their disposal, as well as other, more peculiar, skills. They also only have an intermediary transformation stage and cannot turn fully into a fox.

Banshee: Hailing from Avilar, banshees are often misunderstood creatures. While they do not cause death they *are* drawn to it. Through their essence they passively feed off the death of those around them. When a large surge of energy hits them, they involuntarily scream, especially if they are younger and unable to control themselves. The father often has to be far away from the mother and child at the time of birth. Upon taking their first breath, they scream to such a degree that it can easily kill a being that does not have an enhanced healing factor. While there have been rumors of male-born banshees, the Motherhood would have you believe that they are all born female. What happens to any males, is unknown.

Dragal: Beings that have been blessed by a dragon to carry part of their essence within them. Unless a dragal is an angel or other celestial being, the blessing of essence cannot be undone without extraction or death of the dragal. Likewise, for lesser beings, the blessing must be performed while the being is still young, as the older the being is, the more likely that the blessing will be rejected by the body. Once blessed, the dragal takes on characteristics of the dragon they are connected to. Each dragal has abilities based around what type of dragon they were blessed by.

Dragon: Despite the durability and longevity of the dragon race, there are only seven left in existence. These giant lizards are classified into one of two categories, an arch-dragon or a dragon. Magni the Lord of Destruction and Sirus the Moon Lord are the only two arch-dragons. Leaving five remaining dragons. Ismir the Fire Lord is one of them. Only dragons can create dragals.

Elf: One of the most elusive races in all of Leera, elves spend a majority of their lifetime in Elmora and the surrounding forests. They live long lives, ranging anywhere from five to seven times the length of a typical wyr. Elves are also born with a large pool of mana, although there are of course exceptions to this, leading a majority of them to become powerful castors. In terms of magic, elves mainly specialize in healing and earth magic, but some choose to branch out, especially if they did not grow up in/near Elmora or other elves.

Djinn: Hailing from Sera, Djinn are a rare breed that are mistakenly cast as wish granters. Instead, they are elemental beings. Djinn reside in small objects, but are not bound to any particular item. Their hair ranges widely in color, usually denoting what element they are connected to.

The Fallen: Cursed and eternal beings. While regular angels live, breed, and die, living out normal lives, the fallen do not. They were cursed by Hyn for taking the side of Hoxi, taking a stand against their creator, Bezi. They do not age, but can be corrupted and changed into demons through the corrupted mana that was born into the world by Magni the Lord of Destruction. The Change is one of the only ways to relieve them of their curse, another being if they find someone who will accept and love them for who they truly are. With the increase of malevolence and violence wrought by the fallen and their companions, the latter option has become increasingly difficult to accomplish. But there are some that still cling to the hope that they might be changed back to something resembling what they once were. Their hair now dulled in color and wings painted with ash. They drive out the corruption within themselves where they can, before it has a chance to consume them fully.

Shade: A soul that has been reformed in the dark corners of Dala. Changing even a pacifist soul into that of a devouring beast. They move through the shadows, remaining as a black fog when they can. Light causes their skin to blister and fester as the smoky apparition is turned corporeal. They are beasts of hunger, leaving bloody messes in their wake as whole bodies disappear without a trace. Agents of Dala tend to take shades from the homeland to use them as hunting dogs, because once they have your scent, its almost impossible to get away.

Creatures in Leera

Nemi: A special breed of chicken that cheaply produce "golden" eggs that are rich in both protein and other essential vitamins. Highly nutritious. The eggs appear to be golden but are not made with actual gold. Yolks tend to range in the reddish hues. Very important for wyrs to keep up with their protein intake and the nutrient needs that their abilities impose on them.

Toadstill: Frog-like amphibians that have become one with their natural surroundings. The fungus that grows on them provides most of their nutrients for them by digesting creatures that get caught in the toadstill's sticky mucus.

Children sometimes play with them, but are only in danger if they are largely outnumbered by the toadstills, or are a creature smaller than them. Few cases happen in which children die in the forests and are digested by toadstills. Rarely are the toadstills the actual cause of death.

Imps: Small flying creatures that feed on emissions generated by the environment and people alike. Since there is not much pollution on the mainland, imps remain small and mainly fly around chimneys to inhale the smoke. Imps originated in Dala before being brought to the mainland. Dalian imps differ in the fact that Dala features more pollution and corruption alike. Thus, the imps there are much larger and have lost their ability to fly, despite still having small wings on their backs.

Milithians: Flesh eating bugs that are *extremely* hydrophobic. They have a second set of teeth that allow them to burrow and hollow out solid stone. Milithians are typically found in small groups and typically ingest carrion. However, they can easily be deadly if found in larger hungrier clutches.

Locations in Leera

Klinewal Shoppes: A brand of stores that have made a name for themselves on the mainland for selling meat sticks and other small treats for children and adults alike. They're a big hit particularly with the wyr communities as well as other races that prefer their meat on-the-go.

Bethel's Bazaar: A market that pops up on the days surrounding the summer solstice. The change to Ivis' streets can be so jarring that someone in the area turning a corner can find themselves walking straight into the market where it hadn't been a moment ago. Its seen as its own urban legend around Ivis. Especially given the massive amount of mana it would take to put the whole event on in the first place. Some wonder if the gods are somehow involved, but others point out that while the gods slumber the market simply remains a mystery. One that most just choose to enjoy.

Belvore: One of the largest countries on the Mainland. The capital city of Belvore is Ivis. Home to plenty of humans and wyrs. But other fae and fiends have also made a home there as well. The country's biomes mainly feature plains and forests with some natural lakes and streams.

Dala: The country that makes up most of the Eastern Islands. The name is short for The Darklands. Dala has been the source of a lot of pain and suffering over the last few centuries ever since the fallen made the Eastern Islands their home. Very little grows in Dala since the corruption has lead to barren soil, too acidic for anything of use to grow.

Misc. Others

Ler: The global currency of Leera. Although some countries or even individuals still might prefer trading wares in other ways.

The Theology of Leera

Long ago, Polonus, both father and mother of the gods gave birth to ten. Each god was given dominion over a different part of the world and all were meant to work together to build whatever they saw fit. Bezi and Hoxi, the twin gods of life and death together created the numerous races of fae, fiends, and humanoids that made up Leera. Due to Bezi's fixation with the race known as Angels, she decided it would be best to give each of the other gods a race or races she had created to look after. The only god left out of this arrangement was Hoxi, the God of Death and Endings.

While some races have stopped worshiping the gods entirely, or taken up worshiping another god of the pantheon rather than the one connected more closely to their race, some races are still quite devoted to their patron god.

Here is a list of the gods and their titles:

Yar - God of Earth and Time
Trefunn - Goddess of Water and Depths
Zimm - Trickster God of Air
Sereps - God of Fire and War
Bezi - Goddess of Life and Beginnings
Hoxi - God of Death and Endings
Neron - Goddess of Love and Fertility
Vilt - God of Harvest and Sustenance

Hyn - Goddess of Magic and Curses
Boe - Goddess of Protection and Blessings

The Magic System of Leera

Magic is based around three properties. Those would be a focus, essence, and transformative property. For beings closer to the gods, they may be able to perform magic with simply their mind and their celestial mana being enough to cast most spells. For humans and other such beings who have smaller pools of mana to draw from, they often have to make do with prepared scrolls, enchanted tools or weapons, and other machinery powered by magical stones they can buy from a shop. Humanoids who cross the line of mana into castor territory often have a magic of their own, their specialty. This magic is easier for them to perform and some may not need to use tomes or even words to cast that magic.

A good way to look at the properties is as such (this is not an exhaustive list):

Focus Property

- The castor's mind

- A wand

- A staff

- An orb

- A tome

- A prepared scroll

Essence Property

- The castor's pool of mana

- Magical stones
- Enchanted items
- Blood(or life force)

Transformative Property (sometimes optional)
- An element that ties into the spell (Earth, Wind, Air, Fire)
- Certain body parts from beings that can transform/change shape